# GARY MEEHAN

New York • London

# Quercus

New York • London

© 2014 by Gary Meehan
First published in the United States by Quercus in 2014

Any member of educational institutions wishing to photocopy part or all of the work for classroom use or anthology should send inquiries to permissions@quercus.com.

ISBN 978-1-62365-831-1

Library of Congress Control Number: 2014949435

Distributed in the United States and Canada by
Hachette Book Group
237 Park Avenue
New York, NY 10017

This book is a work of fiction. Names, characters, institutions, places, and events are either the product of the author's imagination or are used fictitiously. Any resemblance to actual persons—living or dead—events, or locales is entirely coincidental.

Manufactured in the United States

10 9 8 7 6 5 4 3 2 1

www.quercus.com

*For Kirby*

# one

Megan had no trouble slipping away from the mill. Her grandfather was at the kitchen table, doing his accounts by the light of the single candle he permitted himself, while Gwyneth was in the living room, needing no light for what she was doing with Holt. She feigned a headache, to which neither her sister nor her grandfather paid more than nominal concern, and after retiring to her bedroom slipped unnoticed out of the window.

She made her way along the riverbank. In the distance, the sun was setting over Thicketford, spilling itself onto the thatched roofs of the village. Across the sparkling waters of the Heledor, fields of wheat swayed in the breeze like an amiable drunk. Beyond them lay the forest, where Wade waited for her.

He had disappeared a week ago, when Megan had told him she was pregnant, leaving her to face the prospects of unmarried motherhood with all its shame and hardships. Despite Gwyneth's advice, she had been on the verge of admitting everything to her grandfather when Alodie had turned up at the mill and told her Wade wanted to meet. Megan had been so relieved, her hug had lifted Alodie off the ground, smearing the little girl's tunic with the dough she had been kneading.

It would have been more direct to wade across the Heledor at the ford, but saturated clothes would have given the game away when she returned home, so Megan headed for the bridge at the village. Planks rattled under her feet as she crossed. A couple of months ago, Megan had been here enjoying the solitude after the evening's service, watching the river burble along, when her sister had slid in beside her.

"You have to come to Cheetham, Meg," Gwyneth had said, dangling her legs through the slats of the bridge.

"What's so great about Cheetham?"

"Grandfather won't let me go alone with Holt."

"That doesn't answer the question."

"We'll only be gone one night," said Gwyneth. "Wade and Holt have their parents' wagon. We can stay with their cousin." She nudged Megan. "Wade really likes you."

"No, he does not."

Wade and Holt were brothers who had moved to Thicketford a couple of weeks ago from Cheetham. Their good looks had prompted much swooning from the village's female inhabitants and even a couple of the male ones. Gwyneth had secured the older brother in no time at all, then given herself the far harder challenge of setting up her sister.

"I've seen the way he looks at you," said Gwyneth.

"He looks at all the girls like that. Even you." *Especially you.* Sometimes Megan felt like a crude counterfeit of her twin. Gwyneth's hair was never an unruly mess; her skin never broke out with acne; her clothes were never splattered with mud.

"Fine," said Gwyneth, extricating herself from the bridge's skeleton. "I'll ask Bliss."

Megan had caught her arm. "All right, Gwyn. I'll come." If Bliss snared Wade, she'd never hear the end of it. "But don't leave me alone with him."

"Would I?"

She had, but Megan found herself not minding. Wade was funny and charming and always knew what to say. Megan continued to see him once they had returned home. He brought her flowers every day, strutted around the village with her, paid her extravagant compliments that Megan in no way believed but brought a smile to her face whenever she thought no one was looking. And she'd be lying if she said she didn't enjoy making all the other girls jealous, especially Bliss.

Jealousy was the last emotion Megan was inspiring now. She reached the temple, whose incomplete sections revealed Brother Rennie instructing some of the younger children in the Book of Faith.

"And who did the Saviors come to help?" he asked.

Alodie's hand shot up. "My family, brother," she said. "My dad's always going, 'Saviors help us.'"

"That's not quite correct." Brother Rennie's expression darkened. "And tell your father to come see me."

"Yes, brother," said Alodie, bowing her head.

"No, children, the Saviors came to help the first king, Edwyn, who unified the counties of Werlavia into a single realm. They brought the Faith, which . . ."

Megan had heard the story too many times for it to warrant another listen and left the priest and his charges to it. She rounded the temple and passed Freya's inn, where the patrons were indulging in more secular matters. For some, it was better to sin and be forgiven than never to have sinned at all.

Skirting the wheat fields, Megan reached the edge of the forest. She wondered if the message was really from Wade. It had not gone unnoticed he had skipped town, nor that Megan had been frantically asking after him. Bliss could be there with her coven, ready with jeers and catcalls, which would only get worse once they figured out Megan was pregnant.

She should have resisted when Wade had pushed for something more physical. Megan had hoped her sister would talk her out of it, but Gwyneth hadn't seen what the problem was.

"It's what happens," she said, with a twinkle in her eye that betrayed experience. "Don't be such a prude. You do like boys, don't you?"

"What about if, you know, things go wrong?"

"Don't let him have any wine beforehand."

"What if I get pregnant?" said Megan.

"That can't happen," said Gwyneth. "Not your first time."

"What about the times after that?"

"You're eager."

It hadn't mattered. Once was enough. Wade hadn't pushed for an encore. He stopped calling on her, and what time they did spend together became shorter and more awkward. Then nausea set in and her period had failed to arrive.

Megan's destination was an old oak tree whose carved inscriptions revealed she and Wade weren't the only lovers to have met here over the generations. She rested against it and brushed leaves and bits of twig from her bare soles. No tormentors; no Wade either. Had he lost his nerve?

There was a rustle from the forest behind her. "Megan."

She composed herself before turning around, swallowing her fear and anger and the need to call him every bad name she could think of. Absence had reduced the once-beautiful boy to a beggar. His tunic was torn, his pants splattered with mud, his bare feet crisscrossed with fresh scars. Megan doubted he had washed since she had last seen him.

The two of them stared at the ground, kicking at the undergrowth, both too nervous to bring up the subject that had brought them here. Eventually, Megan blurted out, "You're not going to marry me, are you?"

Wade shook his head. "We're too young."

"We're sixteen. We're old enough. Grandfather'll give us permission." Megan caressed her stomach. "We were old enough to get pregnant."

"You," said Wade, backing away a little. "You were old enough to get pregnant."

That was it, was it? This was all Megan's fault; she had to deal with the consequences. She and she alone. She had chosen to accept the flattery; she had to pay the price. A lifetime of shame for a few moments believing she was special. Maybe if she prayed hard enough to God and the Saviors, they could undo all this. But why would they? Wasn't she getting what she deserved for her stupidity, her breaking of the Faith?

"What do you expect me to do?" she asked.

"Go north. Eastport maybe. The Sisters of the Faith take in fallen women. They'll look after you."

He didn't even have the decency to run away himself. He expected her to do it, leave Gwyneth and her grandfather for a life in a convent. "Eastport far away enough for you?" she said, contempt sharpening her voice. "How about I keep going north? Slink off to New

Statham? Or the Snow Cities? Perhaps you'd like me out of Werlavia all together?"

Raucous shouts drifted in from the village. Freya's ale must be extra good tonight. Megan wondered if she should pop in, get a tankard to take home to her grandfather. It might help the news he was to be a great-grandfather go down easier.

"I'm sorry," said Wade.

"You're sorry? That makes things better. It'll be something to comfort your child with. Daddy can't be with us, but it's all right because he's sorry."

"Megan . . ."

"Oh, get lost. I didn't want to marry you anyway."

As she uttered the words, Megan realized they were true. She was better off on her own. Sure, the village would jeer and her grandfather would rant and Brother Rennie would rave—sexual immorality was his bugbear unless he was hungover, in which case it was alcohol— but that would fade. Being married to someone who didn't want her, whom she didn't want, wouldn't. Gwyneth had promised to be there for her; she'd help bring up the baby. Megan didn't need anyone else.

The cries from the village were getting harsher, wilder. One was almost a scream. Had a fight broken out? Wade paled and nudged her deeper behind the tree line.

"Wait there," he said.

"What? Why?"

"I'll explain later. Just stay there."

Megan hugged the tree as she watched Wade plunge into the wheat field and head toward the village, the ears of the ripe wheat brushing his waist. A figure peeled away from the cottages and moved to intercept him, the twilight reducing him to a stick figure. Even as he drew closer, Megan failed to recognize him. There was an odd bulkiness about him, a stiffness to the way he carried himself, that matched none of the men she knew.

He and Wade met halfway between the village and Megan's position. Wade held up his hand, said something the wind failed to convey to her. The other man raised an ax. Wade started to turn. The setting sun flashed off metal. Wade's head was struck from his shoulders.

The shock saved Megan, prevented her from screaming; prevented her from revealing herself. She slithered down the chestnut tree, her legs weak as a newborn foal's, as the horror of what she had witnessed played itself again and again in her mind. The blood spurting from Wade's neck, his head arcing into the field, his body toppling into the wheat, his executioner barely breaking stride.

He was coming toward her. *He was coming toward her.* She had to get out of there right now. Megan crawled a couple of feet into the forest. No, she had to go home, back to the mill, warn Gwyneth and her grandfather. She started back toward Thicketford, but it was apparent the almost-screams coming from there were actual screams. The screams of the terrified, the screams of the slaughterhouse. She retreated to the cover of the forest. Who was doing this? Why?

The only way home was the direct way. Megan would have to cross the wheat field and ford the river by the mill. Her legs refused to move. She'd be spotted for sure and then . . . and then . . . She screwed up her face as if trying to squeeze the tears back in. At least make it quick. It had been quick for Wade. She thought again of his execution and wanted to throw up.

She risked a glance out from behind the tree. The ax man was about a hundred yards away, wading through the wheat. Megan had to move now, while distance offered her some protection. She crawled out of the forest and into the field, fast as she dared. Stalks brushed her face as she snaked along, making her want to scratch and sneeze. She tried to keep her progress as soft as possible, placing her hands and feet on the patches between the wheat, praying the grass would reward her care by springing back into position behind her and concealing her movements.

The ax man was close, close enough Megan could hear him tramping through the field. She halted, held her breath, shrank to the ground, hid herself among the long stalks. Something crawled up her thigh. She gritted her teeth and swallowed. Worse things were out here. Far worse things.

She heard a second figure crashing through the wheat. "What are you doing out here?" he said. His accent was refined, like that of the northern merchants who had passed through Eastport when she had been in school there.

"Looking."

Megan assumed this was the ax man. His voice was harsh, raspy, as if someone had slashed his vocal cords.

"There's no one out here."

"I'll decide that."

"The captain says we're to group at the mill."

Fear twisted Megan's muscles. The mill—her home. She had to get there now, had to get her family to safety, but any movement would attract the ax man. He was still here, a faint *whoosh* occasionally coming from his direction. Swinging the ax through the air, seeking his next victim.

"He can wait."

"You know what the captain said he'd do to anyone who disobeyed him. I bet he's got an actual rusty knife. He looks the type."

There was a hesitation. Megan could hear the blood singing in her ears, a blade thwacking at stalks, the chirrup of birds settling down for the night. Then there was a snort and the sound of the two men tramping away.

Megan held herself still until the last trace of them was gone. They were heading for the bridge at Thicketford. They'd have to double back on the opposite bank of the river to get to the mill. Going directly, Megan could arrive there five minutes ahead of them. Five precious minutes to lead her family from danger.

She couldn't bring herself to move though. She was safe here, hidden in the fields of wheat. Surely Gwyneth and her grandfather would have heard the commotion from the village and run? They didn't need Megan. She'd be putting herself and her unborn baby in danger for nothing.

*Coward*, whispered her conscience. She silenced it by dragging herself a yard forward. One yard became another, then another, then her momentum was propelling her through the field. She crawled as fast as she could, ignoring the dirt and stones that scraped her knees and elbows.

Cultivated land gave way to scrub and the thickets that gave the village its name. Megan was nearing the river. She looked through the bushes. Her journey across the field had carried her upstream of the ford, a little past the mill. Home was tantalizingly close, a few seconds' dash were it not for the river.

She was about to squeeze through the vegetation and head down the bank, when a figure emerged from the mill. A strong, reassuring figure silhouetted against the day's last glow on the horizon. Her grandfather had come out to meet someone: a man on horse-back approaching from downriver who had the same bulk as the ax man, a bulk Megan now recognized as armor.

The horse shook its head, shifted from side to side. Her grandfather hoisted his ax over his shoulder and held his ground. That blade had only ever cut wood, but he knew how to handle it. He'd commanded a company in the war against the witches, been rewarded for his bravery by the priests. Pride surged through Megan. You didn't get past her grandfather.

A deep hum split the air. Megan's grandfather staggered, a crossbow bolt sticking out of his chest. He groped for it, tried to pull it out. Another bolt joined the first. Men on foot had joined the horseman. A third one fired his crossbow. Her grandfather keeled over. Megan bit down on her fist to stop herself screaming.

The men drew axes. They rushed past her grandfather's body and into the mill. A boy—Holt, it took Megan a few moments to register—called out Gwyneth's name, but he was cut off before he could get out the second syllable.

*Get out, Gwyneth!* Megan screamed inside her head. She stared at Gwyneth's bedroom window, waiting for her twin to sneak out, waiting for her lithe form to drop to the ground like she had done so many times over the years, like Megan had done an hour earlier. Gwyneth didn't appear. The horseman dismounted and followed his companions inside. Still no one emerged from the window.

There was nothing she could do. Megan couldn't rescue the dead. Hating herself, she fled for the sanctuary of the forest.

# two

Megan stumbled through the trees in a daze, not know-ing where she was going or why. The darkness of the night meant her only guide was the occasional patch of moonlight that broke through the forest canopy, mak-ing the undergrowth shine with an otherworldly qual-ity. Tears blurred her vision, but she plowed on blindly, ricocheting from trunk to trunk, hardly noticing the thorns and branches that slashed at her exposed arms and legs. What were a few scratches compared to what she had witnessed?

This was her fault. If she hadn't let Wade get her pregnant, she wouldn't have been waiting for him. She would have been home, sat by the window that looked out on to the village; ostensibly reading, in reality, day-dreaming. She would have seen what was going on in Thicketford. She could have warned everyone. They wouldn't have been taken from her. And, even if she hadn't saved them, she would have been among the slaughtered and she wouldn't feel this pain.

Who were the soldiers? Why had they done this? Why would they *want* to do this? Were they Sandstriders? They hadn't crossed the mountains since the war with the witches. Her mind couldn't cope with the tumult of questions. Each one felt like a blow.

Megan sank to the ground, left spongy by the early-autumn rains. Spikes dug into her bare soles, making her eyes water. Burrs from the tree. She reached down and brushed them off with a couple of tired strokes. Every year, she and Gwyneth would come out to the forest and harvest them, though they hadn't managed to yet this year. They would take them home to their grandfather and while they roasted he would tell them tales of his battles, tales that grew ever fancier with their retelling. Megan's eyes watered again as she realized she'd never hear his voice again nor exchange sideways glances with Gwyneth as his hyperbole reached new levels.

A smaller chestnut stood a little distance away, maybe an offspring of the one that had just hidden her. She wondered if the elder looked on with pride as its child grew, aching for the day when their branches would grow enough to span the forest that separated them and finally touch. Long ago, before the priests had banished such nonsense, it was said the dead found life again in the trees. The souls of Gwyneth and her grandfather could be out there now, settling into their new homes within freshly germinated seeds. She hoped she hadn't stood on either of them.

There was a low growl—half warning, half threat. Not everything in the forest was friendly. Megan huddled into herself, trying to make herself smaller. The growling got louder. Dry vegetation crumpled under soft footsteps. A black shape slunk toward her. Moonlight glinted off predatory eyes.

She groped around in the vegetation, searching for something to defend herself with. Her fingers brushed a fallen branch. She snatched it up and swung. Another growl, angrier, more savage. Megan swung again.

"Leave me alone!"

Her arm jarred as she made contact. There was a whimper. Megan sprang to her feet and charged, screaming incoherently. Leaves rustled as her would-be attacker scurried away.

Megan composed herself, waited for the panting to subside, her heart to stop thumping. She should keep moving. But where to? She could hardly go back to Thicketford and give birth among the corpses. She knew only one other place: Eastport, the county capital of Ainsworth, where she and Gwyneth had gone to school. Her old tutor, Brother Brogan, had told her to look him up if she was ever back in the city and, while he no doubt said that to all his pupils, he wouldn't turn away an expectant mother; if the rumors were true, he'd been responsible for more than one of them.

But Eastport was hundreds of miles away and she had nothing beyond the clothes on her back and whatever the forest could provide, and what could the forest provide except a few nuts? Her grandfather had always provided for her and he couldn't do that anymore.

Unless . . . A memory came to her, of the last time she had been this deep in the forest. She and Gwyneth had been thirteen and about to go up to school. Their grandfather had often told them tales of the fortune he had seized from the witches during the war and hidden behind a thirty-foot waterfall. Megan had determined to claim it.

"Come down, Meg," Gwyneth had pleaded as Megan scampered up the base of the cliff.

Megan had to shout to make herself heard over the wall of cascading foam. "You heard what grandfather said. It's ours, if we can get it."

"It's not worth killing yourself for a few pennies and a half-eaten apple."

"I'll let you have the apple, Gwyn."

"Grandfather said we were to share everything equally."

"It's all right," said Megan. "I don't like apples."

The cliff steepened. Megan groped for a handhold, enjoying the squeaks of alarm coming from below. She started to pull herself up. Her foot slipped on a stone made greasy by water and algae. She yelped and grabbed on to the rocks, her legs dangling in the air.

Gwyneth screamed. "Meg!"

Megan regained her footing and contemplated the slippery rocks, the roaring water, and the height she had yet to traverse. Her vision swam for a moment. This was silly; she'd never make it up there. She let herself drop the short distance into the pool, splashing her sister in the process. Gwyneth had screamed again, this time in relief rather than fear.

Now there was no witness; what had once been curiosity was now need. Megan had a child to look after. The previous day, the thought had terrified her; now it was something to cling to, something to keep her going and prevent her from curling up in a ball and giving up. If her grandfather had hidden his legacy out in the forest, she would need it to keep herself and her baby alive.

Early-morning sunbeams penetrated the mist rising from the pool and glittered off the quicksilver surface. The opposite bank was barely discernible behind the curtain of vapor and appeared to belong to another world, a ghost land where shades roamed. The hiss of spray as water tumbled over rocks filled Megan's ears. If she closed her eyes she could make out voices buried in the noise. The dead recriminating her for failing to save them.

Megan slipped her tunic off and hung it over a branch. After a moment's hesitation, she did the same with her underclothes. There was no one but the birds to witness her nudity and, even if there was, wasn't she a fallen woman? Strange, how the father of a bastard was never a fallen man.

She clambered up the rocks by the side of the waterfall, grimacing with the exertion. It was impossible to make anything out behind the curtain of foam. She wouldn't know if her grandfather's claims were true unless she could find a way in.

There was a thin ledge, which would just about accommodate her if she went side on. She shuffled out and groped for a handhold. Her hand slipped off a jutting rock. She tried again, this time curling her fingers around it. Her grip held. How had her grandfather managed this? He was twice her size and nowhere near as nimble. Perhaps the rocks had been less eroded forty years ago, or the flow not so fierce. *Or perhaps he hadn't*, she heard Gwyneth remark. *Perhaps it was another one of his stories, like that time he claimed to have slaughtered a dozen—or was it a score?—of witches in single combat.*

A second step took Megan into the waterfall. Thousands of tiny fingers hammered against her, trying to expel the intruder. Spray filled her mouth and nostrils. She had to press her head right against the rock wall to find a place where she could breathe air instead of water.

She stretched out her leg. The ledge narrowed until it was barely wide enough to fit her big toe. She adjusted her weight and slapped at the rocks with her left hand, searching for something to grab on to. Her fingers jabbed into an opening, scraping the skin. The cold dulled the pain and she hauled herself a couple of feet over.

The next step had to bring her to the cave, surely. She slid out her leg again. The ledge narrowed even further before disappearing into the wall. She ran her foot against the wall, looking for an opening. Nothing but slick rock. Another step, then. Well, not a step exactly: she'd have to support herself entirely by her arms.

Megan slid her right hand into the opening and reached out with her left. An outcropping poked into her palm and she wrapped her hand around it. She tested putting her weight on it. It'd hold if she was quick and found another beyond that. She took a deep breath and stepped off the ledge.

It didn't hold.

Megan plunged into the pool. The shock jolted the air from her lungs. She thrashed in the water as she sank, dislodging pockets of air that rushed past her body and headed for the surface. Water filled her nostrils, burning her sinuses. Panic flooded her, making her thrash even more.

Her feet touched bottom, dislodging silt and the creatures living within it. Before the water was clouded by the mud, she glimpsed a gaping black hole where rocks should be. Her grandfather had gotten a detail wrong. The cave wasn't behind the waterfall: it was under it.

Megan kicked for the surface and let the current carry her away to the calmer waters at the other end of the pool. She trod water for a while, telling herself she was waiting for the silt to settle but in reality working up the courage to dive again. Who knew how far the cave went back or what lay within it? She imagined herself getting stuck between its walls, her last actions a desperate attempt to free herself from stone jaws while liquid death seeped into her lungs. Was it worth it for a few corroded coppers? Why not climb out, run away? But then what? The cave gave her a purpose, or at least a distraction, for a few more minutes.

Megan swam back toward the waterfall. Spray pattered her face. She filled her tired lungs with air and dived. Sediment still clouded the water, but she found the entrance to the cave quickly enough and shot into it. The world darkened.

She found herself in a tunnel that, had it been dry, she would have had to crawl through. A little light seeped in through the cave entrance, catching the edges of rocks and the scales of silvery fish that flitted past her, but the illumination only emphasized how black everything else was. Megan swam deeper into the tunnel, using its floor for leverage. She searched for the cache, but there was no glimmer of gold nor any marker laid down to indicate where her grandfather might have hidden his treasure.

She kicked on, trying to ignore narrowing walls and the fact that even with her hands on the floor her head was more often than not scraping the ceiling. Ignorant of their surroundings, her lungs pleaded with her to expel the stale air in exchange for fresh. The top of her lip tickled as a few air bubbles seeped out of her nose. She had to hold on. The treasure had to be here. She had come too far now to go back: she'd never make it before her lungs burst. She found the energy for one last stroke. Light dappled the water above her head. The solid ceiling had given way to a liquid one.

Megan broke the surface and sucked air into her burning lungs. When the purple dots that danced in front of her eyes retired to the sidelines, she looked around. She was in a dim cavern, about the size of a house, with walls made of shiny black stone. Poles of light speared down from holes in the rock, but they were too thin to bring any heat with them.

Although the surface of the cavern was flooded, a ledge at the far end poked a couple of feet out of the water. Megan swam over to it and hauled herself out of the pool. Freezing air enveloped her and she shivered, her teeth rattling. She huddled on the ledge, rubbing her arms and legs in a useless effort to warm them.

The cave was silent apart from the sound of her panting and the *plink* of dripping water. As her eyes adjusted to the gloom, she noticed lumpy shapes tucked up against the wall. Was that it? She pulled the smallest one toward her. It was a pouch the size of a fist, made of some kind of skin and tied with now-rotten leather. More important, it clinked.

She yanked it open. Coins spilled out. Megan counted three gold sovereigns and the equivalent of ninety shillings in silver. Her heart fluttered. It was more money than she'd seen in her life, more money than anyone she knew, save a priest, had ever seen. She picked out one of the sovereigns and held it up. The gold shone as if with its own light, as perfect as the day it was minted. There was a king's head on the front: Edwyn the Fifth, Edwyn the Last, Edwyn the Failed. The king who had led his lords into battle and seen them slaughtered by the witches. The king who had staggered home half dead to find his throne seized by the priesthood. The king who had rotted in a dungeon while others saved his realm.

She scooped the coins back into the pouch and checked the other objects. One was a ball the size of a head, loosely wrapped in skins. She pulled them off and found an iron helmet, crude and undecorated. There was a patch of rust where water had seeped in. Megan rubbed it. Her finger punched a hole in the crumbling metal. She tried it on anyway. Way too big. Heavy metal squeezed her saturated hair. She shuddered as water trickled down her neck.

The final shape was a tube about four feet long. Her grandfather had taken more care wrapping this one. The strips of seal skin were tight and inviolate. Megan's heart thudded as she unwound the strips, realizing what was underneath and the possibilities it offered. She exposed a scabbard, then a hilt and finally a glittering crystal of blue topaz set in the pommel.

Megan drew the sword and held it out, letting one of the shafts of light from the ceiling glint off the steel. She pushed herself to her feet and raised the weapon. It was heavy enough to need both hands and all her strength, but the power inherent in the razor-sharp steel sent a primal thrill through her. She swung. The air almost screamed as the blade sliced through it.

There was a word etched into the sword: KALVERT. It meant nothing to her; some long-dead lord, no doubt. What did mean something was that she now had a weapon. That was good. That was what she needed. The money meant survival. The sword meant revenge.

Eastport was hundreds of miles away, and the only road to it would take her through Thicketford. Would the soldiers still be there, or would they have moved on after their killing and plundering? Not that the village had much to plunder: they hadn't even been able to afford to complete their temple. But if they were there, she'd deal with them. For Gwyneth, for her grandfather, for everyone.

The sheathed blade slapped her as she marched, as if in chastisement. The weapon was too long to strap to her waist, so she had been forced to tie the accompanying belt diagonally across her chest and carry the sword on her back, even though the leather chafed against her skin. She had the money pouch tucked under her tunic and tied to her waist using some of the sealskin wrappings. Some more of the wrappings she had stuffed into the pouch to dull the clink of coins. Her hand kept drifting down to check it was still there.

It was late afternoon by the time she approached Thicketford. A single column of smoke resolved into dozens, each one belching from a neighbor's home. She knew each house: the ones where you could find a playmate or someone to gossip with, the ones where you could scrounge a cake or a slice of pie, the ones where you could find a hot fire and a scary story. Only now the hot fires were part of the scary story, and the story was real.

Megan crept along the road through the smoldering remains, at first scared to disturb any lurking soldiers and then scared to disturb the dead. Smoke and anger made her eyes water, but the tears didn't prevent her from catching glimpses of charred corpses, animals, and people. Everything was destroyed, for reasons she couldn't comprehend.

She reached the bridge, or rather the remains of it. It had been hacked and burned, reduced to a blackened skeleton. The planks had been ripped out and cast into the river; Megan could see a couple the current hadn't swept away, caught in the reeds. There was no way to cross here. She'd have to head upriver to the ford and wade across there. But going to the ford would bring her within sight of home, within sight of her family's bodies. She couldn't face that—the final confirmation she had lost them and was all alone—but she couldn't stay here either. The smell of smoke and burned meat drifting up from the village was making her retch.

Megan set off upriver, conning herself into pretending this was nothing more than a normal trip home, a journey she'd done a thousand times. The air cleared, if not her mood. To her right, the wheat waved at her from the fields. Somewhere in there lay Wade. Megan supposed he'd helped save her life by drawing the attention of the ax man. It was something to tell their child about him, at least; better than revealing Wade wanted nothing to do with either of them.

She reached the ford, where the river's natural shallowness had been built up over generations with earth and stones. Megan picked her way down to the bank, concentrating on her footing so she wouldn't have to look at the mill. Warm mud oozed between her toes, heated by the afternoon sun. A duck glided past, oblivious to the destruction. Megan wished she could share its ignorant bliss.

There was a rustling on the other side of the Heledor. Megan froze. Two men rose from the undergrowth—tough soldiers with coarse skin burned by the sun and inked with strange tattoos. Plate protected their chests and narrow-brimmed helmets their heads. This armor was coated in black lacquer, chinks in which allowed the raw steel to peek through. Underneath it they wore leather the same color and consistency as their complexions.

Blood racing, Megan scrambled back up, mud squelching beneath her feet. The soldiers edged forward. She drew the sword and brandished it two-handed. The momentum of the heavy blade dragged her left then right as she failed to control it. Something black fluttered to the ground. A chunk of her own hair: the blade must have caught it.

The soldiers continued to advance, unconcerned by the threat Megan posed. They reached the river. The taller soldier stuck a boot in, testing its depth before wading out. Megan had two choices: fight or flight. The former option had seemed so simple when she was in the cavern and her enemies didn't tower over her or do anything inconvenient like fight back. She turned and ran.

Her foot slid and twisted in the mud. Megan lost her balance and fell, jerking the sword aside at the last second to stop herself from being impaled. She pushed herself to her feet and hurried up the bank.

"Stop! Get back here or I'll . . ."

*Kill me if I don't stay to let you kill me?* Megan glanced behind her. The soldier on the bank had abandoned his mace and was taking aim with his crossbow, one eye closed as he tracked her movements. Megan dived into the grass, hoping to throw him off. There was a *thrum* and a *whoosh*. She expected pain any second. Instead there was a gargle, the rustle of vegetation, and a splash.

Megan risked lifting her head up. The bowman was sprawled face up in the river, wide-eyed and unmoving, his comrade's ax sticking up out of his skull like the tiller of a boat. The current caught him and he floated away, the water turning pink in his wake.

The other soldier beckoned to her. He'd halved the odds in her favor, for what reason Megan could only guess, but she was in no state to take advantage of them. She scrambled to her feet and dashed back toward the village.

She could hide in the smoking houses, find the right moment to ambush her pursuer. All she needed was a little time. She heard splashing and cursing. The soldier had made it ashore. She increased her pace, wishing she had found time to sheath her sword. She couldn't run properly without threatening to take her own head off.

She was almost at the bridge. Another man in black armor was leaning against the charred remains. He pushed himself off and marched toward her. Megan skidded to a halt. She looked around. The other was making ground behind her; to her right flowed the Heledor; to the left the wheat fields and Wade's body.

It was her only choice. She shot left. Her pursuers moved to intercept her, gaining fast. After everything she had endured, Megan had no strength left. Her legs were giving way, her sides knotting up in stitches. Behind her, the soldiers crashed through the crops. She lurched, swinging the sword as hard as she could. If she could get one of them at least, it would be one small measure of payback for Gwyneth and her grandfather.

She swiped only the ears off innocent stalks. The soldiers had split, coming at her from both sides. Megan jabbed her blade at them. They sneered at her as if she was no more intimidating than a toddler with a twig.

One made a grab for her. She swung at him. He was out of range. It had been a distraction. The other soldier loomed from behind. There was a flash of black and the world went dark. She smelled sweat and mud. Before she could escape the cloak that had been thrown over her, a fist cuffed her behind the ear. Her legs gave way.

She thrashed wildly, but one of the soldiers pinned her arms to the ground and pushed his weight against her, quelling her struggle. She tried to throw him off.

He slapped her through the hood. Megan got the message and was still.

The soldier stood and lifted the cloak. She stared up at them, her focus coming and going. The sun made both men into silhouettes, picking out the edge of their bodies in a fiery halo. She pushed herself backward along the ground. One of the soldiers reached out and dragged her back. Her sword lay in the dirt. Megan made a grab for it. A foot stamped down. She pulled her fingers away just in time. The soldier picked up the sword and examined it. He sneered at the inscription, then lobbed it away.

"Please," said Megan. "Let me go."

She pulled up her tunic and groped for the money pouch. "I can pay you." She tossed the coins into the air as if she was a farmer sowing seed. "Take it! Take it all!"

The soldiers didn't glance at the gold and silver as it rained to the ground, not even when a shilling pinged off a chest plate. Their attention was wholly on Megan as she squirmed in the trampled wheat, staring her down like parents waiting for a child's tantrum to blow itself out.

Megan collected herself, remembered her grandfather's dignity in the face of death. She wouldn't let these bastards see her beg anymore. She wouldn't let them see her fear. When she saw her family again, she wanted them to be proud of her. Her hand drifted down to her stomach. *I'm so sorry I never got to know you.*

She got to her feet, tensing her muscles so her legs wouldn't tremble. Straightening her tunic, she looked into each man's creased face. Unmoved expressions greeted her. They seemed no more alive than the corpses they'd left behind.

"What are you waiting for?" she screamed at them. "Do it!"

"Get the horses," said the tall soldier.

His comrade didn't acknowledge the order. It would have been hard to, what with the arrow sprouting from his neck.

# three

The tall soldier grabbed Megan and whipped out a knife. It stung as he pressed it to her throat. A droplet of hot blood welled up and trickled down her skin.

A hooded archer stood forty yards away, his weapon trained on them. He was slender and a good few inches taller than Megan. A dark-green cloak flapped in the breeze, revealing mud-stained boots and pants underneath. Leather and wool, no metal. He wasn't one of the soldiers.

"Let the girl go."

A woman's voice? Megan peered at the figure. There was a hint of female curves beneath the loose clothing, a glimpse of smooth skin under the hood.

"Did you hear me?" said the woman, drawing her bowstring back an extra inch. "I said let the girl go."

The soldier had another knife stuck in his belt. He'd left Megan's hands free, reasoning—rightly—there wasn't much her fists could do against metal, but his limbs were only covered by leather. There were plenty of gaps through which a blade could cause a lot of damage. Megan stretched out a hand and eased out the knife, fearing any moment the man would notice and draw his own knife across her throat.

She got the blade clear and took a firm grip of the handle, then tensed, preparing to strike. The woman's head flicked downward, attracted by the motion. The soldier's breath warmed Megan's temple as he peered over her shoulder. Megan thrust, hard as she could.

Blood sprayed on to her hand as the knife ripped into the man's thigh, provoking a scream that almost deafened her. She wrenched his arm off her neck and scrambled away from him. She got no more than a step away when his fist crashed at the side of her head.

The world went haywire. The ground swapped position with the sky a hundred times in a second. Dirt filled her mouth. Megan tried to push herself up, but a boot thudded into the small of her back and pinned her to the ground. Something split the air above her head. The pressure against her lessened. She looked up to see the soldier toppling to the ground, an arrow embedded into his eye socket.

Megan clambered to her feet, spitting out soil and rubbing her bruised flesh. She turned to the woman, intending to thank her, only to find an arrow trained on her. She yelped and took a step back.

"Who are you?" demanded the woman, advancing on Megan, her aim unwavering.

"I thought you were helping me."

"Answer the question."

"This is my family's land. I ask the questions." Actually it ended at the river, but if the woman wasn't going to obey the rule of rescuing, Megan could fudge the technicalities of property ownership. "Who are *you*?"

"I am Eleanor of the house of Endalay, Countess of Ainsworth, Baroness of Laxton and Herth, First Lady of Kirkland, Overlord of the Spice Isles, and Defender of the Southern Lands. And you?"

"Megan." And, because she was feeling conspicuously under-titled, she added, "of Thicketford. What are you doing here?"

"I saw the smoke. Did the witches touch you?"

"What?" said Megan. "Those aren't witches."

"Yes, they are. And did they touch you?"

Megan shook her head. "They can't be. The priests defeated them. My grandfather defeated them."

"Look at the tattoos," said Eleanor.

Megan glanced at the dead men. Their faces were inked with a multitude of designs: whorls and waves, suns and moons. None of them was the forbidden symbol, the symbol of the witches.

"Lower."

Lower was covered by clothing and armor. Eleanor jerked her bow, urging Megan on. Megan swallowed

her distaste and crouched down by the soldier she'd
stabbed in the leg. She tugged at the mud-caked scarf
round his neck, exposing the skin below. Etched there,
in faded ink, was a circle whose top was broken by two
five-pointed stars.

Megan shot back as if the body was contaminated.
She had seen the symbol only once before, carved on to
the bridge. The whole village had been hysterical. The
children—Megan and Gwyneth included—had cowered in cellars; the adults resorted to soaking themselves in the ford rather than risk the bridge. When
the culprit, a twelve-year-old boy, had admitted to the
graffiti—a joke, he had claimed—the whole village
turned out to watch him be thrashed by the priest and
his fingers reduced to a bloody pulp as he sanded away
the offending image.

"It's a cheap trick to scare people," Megan said.

Eleanor nodded at the remains of Megan's home.
"You think the people who did this need to resort to
cheap tricks?" She spat on the ground. "These soldiers
are witches."

Megan shivered. The day had gotten colder and
darker in a way the passage of clouds across the sun
couldn't totally explain. She remembered her grandfather's stories, of men who had broken the Pledges
of Faith so absolutely they knew there was no chance of
salvation. Of men who, instead of waiting for death
to condemn them to hell, had given their souls to the

demons Ahebban and Jolecia and brought hell to Werlavia. Better to rule the fires than suffer them.

Edwyn the Fifth had led an aristocratic army against the witches, but his lords were decimated, leaving him a broken man. The Realm was all but lost until the priests rallied the Faithful. The witches had fought hard, but they were pushed back, inch by damn inch, laying waste to the land as they retreated south through Werlavia. The priests' army drove them to Trafford's Haven, where the Endalayan Mountains had prevented any further flight. Rather than surrendering, the witches had chosen to burn the city and themselves with it, condemning themselves to the fate they had fought so hard to avoid.

That had been four decades ago. Was that whom Megan had abandoned her family to? Was this slaughter some kind of sacrifice? Ahebban and Jolecia were said to have slept on a bed of skulls and to have drank the blood of humans. Could they really have returned from death? But what was death to demons?

"How have the witches come back? They're supposed to be dead."

"I don't think anyone counted the bodies," said Eleanor.

"Saviors help us," Megan murmured. The epithet was less a curse than a genuine plea.

Eleanor nodded over to the mill. "That your home?" Megan could manage only the briefest nod.

Eleanor headed for the ford. Megan spun around in confusion. "What are you . . . ?" Eleanor ignored her and started to wade across the river.

Megan didn't want to confront the dead bodies of her family, but neither could she leave them to a stranger. She stumbled to the ford and plunged in, gasping at the shock of the icy water, waded across, and hauled herself up the bank.

Her grandfather lay where the soldiers had shot him down, the arrow holes weeping dried blood, his body far enough from the mill to have saved him from the flames. She knelt down and kissed his forehead. Tears brimmed in her eyes and fell onto his cheek.

"We should say the funeral prayer," said Eleanor.

"We need a priest to lead it," said Megan.

"If God was that bothered, He would have spared us one."

They could at least try. Megan made the sign of the circle over her heart. The words of the funeral prayer came easy to her. They were the first words she could remember, intoned on a sweet summer's day when they had buried her parents, who had succumbed to the sweating sickness when she and Gwyneth were just four years old.

"God, born of the eternal universe, ultimate arbiter of man, take these souls we deliver unto You. Show them Your mercy and love and the wonders of Your creation. Rejoice, for though life ends in death, out of . . . out of . . ."

Her voice gave out. Eleanor placed a hand on her shoulder and finished the prayer. "Out of death comes life."

Together they recited the Pledges of Faith. "I pledge obedience to God and His priests. I pledge to uphold the Faith and destroy its enemies. I pledge to accept no other God. I pledge my body and all that I am for God's purpose." *Sorry about that*, Megan added silently, her hand drifting to her stomach. "I pledge to defend His people. I pledge truth in all I do."

The mill that was once her home was a blackened shell. The wheel had slumped into the river and although water flowed through the slats, it failed to turn. Megan had to go inside, but the prospect terrified her. The glimpses she'd had of the villagers, the charred corpses and contorted faces, were haunting enough. To see her sister like that—the girl with whom she had shared her sixteen years in the world and before that their mother's womb—made her want to throw herself in the river and hold her head under the surface until oblivion took her.

She forced herself to enter. Dust motes swam in the hazy columns of light that spilled in through the punctured roof and illuminated a burned body with a knife in its chest. It had enough of its features for Megan to recognize it wasn't Gwyneth. It was a man, or rather a boy: Holt. She fled the room, eyes squeezed shut, trying to excise the image from her mind.

Megan advanced through the house, her stomach lurching every time she entered a new room, expecting to find Gwyneth dead on the floor. There was a heavy smell that reminded her of hams being smoked. Residual heat trapped in the floorboards warmed her soles. Odd bits of wall and furniture had survived the fire and she could make out scraps of paint and varnish on otherwise blackened wood. The fragments of familiarity hit her hard, a reminder of what she had lost.

Gwyneth wasn't here. The walls groaned as if in empathy. There was a scuffle up on the fragments of roof. A whisper of soot dropped on to her shoulders. Some bird disturbed at the destruction of its resting place.

"This place isn't safe," said Eleanor. "We should leave."

Megan turned. The countess had followed her inside. Water dripped from her cloak, soaking the ashes that carpeted the floor. The bow was now strapped to her back, but she kept her hand on the hilt of a short sword hanging from her waist. Her hood was still up, leaving just a hint of a pale face visible in the shadow.

"I'm not leaving until I've found her," said Megan.

"Who?"

"My sister."

"They'll have taken her with them."

"What?" said Megan. "Why? That doesn't make sense. Why cart her body around with them?"

"Body?" said Eleanor. "You think she's dead?"

"You think she's alive?"

"I . . ."

"She was in here. Holt called her name but she didn't get out, and I waited and waited and she still didn't come out. That's when I . . ."

"Ran?" said Eleanor.

Megan nodded. She recalled the witch at the ford, the one who had killed his compatriot rather than have him shoot her. "They were waiting for me. They wanted me alive. They wanted *us* alive."

"It would appear so."

"But why?"

"You must have heard what the witches do," said Eleanor.

Megan's stomach churned, and not just from morning sickness. She couldn't think about that. Gwyneth was alive. That's what she had to concentrate on. But if she was, it led to an awful implication. "I could have rescued her," she said. "I *should* have rescued her."

"There was nothing you could have done," said Eleanor, reaching out.

Megan knocked her away. "I should have tried!"

"You did the right thing."

"By saving my own skin?"

"If the roles had been reversed, what would you have wanted for your sister?" said Eleanor. "At least one of you got away."

It was the logic of a coward, impeccable but wrong. Megan had been the one person Gwyneth should have always been able to count on, but instead she had abandoned her. Somewhere out there, Gwyneth was suffering and wondering why Megan didn't come for her. There was only one thing to do now.

She stormed out of the mill and headed for the ford. Eleanor hurried after her. "Where are you going?"

Megan spun on her feet. She saw her grandfather's corpse out of the corner of her eye. She should bury him properly, but there were no tools to do so and she didn't have time. He would understand what she had to do.

"I failed Gwyneth once," she said. "I won't fail her again. I'm going to find her and rescue her, and God help anyone who tries to stop me."

# four

The coins lay where Megan had scattered them, among the trampled stalks. She interrupted the pouch from its dance with the breeze and scooped the coins into it, counting them off against the tally she had made in the cavern. She was three shillings down. There was only one place they could be. She screwed up her face and rolled the soldiers' corpses over. The silver winked as the sun caught it, a cheeky gesture as if this was nothing more than a game of hide-and-seek. Megan grabbed it and went to retrieve her sword.

She heard splashing and cursing. Eleanor had followed her across the ford and was now wringing water from her cloak. Before the priests abolished the aristocracy, the countess would have had servants to bear her across the river. Now she had to get wet with the rest of them.

"You really think you can take on the witches by yourself?"

Megan glanced at the dead soldiers. "I seem to be doing all right so far." She should check their bodies for supplies, but the thought of touching them again revolted her. Better to leave them here to rot. *Like you did to grandfather*, Gwyneth whispered to her.

"Oh, I forgot. You defeated them all in single combat."

"Thank you for your help, *my lady*." Megan slipped the sword into its scabbard. The belt began chafing again. "Do you want to be paid? Or do I have to kneel and accept you as my liege?"

"I want you to listen to reason. We can get help. Come with me to Eastport."

Megan knew what she was suggesting. The High Priest there, Father Galan, controlled a garrison of a thousand soldiers. They could deal with the witches—maybe—but it'd take a week to get to Eastport. "I don't have time," she said. "I don't know where they've take her, *why* they've taken her. I need to find her before I lose the trail."

"You'll get yourself killed."

"What's it to you?"

"Nothing," snapped Eleanor.

She stood there, her hooded face hidden in shadow, hand clenching and unclenching on her sword hilt. The priests had told many tales of the aristocracy's caprice. Had Megan angered the countess with one impertinent remark too many? She became all too aware of their relative sizes, their fighting abilities, the knowledge one more corpse among the slaughter would bother no one.

She backed off and headed to the village. After a few moments she heard feet squelching inside soaked boots as Eleanor hurried after her and drew level. They marched on silently.

"The men . . . The witches said something about horses," said Megan. "Have you seen any?"

Eleanor put her thumb and forefinger in her mouth. A whistle shrieked across the fields. From a distance came a faint whinnying. Along the Heledor, downstream from the destroyed bridge. Megan adjusted her direction.

They found two horses wandering by a small brook that trickled into the river, their ragged tails swatting at the flies that buzzed around them. Long reins secured them to the trunk of a tree winter storms ten years ago had uprooted. Their coats were rough and patchy, in desperate need of a groom. Burst blood vessels colored their eyes pink.

Megan edged toward them. One bared stained teeth. She shrank back.

"You ever ridden a horse?" asked Eleanor.

"Yes," said Megan, neglecting to specify just how many times, and classing ponies as horses. These beasts towered above her, their legs powerful and poised to kick her to death.

She stepped over the brook and approached the more docile of the pair, docile in that it hadn't tried to bite her head off. It tossed its head when she reached out to pet it, but it made no further attempt to drive her away. She stroked it. The horse was warm under her palm, a film of sweat covering its coat.

"Good boy."

"It's a girl," said Eleanor.

"You sure?"

"It's the world's unluckiest stallion if it's not."

"Oh." Megan patted the mare's neck. "Sorry."

Satisfied the horse was calm, she unhitched it and hooked her foot into the stirrup. Eleanor folded her arms, her body language that of a woman expecting humiliating failure. Megan wrenched her sword into a diagonal, bounced on her standing foot a couple of times, and hauled herself into the saddle. The mare bucked a little, throwing her forward into its matted mane. She clutched its neck. "Calm, calm."

The horse got over its initial antipathy and shuffled its hoofs. Megan tugged on the reins and gave the animal the gentlest of kicks to its ribs. The horse humored her by ambling over to the path by the river.

"Do you even know where you're going?" Eleanor called after her.

"Follow the road south."

"How do you know they didn't go north?"

"Why leave your horses on the wrong side of the river when you burn the bridge?" Besides, north led to Eastport and the massed ranks of the priests' soldiers. The road south was wilder and terminated at Trafford's Haven, the dead city, which promised resistance no fiercer than weeds or cockroaches.

Megan spurred the horse on, leaving Eleanor behind. It broke into a trot, jolting her in the saddle. She clamped her legs to its midriff, steadying herself, then dug her heels in. The animal broke into a gallop. Megan clung for dear life.

As the fear of being flung off and every bone broken faded, euphoria gripped Megan. The world sped by, the familiar environs of the village and the pain it now represented giving way to the unfamiliar of the world beyond. The wind whipped her hair and dried her tears. For a while she forgot everything and lost herself in the journey.

Ten minutes in, the horse slowed down, sometimes even stopping to munch at the grass and take in the scenery, its willingness to go beyond a canter becoming less and less as the miles ticked by. Megan's own tiredness caught up with her and she slumped in the saddle. The constant rasp of leather and the stirrups digging into her bare soles kept her awake, for now at least.

The road curved to the southwest as it cut its way through the forest, bringing the setting sun into view.

Megan closed her eyes to avoid the glare, but, once dropped, her lids proved too heavy to lift. She drifted off: back to the cavern, back to the forest, back to the mill. Gwyneth screamed. Megan slapped herself awake. How would a sleeping girl rescue her sister?

The day's heat fled the approaching night. Megan shivered. The bottom half of her tunic and her under-clothes hadn't completely dried after their repeated soakings and weren't likely to now. She reached a cross-roads, if that wasn't too fancy a term. The road that crossed hers was nothing more than a dirt track, and an overgrown one at that. Still, someone had seen fit to build an inn here—the Old Warrior, according to its peeling sign—a two-story stack on the verge of falling down. Light glowed from a couple of the dirty windows on the ground floor. A wisp of smoke snaking its way out of the chimney was just visible in the twilight. Megan fantasized about a warm fire and a soft bed.

The mare sauntered past the inn and pulled up outside a ramshackle stable. A decrepit pony was chewing on some hay with all the enthusiasm of a child faced with cold vegetables. It cast a disinterested eye toward the newcomers before resuming its mastication.

Megan knew she couldn't afford to stop. There was still light, time to make another mile or two. She pulled her horse away from the stable—wishing for once it hadn't obeyed her so readily—and plodded on down the road. She tried to lean forward and hug the horse's neck, to share its body heat, but the pommel dug into her belly so she had to sit upright, exposing herself to the cold air.

Hoofs clattered behind her. The prospect of fighting or running again provoked only desperate weariness. Had she overtaken the soldiers somehow? No, they'd been lying in wait for her, like they had in the village. How could she have been so stupid as to use the road? She should have stuck to the safety of the trees, even if it would have slowed her down.

Megan yanked the horse around and groped for her sword. It took her four attempts to get a grip on it. When she did manage to draw it, she didn't have the energy to hold it up one-handed and had to let it dangle by her side.

The silhouette of a hooded rider hove into view: Eleanor. She pulled her horse alongside—she had tamed the other at the brook, it would seem, though considering how long it had taken her to catch up, it hadn't been an easy process—and examined Megan.

"When did you last sleep?"

"I . . ." Megan might have dozed in the cavern, but before that? "Does it matter?"

"There's an inn half a mile back."

The reunited horses nuzzled each other, whinnying softly as if exchanging gossip. *I see you got the crazy one*, Megan imagined Eleanor's saying. "I've got to keep going. Gwyneth needs me."

"Until you drop? What good's that going to do?"

Megan dragged up the energy to sheathe her sword. "Why do you care, countess? Shouldn't you be off somewhere, I don't know, counting?"

"What about your horse? How much longer do you think it's going to last? It wasn't exactly fresh when you started."

"It's . . . She's . . ." Megan was too exhausted to argue anymore.

Eleanor wrapped a gloved hand around Megan's and gave the reins she was holding a tug. The horses began to clop in unison—back toward the Old Warrior.

The welcome at the inn was friendly inasmuch as the landlord didn't actually hit them with the cudgel he brandished in front of their faces. He had been warming himself at a meager fire when they had entered and his immediate response had been to back off and snatch up a club with rusty nails driven through it. Megan suspected the hospitality industry wasn't his natural calling.

There was no one else there. Tallow candles illuminated the smoky room. There was a stench of stale beer and rotting vegetables. A bar stretched the length of the wall opposite the fire, littered with greasy glasses and a bowl filled with the congealing remains of a stew. A miscellaneous regiment of bottles lined the shelves. Years of

grime had clouded the glass, but here and there finger-
prints revealed a glimmer of blue or green. There were
casks of ale too: some barely larger than Megan's head,
others large enough for her to hide in. Liquid dripped
from one of the taps, forming a slick on the dirty
floorboards.

"We want food and a room for the night," said Eleanor, tugging off her gloves.

"We ain't got no rooms," said the landlord. He was
a scrawny man with a bald pate that made him look
older than he was. Megan guessed from his age and the
inn's name he had fought in the war and had invested
his pay in this place as her grandfather had the mill.
A sensible decision had Trafford's Haven been rebuilt,
but it hadn't and he'd found himself in the middle of
nowhere.

"You're telling me this hovel is full up?"

The landlord shifted his weight. "Holiday season."
He shrugged and added, "Sorry," without even beginning to feign sincerity.

The room went silent until all that could be heard
was the crackling of the fire. Megan wanted nothing
more than to curl up in front of it.

"We can pay," said Eleanor.

The landlord's eyes flicked between them. "Don't
want any strangers."

"How do you hope to keep your business going?"

"Don't want any business."

Eleanor lowered her hood. The landlord swallowed and looked away, but his gaze kept drifting back to her. Eleanor was beautiful: smooth, white skin with a smattering of freckles across her nose and her high cheekbones; sapphire eyes that shone in the candlelight; copper tresses that tumbled down her neck; lips that promised kisses and laughter. If you'd asked Megan what a countess looked like, she couldn't have painted you a better picture.

"We're very tired and very cold and very hungry," said Eleanor, her voice soft and alluring. "We won't hurt you."

The landlord jabbed a finger at the weapons they were carrying. "You're not walking around like you're not going to hurt me."

"We have to defend ourselves," said Eleanor.

"The wi—" started Megan.

Eleanor placed a hand on her arm and cut her off with a shake of the head. "Can we stay, please?"

The landlord licked his lips. "One night," he said. "Five shillings."

Eleanor snorted. "Five shillings? I wouldn't buy this place for that, not even if you threw in a six-shilling rebate. We'll give you one. Our horses are in the stables."

"Horses?"

"Four legs. Go 'neigh.' Shit a lot."

"Three shillings."

"Two. And we want some clothes as well. For my . . ."

"Subject?" said Megan.

"... friend. You must have some left behind by guests who fled without paying the bill. Adulterers escaping avenging husbands—" she glanced at the stained tables —"murder victims ..."

"Might have a few odds and ends. Not for a girl though."

"That's fine. We didn't expect high fashion."

"I want the money in advance."

Eleanor nodded. "Of course."

She led Megan to the warmth of the fire, then bent over to whisper in her ear, "You'll have to pay the man."

"Why can't you?"

"Do I look like the kind of woman who has two shillings on her?"

"Why would you need to when you can get the peasantry to cough it up for you?"

Megan was too tired to care. She reached under her tunic and pulled out the pouch. She tried to open it carefully, but weariness played havoc with her coordination and she used too much force. The pouch fell from her hands, spilling the coins onto the floor. The landlord's eyes widened. He abandoned his club and dropped to his knees, retrieving the gold and silver with more enthusiasm than was strictly necessary.

He plonked the last of the coins into the pouch and handed it back to Megan. "And the rest," said Eleanor.

"What?"

"The five-shilling piece you palmed. We want it back."

The landlord's head darted to the side as he eyed up the distance to his cudgel. Eleanor's hand moved to her sword. "I'll have your guts steaming on the floorboards before you're halfway there."

"You wouldn't."

"It could only improve the decor of this place," said Eleanor. "And the smell. Did something die in here?"

"Hope," muttered Megan.

The landlord dove under a table. "Look what I've found," he said, crawling back out. A five-shilling piece glittered in his palm. Eleanor exchanged it for the two shillings he had been promised.

"Don't forget the horses," she said.

The landlord craned his head toward the door. "Bo—!" He checked himself. "I'll see to 'em myself."

He shuffled off. Megan and Eleanor sat close to the fire. Their table appeared to have been constructed by someone with only a passing acquaintance with the concept of carpentry, or even furniture.

"Why didn't you want me to tell him about the witches?" Megan asked.

"Do you think he would have let us stay if he'd known?"

"You don't think he deserves to be warned?"

"The witches have already passed. He's safe."

"What about everybody else?"

"The post horse'll be down here in a few days' time. They'll get their warning then."

"I suppose . . ."

Megan picked at a scar in the wood where some blade had gouged it. A splinter slipped under her fingernail. She winced and shook her hand.

"Here," said Eleanor. "Let me."

She took Megan's hand in her own, the aristocratic paleness of her skin contrasting with Megan's peasant olive. She examined the wounded finger. A sliver of wood was visible in the candlelight. Eleanor plucked it out with her teeth, making Megan shudder as her lips brushed her fingertips.

"Why are you doing this?"

"You don't want it getting infected."

"No," said Megan. "Helping me."

"I'd be camping on open ground if it weren't for your generosity."

That wasn't it. If she'd wanted money she could have helped herself or taken it by force. They stared into the flames, listening to the distant thumps of the landlord going about his business, until Eleanor spoke up again. "Everyone in Ainsworth is my responsibility."

"We're back to the countess thing?"

"I have to protect my people."

"No, you don't," said Megan. "You have no people. The priests abolished you." The priests had used winning the war as evidence they should rule the Realm as well as tending to its spiritual needs and providing the administration. Did not the first Pledge of Faith demand obedience to God and them? The aristocracy's titles had been declared void, their lands forfeit, the link with Edwyn the Unifier severed.

"If the priests abolished winter, would that stop the cold? If they abolished the moon, would that stop the tides?" Eleanor jabbed at the fire with an iron poker, coaxing a little more life from it. "My father taught me our titles meant duty, not power. We have to help those under our care, not exploit them."

It wasn't what the priests taught. "That's . . ."

"Idealistic?" Eleanor forced out a laugh. "My father was all about ideals. He preached them every day but was too scared to put them into practice. He was convinced the priests would have our heads if we dared show our faces, so we skulked in the mountains for forty years, convincing ourselves it was good enough to know what the right thing was."

Forty? Megan snuck a glance across the bench. There were small lines at the corners of Eleanor's mouth and eyes, strands of steel in the copper of her hair. Yes, maybe that old.

"What changed?" she asked. "Why did you . . . ?"

"My father died."

"Oh."

"I inherited another bunch of empty titles. I didn't want them to remain empty, so I decided to explore my ancestors' lands, help wherever I could. There might be no lands or castles, but I'd be doing something." Eleanor shrugged. "Besides, I was beginning to talk to myself."

"What about your mother?"

"She died not long after I was born."

"The war?"

Eleanor swatted away a fly that buzzed in her face. "When the witches routed the king's army, they descended on Eastport. My nanny smuggled me out of the palace while my mother distracted the witches."

"What did they do to her?" asked Megan.

"I hope to God I never find out."

"Then what the hell are we sitting here chatting for?" said Megan. Fear and adrenalin jolted her to her feet. "Do you want what happened to your mother to happen to Gwyneth?"

Eleanor yanked her back to her seat. "Of course I don't," she said. "And do not use my mother as an excuse to do something stupid ever again."

Megan saw the fire in the countess's eyes, and the pain she tried to conceal. She hung her head and stared at the dusty floorboards. "I'm sorry," she mumbled.

The landlord brought in two earthenware bowls filled with a stew. It looked to be a concoction of barley and root vegetables, not so much cooked as boiled into submission until it formed a thick gray sludge. Black flakes were sprinkled in it: herbs if Megan was feeling generous; the burned remains of a hundred other dinners if she wasn't. She tried a spoonful. She'd eaten worse, though only as a dare. But at least it was hot, and the energy it gave her would give her the strength to go after Gwyneth.

Eleanor lifted her spoon out of the stew. It came free with a *plop*. "Is there any meat in this?"

"No," said the landlord. "Got some barbequed squirrel if you want."

"I'll pass."

They ate and drank the beer the man poured for them—Eleanor warned Megan it'd be safer than the water. The warmth returned to Megan's body but unfortunately so did feeling. Where she didn't ache she stung, and where she didn't sting she throbbed. Part of her wanted to step back out into the night and let the cold air numb her mind and her body once more.

The landlord fetched a crate filled with rags. It was the clothes they had asked for, slashed and torn and smelling of old sweat. None of the garments was wearable in its own right, but by doubling up and folding Megan was able to ensure none of her skin was exposed to the elements. Eleanor shooed the landlord out while Megan changed. She found a pair of boots made of cracked leather and padded them with strips of underclothes until they fit snugly around Megan's feet.

"Do you want to talk about what happened?" said Eleanor. "Back in Thicketford."

"No."

"It'll help."

No, it wouldn't. To talk about it, Megan would have to remember, and if she remembered it would cripple her, and how would that help Gwyneth?

"I'm going to find a bed," she said. Eleanor's insistence on always being right was beginning to grate. It reminded Megan of Gwyneth's bouts of bossiness, but at least her sister had earned those.

"I'll wake you at first light," said Eleanor.

"Make it before," said Megan. "We'll need breakfast before we go."

"We have to eat in this place twice?"

Megan climbed the stairs. It was dark on the landing. Icy drafts stung her skin and every step prompted a groan from stressed floorboards. She tried a door at random and found a musty room illuminated by the moon. There was a bed shoved against a wall, old and rickety, with the blankets in a crumpled heap at its foot. The mattress was packed with straw and when Megan pressed down on it there was a faint squelch. She spread the blankets across it and collapsed on top of them, curling herself into a ball.

Pressing her arms across her belly, she thought about the baby growing inside her. Her grandfather would have loved a new child around the mill. If Megan got through this alive, she'd name the child after him, unless it was a girl, in which case Gwyneth would no doubt insist it be named after her. She smiled as she imagined her sister muscling in on the raising of the child. Gwyneth would be more a father than an aunt, certainly more of a father than Wade would have been. No, that was unfair. Wade might have come around. He was still at the panicking stage and, unlike Megan, he could escape the child.

Megan fell into an uneasy sleep. The soldiers came again, only this time they were eight feet tall and their eyes burned red. Her grandfather died again and again; Wade rocked his decapitated head in his arms before getting tired and throwing it away; Gwyneth screamed for someone to save her. Megan kept chasing after her sister, but she was always out of reach. Her legs gave way, reducing her to a crawl. The men were on top of her, raking her with thorns. Fetid breath prickled her skin, fat fingers pawed at her.

The last wasn't a dream. Megan's eyes snapped open. The landlord was on top of her. He had a dagger against her face.

# five

Megan's skin crawled as the landlord patted her down. She wanted to hit him, throw him off, but her body was still stuck in sleep and refused to obey her bidding. Sword—where was the sword? Downstairs with Eleanor. She was defenseless.

Coins tinkled as the landlord slapped the purse that now lay beneath two layers of clothing. He grunted and searched for a way under her jerkin. The too-large garment had been secured with a leather belt, and as the landlord fumbled with the buckle it became obvious he wasn't going to release it with only one hand. He slipped the dagger between his teeth and brought the other hand into play. Megan found the will to strike. She grabbed the dagger and jerked. The blade ripped into flesh, slicing into the corner of the man's mouth. He howled. Warm droplets splattered onto Megan's face.

She squirmed out from under him and tumbled onto the floor. He made a grab for her. She swiped at him with the knife. He cried out as the point raked across his palm. Megan scrambled for the door. Her feet flew from under her as the landlord shoved the bed into the back of her legs. She smacked into the hard floorboards, the impact jarring the knife from her hand.

The landlord scurried over to her. Moonlight caught his face. Blood trickled from his cut mouth, as if he had just feasted on flesh. Megan kicked him in the shins. He backhanded her across the cheek, making her head spin, then started to pull at her clothes.

"Where's . . . the . . . gold . . . ?" he said, every syllable followed by the sucking of saliva.

The dagger lay just within Megan's reach. She stretched for it. The landlord shoved up her jerkin, exposing the bare skin of her stomach and the hidden money pouch. Spindly fingers tugged at the knot.

Acting on instinct, Megan whipped the knife around and drove it into the man's arm. He shrieked, his face contorting in pain as he wrenched it out. Blood pumped from the torn flesh. He staunched the wound with his palm and sank to the floor. He started sobbing.

Megan stared at him, panting as she got her breath back. He was a pathetic bloody mess; a pathetic bloody mess she had made. She swallowed and took a step toward him. "Are you . . . ? Are you all right?" The landlord struck out at her, swinging the knife in a wild arc. Megan jumped back.

She stumbled downstairs. The remains of the fire cast long shadows, picking out edges in a dull red. Megan's sword was propped up against the crate containing the rags even her desperation hadn't made her wear. Eleanor was slumped over one of the tables, a flagon by her elbow. Megan sniffed the liquid inside. The fumes made her head swim.

Eleanor's head lolled from side to side as Megan pulled her upright and slapped her. Eleanor groaned. Her eyelids fluttered. She mumbled something unintelligible.

"Come on, your countessness. We need to get out of here."

Eleanor wiped her mouth on the back of her hand. "Just as I was getting fond of the place," she slurred, her breath thick with alcohol.

Megan tugged her up. "Can you walk?"

"Sure. My father taught me. See . . ." She took a step forward and swooned. Megan caught her just in time.

"What have you been drinking?"

"Don't know, but I want some more."

Eleanor lurched for the flagon. Megan smacked her hand away. "You've had enough." Footsteps clomped down the stairs. "The landlord's going to be here any minute, and when he does he's going to be . . . pointing a crossbow at us."

The landlord was stood in the doorway, eyes burning with rage, his skin pale and experimenting with green in places. He had torn a strip from his tunic and bandaged his wounded arm with it. There was nothing he could do for his cut mouth though. Blood continued to dribble down his chin.

"I see you had the squirrel," said Eleanor. She leaned forward and peered at the landlord's weapon. "Crossbow?" She flicked her hand. "Peasant's weapon. Takes forever to load. Longer even. Get yourself a good longbow." She looked at Megan, her brow creasing. "Why is he pointing a crossbow at us anyway? Did I miss something?"

"The gold," slobbered the landlord. "Now."

"Or?" said Eleanor. She drew her sword and brandished it, a threat that might have been impressive had she any control over the weapon.

The landlord jiggled the crossbow and sidled behind the bar. Megan reached under her jerkin for the purse. "I think we should give him the money."

"Nonsense. We're not going . . . We're not going to be robbed by him. He's *awful*. Who robs two people with a one-shot weapon?" Eleanor went pale, quite a feat considering her complexion. "I think I'm going to be . . ."

She bent over the corner of a table and retched. Vomit splatted onto the floorboards. Megan couldn't help but notice it looked exactly like the stew the landlord had served.

"Are you all right?" she asked.

Eleanor held up a finger then threw up once more.

"That was ladylike."

Eleanor wiped her mouth on her sleeve and pushed herself upright. She clutched her stomach. "I am always ladylike. I'm Eleanor, Countess of Ainsworth, Baroness of . . . lots of places."

The landlord waved his crossbow. Eleanor regarded Megan with bleary eyes. "What's happening again?"

"He's trying to rob us."

"Why?"

"He wants to get out of here."

"Don't blame him. This place is a dive. Look at that pile of sick there. Disgusting."

"He wants to get away from the witches."

"How does he—"

"Put the sword down and the money on the table," said the landlord.

Eleanor looked at the short sword in her hand, then across to the landlord, who was half obscured by the bar. "You're right. Sword's no good in a situ . . . in a sit . . . in these conditions." She sheathed the blade, then slipped her hand beneath her sleeve. "You need something with a bit more range."

She whipped her arm out. There was a flash of steel as a knife hurtled toward the landlord, too fast to dodge. He didn't need to. It clinked on the bottles behind him and clattered to the floor.

"Damn. I can never get the knack of throwing knives."

Megan was anticipating the landlord's response even before his knuckles whitened. She grabbed Eleanor by the shoulders and pulled her to the ground behind the table. There was a *thrum* and a *thwack* as a crossbow bolt flew over their heads and embedded itself in the floorboards. As if the world didn't hate her enough, now she had a homicidal landlord and an aristocrat out of her head on booze to deal with. She would have laughed if the situation wasn't so desperate.

They poked their heads above the table. The landlord was fumbling with his crossbow, trying to set another bolt in it. "Told you," said Eleanor. The landlord threw the crossbow at her. She ducked just in time.

Bottles followed the crossbow and shattered all around them as the man hurled the contents of his shelves at them. Megan's cheek stung as a shard caught her. She buried her head in her arms and crawled under the table, sweeping away the worst of the broken glass.

The landlord's aim grew wilder. One bottle smashed into the fire. The flames shot up as they drank its contents. Another bottle scattered burning embers over floorboards soaked with fuel. A dozen fires sprung up. The crate of rags began to smolder. Wisps of smoke wafted from the scabbard of the sword Megan had leaned against it.

No, she wasn't going to lose it. It was the only connection she had left with her grandfather. He had stashed it knowing his granddaughters might need it one day, and she had been through too much to abandon it. She crawled over to it. A bottle whizzed past and shattered on the side of the crate. There was a *whump* as wood and cloth erupted into flames. Megan yelped and made a grab for the sword. Too hot. She pulled her sleeve down over her hand and made another attempt. Bearable this time.

Megan drew the sword. The landlord's throwing arm halted midstroke. He had an opponent who was both armed and sober, and who had already showed no compunction in acting against him. Megan charged him, forcing his hand. He dropped the bottle he was about to fling and disappeared under the bar. Megan's momentum carried her into the wooden barrier, the impact winding her. She swung the sword up two-handed to protect herself from the expected blow but none came. She craned over the bar. The landlord really had disappeared. She frowned, wondering what was going on, then noticed the trapdoor. He had fled to the cellar. Fine by her.

Flames were claiming the inn. Smoke billowed up, making Megan's eyes water. She sheathed the sword and dropped to her hands and knees. Where was Eleanor? Coughing, she crawled back to the table. The countess was curled up under it, her snores audible over the crackling of the fires. Megan yanked her hair. She woke with a yelp.

Keeping low, Megan half led, half dragged Eleanor across the inn. The flames cackled at their retreat. Smoke invaded Megan's lungs, smothering the precious air contained inside. Megan's head swam. Her vision blurred, separating into two distinct images. She tripped and smacked into the floorboards. They were seductively warm. Megan rested her cheek against them. She didn't want to get up.

Tugging forced her to move again. She grabbed Eleanor's proffered arm and lurched the final few yards to the exit. There was an ominous groan. Megan rolled out of the way just as a flaming timber crashed down from the ceiling and blocked the route to the door.

They needed another way out. Megan looked around. It was getting too smoky to see. If this place had a back entrance, they'd never find it. From what she remembered of the windows, they were too small to crawl through. They were trapped. They would burn alive with the landlord.

Wait—the cellar. It'd open to the outside to allow deliveries. Spluttering, Megan hauled Eleanor to the bar and felt her way around it until she found the gap that led behind it. She yanked the trapdoor open and bundled Eleanor down the stone steps that led down to the cellar. She followed, slamming the trap shut behind them.

The air was clearer down in the basement. Megan bent over and coughed up the poison smothering her lungs. She wiped the tears streaming from her eyes. Blades of orange light sliced down between the gaps in the floorboards. The way out should be . . .

She screamed and scurried back. There was a man tied to a table. His face was contorted in agony. The star-broken circle had been carved into his forehead. His ribcage had been ripped apart and his insides scooped out. Bloated flies crawled around the exposed cavity. A thick black gloop glistened on the floor underneath.

Now it was Megan's turn to throw up. Sour vomit burned her already raw throat. She had slept over that? She had eaten over it? Her stomach lurched again.

A shaft of light at the far end of the cellar indicated the exit she had hoped for. Unfortunately, the eviscerated body was between them and it. She groped for Eleanor and pulled her to her feet. Hugging the wall, they edged their way through the cellar. Above their heads, the fire continued to crackle away. Wisps of smoke hugged the low ceiling. Any moment now, she expected the corpse to strain against its bonds, plead to be rescued from its torment.

Megan tripped over something, only just managing to keep her footing. The reflection of the flames danced in the gilt of a book title: *The True History of the Witches* by Brother Deogol. She grabbed it and kept running.

They reached the end of the cellar. The two women raced up the steep ramp and flung themselves outside. They collapsed onto the road. The night air was fresh and cold and sweet relief to Megan's clogged airways. She rolled onto her back and stared up at the stars, taking deep breaths and giving thanks to God.

A repeated banging made her lift her head. The stable door was open and slamming into the wall of the inn. Inside it was empty. Megan staggered over to Eleanor, who was dry-heaving into a ditch.

"The horses ran away!"

"Don't think I'm in a fit state to ride anyway," said Eleanor.

"We have to go after them."

"Or walk." Eleanor held her head in her hands. "I feel awful."

"*You* feel awful. Do you know how I feel?"

"No, but I've got a suspicion you're going to tell me. You haven't seen a willow tree, have you?"

"A what?" said Megan. "Get up. We have to get the horses back."

"That landlord will have nicked one, the others, well . . ." Eleanor looked at Megan with hooded eyes. "You know the chances of catching up with a spooked horse?"

"Zero?"

"Not even that much." Eleanor used Megan to haul herself to her feet and then as a prop to keep herself vertical. "We might get lucky. They might be around the corner, grazing. Animals get easily dis . . ." She sniffed. "Why do you smell of feet?"

It was the scavenged clothes, whose odor wasn't improving with the wearing. "Does it matter?" Megan asked. "Will you focus?"

"I would if I could. I feel strange. Fantastic and awful at the same time."

"Have you never been drunk bef . . . ?" Megan started to ask and then realized. "Oh, Saviors, you haven't, have you?"

"My father wouldn't have approved." She pointed to the book in Megan's hand. "What've you got there?" Megan showed her. The countess grimaced. "*The True History of the Witches*? I'm more of a romance girl, myself."

The book fell open at a page showing a woodcut of two horned demons cavorting around a disemboweled victim. Megan flicked through a few more pages. The images of screaming victims made her skin crawl. That was what they wanted Gwyneth for? Please, no. Please God, no.

"Why . . . ?"

"The witches want to make the Faithful suffer, to make them abandon God or send them to Him." Eleanor plucked the book out of her hands and hurled it into the burning inn. "I don't think that's going to do you any good."

"The landlord? He was a witch?"

"That or he was currying favor."

Megan pointed in the direction of the cellar and its grisly contents. "By . . . ?"

"I'm not sure the witches would have settled for a discount on their room and a free breakfast." Eleanor groaned and squeezed her temples. "They left him alone for some reason."

"Perhaps he hid."

"Perhaps."

Megan looked down the road, stretching out to blackness. They had to keep going after the witches, after Gwyneth. With any luck, they'd come across a village, somewhere they could buy another ride.

Megan and Eleanor walked for hours after leaving the Old Warrior—mile upon countless mile until they had come across the next village—and realized that the only way they'd get another ride was if they harnessed rats. Halliwell was nothing more than a hamlet, half a dozen cottages clustered around a bend in the river. The houses had been ransacked, their inhabitants reduced to corpses. The air was thick with the buzzing of flies and the sweet stench of rotting meat. A little way from the dwellings, Megan came across a teenage girl sprawled in a pool of dried blood, the remnants of a posy scattered by her hand. Her features were set in state of bewilderment. She hadn't been scared by what happened to her, just confused.

Eleanor was slumped at the base of the tree, hood up and facing away from the village, perhaps so she wouldn't have to confront the horrors. She was chewing on bark. Woody saliva dribbled down her chin. Sometimes she found the energy to wipe it away.

Megan collapsed beside her. Her feet were raw, throbbing in time to her heartbeat.

"Why?"

"The witches worship death," said Eleanor. "Why they couldn't do it in the form of suicide is beyond me." She proffered the bark at Megan. "Willow?"

Megan shook her head. "There's a dead girl back there. Pretty. My age."

"Poor thing."

"Why didn't the witches take *her*?"

"I don't know," said Eleanor.

They must have been wrong about the witches wanting Megan and Gwyneth alive. It didn't make any sense. Other girls in Thicketford were dead too. And Gwyneth could have nipped into Thicketford while Megan was meeting Wade; Megan could have passed her body without knowing it. This could be a fool's quest, a way to assuage her conscience and stop herself going crazy. No, she couldn't think about that; she couldn't give up on her sister. Not while there was still a chance.

"We should think about breakfast," said Eleanor. "I wonder if they left any food back there."

"I'm surprised you can think about food in your state."

"I meant for you."

Megan had spotted the butchered remains of a few farm animals in the village. The meat would have spoiled by now. "I'm not sure I want to go back."

"Me neither. But if we're to keep going, you have to eat and there's not much this far south since the sack of Trafford's Haven." Even less in the aftermath of the witches. "Take your opportunities when you get them."

She struggled to her feet and held out a hand. Megan patted it away. "I'll manage."

Eleanor swayed and fell against the tree. "I won't."

The witches had stripped the village like a plague of locusts, but Megan and Eleanor were able to scavenge a few supplies—a jar of olives, some stale bread, a couple of cured sausages, a few oranges—which Eleanor stuffed into a blanket she formed into a makeshift pack. She suggested Megan find some better clothes than the smelly rags she was wearing, but Megan refused. Perishable goods were one thing; helping herself to a dead girl's clothes was too much like grave robbery. She didn't object, however, when Eleanor spied a cloak hanging on a door hook and draped it over her shoulders.

They resumed their journey, unsure if they were even going in the right direction, never mind if they would catch up with the soldiers, though Eleanor occasionally poked at a pile of dung on the road and declared it fresh. The road became more and more unkempt as they traveled south. Weeds pushed their way through the packed dirt, and the trees reached out to form a canopy across the highway. Sap oozed from dismembered branches. Someone had been there recently, slashing a way through the low-hanging vegetation.

A path branched off from the road, not something intentionally laid but formed by the tramping of feet. Eleanor considered it for a moment, then started down it. Megan frowned—it wasn't wide enough to accommodate the soldiers' horses—but she followed the countess anyway.

The path rose, gentle at first but becoming ever steeper. The muscles in Megan's legs burned and the effort made her woozy. Some of the trees were already shedding their summer finery, and brittle leaves fluttered around them like amber snowflakes. Squirrels and birds scampered in the undergrowth, harvesting food and bedding for the oncoming winter.

They reached the top and broke out into a clearing. The withered stumps told Megan this was a man-made clearing, not natural, and when she looked around she could understand why. You could see for miles. The forest spread around them, the tops of the trees forming a multicolored mattress bisected by the just discernible ribbon of the road they had traveled. To the south, the Endalayans stretched across the horizon, their peaks smothered in cloud; beyond them lay Andaluvia, the desert lands of the Sandstriders, who had seceded from the Realm after the death of the Unifier. To the west lay the Harris Sea, at this range a shimmering blue expanse. And there, between the forest and the coast, a few miles up from where the mountains dropped into the sea, huddled the remains of Trafford's Haven.

The city had been built sixty or seventy years ago. It had been intended to protect the southwest corner of Ainsworth from Sandstrider pirates, but instead had provided a handy one-stop establishment for all the pirates' pillaging needs. That was until the witches had come. They had made their last stand here, besieged by the priests' army. They, like the city, had perished in an orgy of blood and fire. Now no smoke rose from its chimneys, no ships moored at its jetties, no people trod its streets. It was a corpse inhabited by corpses.

Eleanor nudged Megan and pointed out activity on the beach between the dead city and the Endalayans. Black spots darted across the sand like flies. A smudge marred the surface of the shimmering water—a ship anchored a couple of miles offshore.

"Is that them?"

"I guess so."

Megan strained her eyes, trying to make out whether any of the figures scurrying across the sand was Gwyneth. They were too far away to distinguish anything but their number. A couple of dozen or so. Were these the only surviving witches, or were more lurking out there?

Eleanor folded her cloak underneath her and sat on the scrubby grass. She pulled an orange out of her pack and split the skin with her thumbnail.

Megan couldn't believe she could be so calm. "We have to go!"

"We need to stop flapping around. We'll draw attention to ourselves. And when I say *we*, I really mean *you*."

Megan crouched. "But—"

"That camp's miles away. I don't think a few minutes' rest will make a difference." She ripped a length of peel off the orange, spraying juice into the air. "Besides, we don't want to get there too early."

"How can we be too early?"

"If they can see us sneaking around in the daylight. Or were you planning a full-frontal assault in the glare of the afternoon sun?"

Megan hadn't thought that far ahead because she had never thought she would have to. Now she was in sight of her quarry her stomach sank. She didn't have a clue how to rescue Gwyneth. How had she ever thought she would have the courage to execute her non-plan?

"I preferred you when you were drunk."

"*I* preferred me when I was drunk."

Megan stretched out and stared up into the sky. Raptors rode the thermals, some squawking to one another, others silent as they scoured the skies for prey. She wondered if they had lost anyone and, if they had, would they even remember. Life would be so much simpler without the concept of loss, but without it, could you have love?

Eleanor twisted her orange into two halves and handed one over. Megan sat up to eat. She peeled off a segment of the fruit and popped it into her mouth. It exploded when she bit into it, filling her mouth with sweet juice and kicking her brain back to life.

"What do you suggest we do?" she asked.

"We'll have to stay off the road from now on," said Eleanor. "They'll have scouts posted."

"Scouts?"

"I ran into one outside Thicketford. He managed to get a warning off before I could deal with him. We'll find a nice hidden spot to observe them, see if we can find your sister, then . . ."

Megan had stopped listening. Her attention was fixed on the beach. The column of smoke was fading. The dots were swarming and gathering at the water's edge. A black blob pushed into the sea, disturbing the blue—a landing craft heading for the anchored ship.

The witches were leaving, taking Gwyneth away. And Megan had no chance of following.

# six

Megan crashed through the forest, arms and legs pumping as she called on reserves she didn't have. The trees fought back: branches whipped her face, roots attempted to trip her. She dodged when she could, took the punishment when she couldn't. She had to keep going, she had to. Not everyone had got on to the landing craft—at least half had been left behind. Maybe Gwyneth was one of them. Maybe they were waiting for the craft to come back and pick them up. Maybe she could distract the witches long enough for Gwyneth to make an escape. What would she do once they set sail? Swim the high seas?

She stumbled back out onto the road and paused to get her bearings. Her stomach took advantage of the respite to lurch. The orange came back, burning a bittersweet trail up her throat. Megan bent over, hands on her knees, coughing and retching. A cramp twisted her insides. Her legs started to buckle. She had miles to go but nothing left to give. *I'm sorry, Gwyneth.*

Thunder rumbled, intensifying with every second. Megan lifted her head. Horses approached from the west, from the beach. Still hundreds of yards off, but they'd be on her within a minute. She had to move before they saw her. Her abused body refused to obey. Maybe they would capture her rather than kill her. At least that way she'd see Gwyneth again.

Someone grabbed her and yanked her into the trees, too quick for Megan to register a protest even if she'd had the energy to. A pale hand clamped over her mouth. A body pressed into hers and dragged her to the ground.

Eleanor spread herself across Megan. They watched through the gaps in the undergrowth as horses galloped past. The sound of hoofs faded, then suddenly dropped off. There was a steady *clip-clop, clip-clop*. One of the horses was coming back.

The mount drew level with where Megan and Eleanor were hiding. It turned in a slow, deliberate circle, snorting and panting. Megan could make out the bottom half: legs spattered with mud and sand; the boots of its rider coated likewise; sun flashing off a dangling ax head. Her heart thumped hard enough to hammer a hole in the ground beneath her. How hidden could they be? The horseman must be able to see the disturbance in the undergrowth, hear their quickened breathing. Only Eleanor's weight on top of her prevented her from running.

There was a whinny and the horse galloped off. Only when the clatter of hoofs had been replaced by silence did Eleanor roll off Megan. Megan felt vulnerable again, robbed of the intimate protection the older woman had afforded her. She stretched and pushed herself to her feet. Her muscles objected, but didn't rebel.

"They're going after me, aren't they?" said Megan. Off to help their comrades in Thicketford. Not many of them, but how many men did you need to handle a confused, frightened girl?

Eleanor neither confirmed nor denied Megan's suspicions. "They're gone now. We need . . ."

"Wha—?"

Eleanor pressed a finger to Megan's lips, silencing her. She drew her sword. Megan nodded and heaved her own out of its scabbard. The heavy steel dragged her arm to the ground, kicking up dead leaves.

Eleanor pushed Megan behind her and waved her sword, as if the blade could cut away the forest obscuring her vision. Megan strained her senses, trying to discern the intruder Eleanor thought she had detected.

"Drop your weapons."

The women tensed, knuckles whitening as they clenched their weapons. "Please tell me your voice just broke," said Eleanor.

"I think there's a man," said Megan.

"Uh-huh."

"Behind us."

"It's that kind of tactical awareness that gives me grounds for optimism."

"Drop your weapons and get on your knees."

Eleanor let her sword fall to the ground and gestured to Megan to do the same. The two women knelt. Eleanor placed her hands on her head, then slipped them beneath her sleeves. Megan copied her.

The man tramped through the undergrowth until he was standing in front of them. His eyes were bloodshot and circled with dark rings, his skin like a leather jerkin to which someone had taken offense. His black armor matched that of the soldiers who had desecrated Megan's home, and he had discarded his helmet to reveal hair that looked as if it had been hacked through with a knife. A tattoo of the star-broken circle, the sigil of the witches, snaked out from under his collar.

He slipped the flat of his ax under Eleanor's chin. The blade was speckled with dried blood. He bent forward to get a better look at her, his brow furrowing. Eleanor's hand shifted beneath her sleeve. The soldier moved in a little closer.

Eleanor whipped a knife out and jabbed at the witch soldier's face. He jerked out of her range. She made to thrust again. This time he caught her wrist in his free hand and smashed it with the shaft of his ax. Eleanor cried out and dropped the knife.

Megan snatched her dropped sword and swung, hard as she could. A *ting* echoed through the forest as she struck the plate protecting his chest, the impact jarring her arms enough to make her drop the sword. The soldier grabbed her collar and pulled her close. Megan raised her hand to strike him. His fist jabbed into her face. She went down, spitting blood.

The soldier shoved Eleanor down onto her front. She tried to scramble to her feet, but he placed his boot between her shoulder blades and pinned her to the ground. He scraped the copper hair away from her neck with the edge of his ax. The veins beneath her reddened skin fluttered at an alarming pace.

The soldier took his ax in both hands and raised it above his shoulders. Megan looked around, frantic. Eleanor's throwing knife glinted among the dead leaves. She snatched it up and hurled it at the man. It struck him in the eye—handle first, but it was enough to distract him. Eleanor bucked, throwing him off. He stumbled and flailed, slicing the air.

Eleanor scurried to her sword. She grabbed it and pushed herself up into a crouch. The soldier advanced on her, ax held across his body. One eye burned fierce; the other was red from where Megan had hit it. He came within range and brought down his weapon. Eleanor was already rolling away, her own weapon swinging in a graceful arc. The blade slashed him above the knees. He arced his back and cried out, dropping his guard.

Eleanor pivoted and thrust. The point of her sword opened up the soldier's cheek. He fell to his knees. Eleanor stood above him and prepared to administer a final blow.

The soldier turned his gaze to Megan. "Stop resisting," he said. He cupped his palm to his cheek to staunch the blood pumping from the wound. "You cannot escape your fate, Megan."

Megan froze at the sound of her own name. They knew who she was. Had they come to Thicketford especially for her? Was she the reason they had taken Gwyneth? Was she the reason everyone else was dead?

Before Megan could speak, Eleanor brought her sword crashing down on the soldier's skull, silencing him forever.

Eleanor started to drag the soldier's body away from the road. Megan was still too numb to move, the questions in her head demanding all her attention.

"How did he know my name?"

"I don't know," said Eleanor. "Perhaps Gwyneth told them. Are you going to give me a hand?"

Megan grabbed the soldier's legs. "What if they were—"

"Speculating is not going to help your sister, is it?" snapped Eleanor.

Maybe it wasn't, but Megan couldn't help it, albeit now in silence. They relieved the soldier of his provisions and scattered leaves and branches over his body. He'd be hard to spot. If it was dark. And you were drunk. And blind in one eye, or preferably both. It would have to do. There was no time to dig a grave. Not that the bastard deserved one.

They trudged through the forest, keeping to the trees but close enough to the road to navigate by it. A path branched, its patchy grass showing signs of being recently trampled. Eleanor drew her sword and led the way down it. Megan struggled against tiredness to keep her senses alert for the approach of soldiers. None came. There was only the chatter of birds and the roar of distant waves.

They reached the edge of the forest. Eleanor nudged Megan to her belly. They crawled the rest of the way, aiming for the faint plume of smoke that reached for the heavens. Trees and dirt gave way to sand, level ground to an incline. They dragged themselves up the dune. It wasn't far but it was hard work. The sand kept resisting their attempt to get a hold, going from solid to liquid in the time it took for them to squeeze their fingers.

They reached the top. Eleanor placed a cautionary hand on Megan's shoulder. Megan nodded, indicating she had understood the warning, and together the two women peeked over the dune. A desolate beach sloped down to the water's edge. Out to sea, the sun brushed the horizon, taking with it its twin gifts of light and heat.

They must have gotten disoriented, come too far north, too far south. No, there were the remnants of a fire, continuing to smolder, piles of dung from the horses, tracks in the sand leading to the sea. The soldiers had already sailed, taking Gwyneth with them.

Megan started to get to her feet. Eleanor pulled her down again. "They may have left someone behind," she said.

"I don't care," said Megan. She plucked Eleanor's hand away and staggered out on to the beach. Foaming water worked at the sand, smoothing it out into a uniform plane, cleaning away the evidence of the soldiers' presence. It could clean her too, if she gave herself to it. Absolution in exchange for her life. An easy bargain. Why did she want her life anyway?

Would God accept the sacrifice if she offered it, exchange Gwyneth's life for hers? If she could be sure, Megan would gladly do it, but as always with God, it was hard to separate His desires from her own. The sea offered her an easy way out, and surely that was what she wanted rather than Him?

A voice disturbed her thoughts. Megan thought it was Eleanor until she realized it was male.

"Hey! Over here!"

She turned around. A head lay on the beach, about a hundred yards away. It was shouting at her.

# seven

Megan inched toward the head, one hand stretched back, hovering over her sword. What the hell was it? Her grandfather had told tales of the witches bringing the dead back to life to serve in their armies, but why reanimate just a head? Did they hope to terrify their enemies with the prospect of nipped ankles?

"Please tell me there's a body under there," said Eleanor, advancing with her own weapon drawn, "otherwise I'm going to freak out."

Coming closer, it became clear that a man had been buried in the sand up to his neck. He looked eighteen or so, with a light tan and a few days' worth of blond stubble peppering his face and shaved head. His nose had a kink in it: an old break, Megan guessed. The setting sun glinted in his eyes, a burned orange contrasting with their pale green.

"What are you doing in there?" said Eleanor.

The man looked down. "Not much," he said in a northern accent.

"You're not from round here."

The man jerked his head at the incoming tide. "Is this really the time for xenophobia?"

"You're being very evasive."

The man looked to Megan. "Please get me out of here."

Eleanor smoothed the back of her cloak and sat down. "There's no rush."

"That's not a position I necessarily agree with."

Each surge brought the sea a few more inches closer to them. The water would be lapping their feet in minutes. "I think we should . . ." Megan started.

Eleanor shook her head. "Who buried you here?"

"It was just a lark, a prank taken a little too far."

"Why did the witches bury you here?"

"Don't be crazy. There's no witches. Not anymore. They perished at Trafford's Haven. Everyone knows that."

"There's a prophecy the witches will return," said Eleanor.

"What prophecy?" said the man. "Look, whoever did this, they're not coming back. You've got no reason to be frightened. I, on the other hand . . ."

Megan was only half listening. The idea the man might know about Gwyneth dominated her thoughts.

She knelt down in front of him. "Soldiers did this to you, right? Soldiers in black armor?" The man nodded. "Did they have a girl with them?"

"A girl?"

"My size. My age. She would have looked a bit like me." Although they weren't identical twins, Megan and Gwyneth could arrange themselves to pass for the other, enough to fool anyone who wasn't their grandfather. "Did you see her? Was she . . . ?" Megan couldn't bring herself to use the word "alive."

"There was a girl, yes."

"What happened to her?"

"They took her with them," said the man. "I think."

"You think?"

"I was kind of occupied at the time."

"Where did they go?" said Megan.

"I don't know; they didn't leave an itinerary. Look, I've answered your questions. Can you please—"

"Why did they do this to you?" said Eleanor.

The man licked his lips and glanced nervously at the onrushing water. "They attacked my village. Killed everyone else. Took me prisoner. I tried to escape. They made sure I couldn't."

"Your village?" said Eleanor. "We've established you're not local."

"Says the redhead."

"My mother was from Keedy."

"Nice place. Apart from the constant rain. And the constant cold. And the constant . . . what's that stuff you eat?"

"That's hardly relevant."

"I'm glad you're capable of noticing such things."

The sea licked the beach, as if aware of the dish that had been laid out for it. The man's face grew red as his body exerted itself under the surface. He could do nothing to counteract the weight pressing on him.

Megan knelt and motioned to scoop away the sand. "I really think we should . . ."

Eleanor held up a finger. Megan paused, her hands halfway in the beach. "What village was this?" the countess said to the man. "Thicketford?"

He glanced at Megan. She tensed at the mention of her destroyed home. "No," he said. "It's small. You won't have heard of it."

"Try me."

"Halliwell. I was looking for work."

"Work? There were barely three people and a dog there."

"I never said I was successful, did I?" The sea was a stride away now, foaming as it crashed upon the sand. "Please . . ."

Eleanor cocked her head at Megan. Megan nodded back. They started to dig the man out. Lacking tools, they had to use their hands, scooping up chunks of damp sand and flinging them over their shoulders. Seawater trickled into the hole they created. The man squirmed and stretched, trying to gain a precious advantage on the flood, however slight.

"Please, don't rush," he said. "If worse comes to worst, I'm sure I can hold my breath for a few hours until the tide goes back out." Megan stopped digging and rested her aching arms on her thighs. "That was sarcasm, by the way. You do have it this far from civilization, don't you?"

There was something shifty about the man. Megan thought he was trying to distract them, but she had no idea what from or why. It didn't mean they could let him die though. She resumed helping Eleanor to dig.

They cleared the sand down to the man's shoulders. Eleanor slipped her hand under the man's arm and urged Megan to do the same. They heaved.

"Ow! Ow! I'd like to come out in one piece."

"We can leave you, you know," said Eleanor.

"Arms? Overrated."

They heaved again. The man's arms burst out of the sand. His wrists were tied with a thin rope. Eleanor pulled a knife from its scabbard and sawed away while the sea continued its remorseless advance. Fibers surrendered to the blade. The man pulled his arms apart. The rope unraveled. His hands sprang free.

All three of them dug now, their actions frantic. They cleared a space around the man's torso, then

Megan and Eleanor hauled again. The man came free a little. He wriggled and jerked and then broke out. A final tug and he was released from his would-be grave.

The man scrambled up the beach and collapsed, panting. Eleanor and Megan followed at a more sedate pace. They sat on either side of him and watched as the water rushed into the hole he had vacated, their breathing and heart rate slowly returning to normal.

"You two look how I feel," said the man, beating wet sand off himself. He wore a simple tunic and pants, a dirty brown in color and torn in several places. His feet were bare and filthy. "What's with all the bruises and dried blood?"

Megan rubbed her face, catching her swollen lip. It was the least painful part of her body. "We—"

"Sports," said Eleanor.

"You girls play rough." The man pointed out to the waves. "Thanks for . . ."

"We were just doing God's work," said Eleanor. "He's trying to postpone the time He has to meet you."

"Is that a compliment or . . . ?"

"The other one."

The man turned to Megan. "You must be the nice one." He held out his hand. "I'm Damon."

"I'm Megan and this is . . ."

She looked across to the countess. "Eleanor." The expected litany of titles didn't come.

Damon patted their knees. "Meg and Ellie—my saviors." He caught Eleanor's glare. "No touching?"

"No diminutives."

"Oh." Damon turned to Megan. "You?" She shook her head. "All right, a full set of syllables it is. You don't have any water on you, do you?"

"Here," said Megan. She handed Damon a skin they had taken from the soldier in the forest. He guzzled down its contents.

"We've stayed here long enough," said Eleanor. "That soldier—his friends might be back. We should move."

"What soldier?" asked Damon. Eleanor ignored him.

The reality of the situation slammed back into Megan. Where could they move to? Gwyneth was out there, on the high seas, if Megan could trust Damon, though she wasn't sure he viewed reliability as a virtue. "Are you sure you saw my sister?" she said to him.

"Your . . . ? I saw a girl, that's all I can say. She looked a bit like you, but no one was exchanging family trees."

It was her. It had to be. Relief flooded through Megan. She hadn't lost Gwyneth. There was still hope.

"How is she?" she gabbled. "Did they hurt her? Why did they take her?"

"I don't know," said Damon. "I was kind of tagging along in a prisoner-y kind of way. I didn't see any obvious signs she'd been . . . you know . . ."

Some harm didn't leave physical marks, but at least Gwyneth was still alive. Alive and in desperate need of help.

Megan grabbed fistfuls of sands and squeezed. She would get that help, anything Gwyneth needed. The witches had a ship; she'd get a navy. The witches had soldiers; she'd get an army. The witches had her sister; she'd kill every last one to get her back.

"Looks like we're going to Eastport after all," she said. "The priests keep boasting how they defeated the witches the last time. Let's see if they're up for a return match." They would be; they *had* to be. The priests wouldn't stand by while the witches threatened the Realm.

"Wait," said Damon. "You want to go after the witches?"

"Yes," said Megan.

"Are you stark raving bonkers insane?"

"They have my sister." Megan got to her feet. "We've still got a bit of daylight left," she said to Eleanor.

Eleanor pushed herself up. So did Damon. The two women stared at him. "What?" he said, spreading his palms. "I'm not invited?"

"Well . . ." said Eleanor.

"Where else am I supposed to go? The dead city? Even the witches wouldn't go there."

He was right. The witches had preferred to beach their boats rather than use the long-abandoned moorings of

Trafford's Haven. It loomed to the north, a malevolent husk. Megan could just make out the piers, spindly silhouettes stretching out into the sea like insect legs. Maybe the witches had tried them and found them rotten. Or maybe they thought it prudent to let the city's ghosts rest in peace.

Eleanor stood beside her and contemplated the city. The quickest way to Eastport was to follow the road up the coast, but it blocked their path. "We'll have to find a way around."

"It'll be quicker to go through," said Megan. "Besides, we need somewhere to camp for the night. And if the witches won't go there . . ."

"For very good damn reasons," said Damon. "You want to get to Eastport, take the inland road. Nice, safe, good chance of a lift."

"Good chance we'll run into the witches," said Eleanor. "They won't be looking for us on the coastal road."

"Why would they be looking for you?"

"I don't know," snapped Megan. "I'm going to Trafford's Haven, and that's that. What can hurt us there?"

"Can't say I'm desperate to find out," said Damon. Neither was Megan, but they couldn't afford to lose time, time Gwyneth didn't have. Who knew how long the witches would hold off whatever they had planned for her?

She and Eleanor set off toward Trafford's Haven. "Nice meeting you," Megan called out to Damon. "Watch out for wolves."

"There're wolves around here?" asked Eleanor.

"Only common grays," said Megan. "Usually timid. Won't attack groups."

Behind them came cursing and the kicking of sand as Damon struggled to catch up.

# eight

"Great," said Damon. "Not only do we come to a haunted city but we do it at *night*?"

"Don't worry," said Eleanor. "I think your smell is enough to drive anything off."

"Hey, that hole didn't come with toilet facilities, you know."

They were supposed to be looking for somewhere to shelter for the night, but this idea had become less and less attractive the further they advanced through Trafford's Haven. There was a tacit agreement among them—keep going and hope to come out the other side. Preferably alive.

Empty shells of buildings loomed above them, their stonework blackened by soot. It was as if they were inside the skeleton of a leviathan whose flesh had been picked clean. Wind whistled through the gaps, disturbing the weeds that had forced their way through the cobbles and shifting dust from curb to curb. Whenever they paused, a faint scratching could be heard. Rats scrabbling for food, or spirits still trying to claw their way out of the blaze forty years after it had been extinguished?

"What happened here?" said Megan, keeping her voice low. She didn't want to disturb anything or alert anyone to their presence. The bravado she'd shown on the beach was well and truly gone.

Eleanor crouched down and examined the remains of a shoe. Fire and sea air had reduced it to a few strips of shriveled leather. She tossed it aside. "It's said Jolecia and Ahebban summoned a thousand devils, who burst out of the ground here and devastated the city with hellfire."

Damon prodded one of the cobblestones with his toe. "Not that literal spot," Eleanor said.

"How do you know?"

Something fluttered between the roofs. An owl. Possibly. "Where are all the bodies?" said Megan.

"Do you really want to know?" said Damon.

It was worse than Thicketford and Halliwell. There, despite the blood and corpses, you could close your eyes and convince yourself that someone would walk around the corner and life would return to normal. It was hard to believe life had ever existed here, never mind could again.

A cloud drifted across the moon. The buildings took advantage of the dark to press in on them. Megan imagined herself being squashed by them. Adrenalin surged. She darted forward. A jutting cobble caught her foot. She tripped and stumbled into Damon. Eleanor let out an indignant cry as he did the same to her.

The moon came back out. A shape flitted across the street in front of them, but it was gone before Megan could even begin to figure out what it was. She swallowed and reached back for her sword, even though she knew steel was useless against the incorporeal.

A croaky voice echoed down the street. "Fear not, O True. God will watch over you."

Megan froze. Her skin prickled in waves, as if spectral fingers were brushing against her. She started to move closer to Eleanor, only to find the countess had pre-empted her.

"The ghosts are doing poetry now?" muttered Damon.

"When the world has gone four score times around the sun. My sisters will be born again to clean the world of its stain."

"And bad poetry at that. If they start with the folk music, I'm out of here."

Megan caught a flicker of movement out of the corner of her eye. Something rushing through the remains of the house to their right. She drew her sword and spun on her heel. The structure was empty, but anything could be hiding in its shadows.

"What is it?" whispered Eleanor.

"I saw something. In there."

"Why are we not running away very fast?" asked Damon.

"Because we're not cowards," said Eleanor.

"Speak for yourself." He took a few steps down the street, head jerking from side to side like a nervous squirrel's.

"I wouldn't go that way," said Megan. "That's the way it was—"

Something hissed through the darkness. Damon yelped. His hand flew to the back of his neck. A figure rushed across the street and down an alley. Man, woman, or something else? Damon lurched away from it. Megan was tired of being scared. She charged after it.

She clattered down the alley, bouncing off its walls. She couldn't see anything. It was too narrow for the moon to penetrate. The only evidence of her prey was a skittering against the cobbles, a shimmer in the black that could be whirling robes or her eyes playing tricks.

Megan emerged from the alley. Behind her, leather slapped upon stone. She spun round, hand reaching for her weapon. Eleanor skidded to a halt. Megan let her sword slide back into its scabbard.

"Where . . . ?" she started, panting.

Eleanor held a finger to her lips, then pointed. A scratching, like claws against stone, came from a building down the street. Business premises once—two stories of thrown-together limestone, soot staining the area under the windows like tears. A rusting pole stuck out over the doorway, the sign it had once held long since consumed by fire.

They approached, weapons at the ready. Megan peered into the doorway. It was pitch black inside. No sound came from within. She made to advance. Eleanor pulled her back.

"Let's leave it."

"And let it attack us while we're sleeping?" said Megan.

"I don't think any of us are going to be sleeping in this place," said Eleanor. She adjusted the grip on her sword. "I'll go in."

"You can't go on your own."

Eleanor ducked inside. "I'll scream if I need you." The darkness swallowed her.

Moments later, she screamed.


Megan stared into the blackness. "Eleanor!"

Silence came back in return. Megan swallowed and leaned into the building. A chill enveloped her as if she had fallen through ice on a frozen lake. "What's happened? Where are you?"

There was a groan: low, deep, distant. "Eleanor! Is that you? Are you all right?"

After a few agonizing seconds Eleanor called out, her voice strained. "Floorboards gave way."

Megan inched into the gloomy hallway. "Where are you?"

"Down. Don't come any further."

"Are you hurt?"

"I landed in something soft."

"What?"

"I'm in no hurry to find out."

Megan spread herself on the ground and crawled inside, sweeping her palm in front of her. There was stone, then splinters of wood and then nothing. She groped around and found the crossbeam that formed the edge where the floor had given out from under Eleanor's feet. Charred wood peppered it like scabs, but underneath the fire damage it felt solid enough.

She pulled herself along and dropped her arm into the cellar. "Can you see my hand?"

"I can't see anything."

"Follow my voice." Banging and grunting came from down below. "Over here." Something brushed Megan's dangling arm. "That's it." A thought came to her. "That is you, isn't it?"

Fingers locked round her wrist. "I hope so, for both our sakes."

Megan gripped Eleanor's arm and prepared to haul her up. A scream echoed through the city. A man's scream. It cut off.

"Damon . . ."

"Hurry!"

Megan braced herself and heaved. Beads of sweat broke out on her brow despite the chill of the night. Her arm felt as if it would be wrenched out of its socket. Her fingers burned as they slipped across the rough fabric of Eleanor's clothes. She was losing her, she was losing her . . .

The strain halved. There was a pawing around her knees. Eleanor had gained a handhold. The knowledge inspired Megan, and she yanked as hard as she could. The exertion almost killed her, but she managed to haul Eleanor up.

They stumbled out of the building. Megan massaged her throbbing shoulder and blinked. The moonlight was as strong as sunlight after the darkness inside, the air fresh after the staleness. No time to enjoy either. Damon needed them. They stumbled through the streets, back to where they had left him.

He was gone.

"Let's get out of here," said Eleanor.

"We can't leave him."

"It was his choice to run off. We've saved his life once; I don't think we're obligated to repeat the exercise."

"I thought you were obligated to *all* of your people," said Megan.

"He's a foreigner."

"Fine. I'll go after him myself."

"And who'll rescue Gwyneth once you're dead?" said Eleanor. "You don't know what's out there."

"Do not use my sister as an excuse to do something cowardly ever again."

Megan regretted her words the moment they left her lips. Eleanor was silent. Had she pushed her too far? She didn't want the countess to storm off, leave her in this city all alone.

"I'm—"

"Shush."

"Don't shush—"

"Listen."

Megan closed her eyes and moved her head slowly from side to side, taking in the sounds of the dead city: the wind rushing through the gaps in a never-ending search for companionship; the distant crashing of waves against long-abandoned jetties; the faint scuffle of dragging and footsteps.

Megan raised an arm and swung it like a compass, trying to fix the position of the scuffling. *There.*

Eleanor nodded. "Let's be more careful this time," she whispered.

They tiptoed through the city, trying to regulate their breathing. Megan imagined ghosts staring at them from the glassless windows, consumed by rage. The intruders enjoyed life while they knew only the agony of the flames. Any minute now, she expected hands to reach out and pull them into the blackness.

A clang of metal on stone made them jump. Megan realized her own tired arms had let her sword slip and hit the cobbles. She whispered an apology and hoisted the blade up so the flat rested upon her shoulder. Damon was right. They should have stayed away from Trafford's Haven. Now there was another soul paying the price for Megan's bad decisions. Perhaps if she rescued him God would mark it off against her sins and allow her to see Gwyneth again.

They emerged into a large square dominated by the city temple. It was still being built when fire had come to Trafford's Haven and lay in ruins before it had even been born, forever to remain an architect's dream. The outer ring had been completed, but only one of the towers had been erected—the other five were no more than stumps. Heaps of bricks and stone lay scattered in piles, cement had calcified into lumps on abandoned mortar boards, remnants of charred scaffolding threatened to give way if anything heavier than an insect landed on them.

An arched passage led them through the walls of the temple to the exposed theater inside. Moonlight spilled down the stone terraces that radiated away from the center. The Faithful would have sat there—enduring the elements, whether sun, rain, or snow—while the priests prowled the circle, preaching their lessons. Now it was a monument to God's unwillingness, or inability, to protect His people.

There was a heap in the middle of the stage. Damon was stretched out across the stones, his eyes open but his body rigid. His tunic had been pushed up to expose his belly. A creature clad in rags hunched over him, its mouth hovering over a cut down his stomach. Its tongue darted out, penetrating Damon's flesh and lapping up his blood.

Megan's stomach turned. She groaned in revulsion. The creature's head snapped up. It was human, just about. Its face was wizened like a rotten piece of fruit and its eyes had sunk into its skull until they were nothing more than dots blacker than the night.

Eleanor charged. The creature fumbled with a small tube and brought it to its lips. Eleanor swung. Her sword knocked the blowpipe from the creature's fingers, taking skin with it in the process. The creature howled and scuttled away, disappearing down one of the passageways that led to the outside.

Megan hurried to Damon and checked his wound. He'd survive: the blood was already clotting. She cupped a hand under his head and tilted it to check out his neck. There was a swelling the size of a walnut, a speck of dried blood marking its center.

Damon managed a couple of strangulated grunts, but remained still.

"What's happened to him?" Megan asked.

"Some kind of poison," said Eleanor, crouching beside them.

"Is it permanent?"

"We can but hope," she said. Damon squealed. Eleanor stroked his cheek with the back of her hand. "Relax. It should wear off soon."

The croaky voice sounded again. "No more the liar, the priest. Only His eternal peace." It was the creature, rocking back and forth as it hunched in the mouth of the passage. It was squeezing its injured hand between its knees.

"Quiet," said Eleanor.

"You had no right to come here," said the creature. Its voice had a sucking quality—it was lacking teeth.

"I have more right than anyone. My ancestor built this city."

The creature snorted. "Trafford Endalay? He was a fool."

"He was a great man."

"A fat fool at that. This city's first victim. He stuffed himself so much at the inaugural feast his stomach burst open. You could have fed a village with the undigested food that spewed out."

"You don't know what you're talking about," said Eleanor.

"I was there. A serving girl, all of six." It was a she, then, a decrepit old crone clinging to life by God knows whatever means. No, not that decrepit: she had incapacitated Damon and outrun Megan and Eleanor. "Oh, the courses they had, it makes my mouth water to think of them. There were stuffed quails—"

"We're not interested in the menu," snapped Eleanor.

"What I wouldn't give for a morsel from that table. I'm hungry, so hungry."

Megan stared at the crone. She was pathetic, an ancient creature. Her earlier revulsion dissolved into something approaching pity. She rooted around in their pack. They had a couple of dried sausages left, plus one of the oranges. She selected the orange and stepped toward the creature. Eleanor grabbed her.

"Don't. It's—"

"I'll be fine."

Megan went over to the creature and placed the fruit in front of her. She backed off. The crone eyed the fruit and then Megan.

"It's for you."

"I know. Do you think I'm stupid, girl?"

The crone snatched up the orange. She ripped it apart and sucked on the juicy flesh with the same eagerness she had feasted on Damon. Megan swallowed the bile that rose in her throat and turned away.

"Does anyone else live here?" asked Eleanor.

"Only rats," said the crone between slurps. "Hard to catch. Everything else is dead. Dead, dead, dead. Happens to everyone who steps in this place. Lords and peasants. The True and the Faithful."

"The True?" said Megan.

"It's what the witches call themselves," said Eleanor. "There's irony for you."

The crone tossed the gnawed peel aside. Juice mixed with congealed blood dribbled down her chin. "Why did you fools come here?"

"We thought we'd be safe," said Megan. "The witches wouldn't come here."

The crone snorted. "No one comes here. Even the priests burned it from afar."

"What are you talking about? The priests didn't burn it, the witches did."

"What do you know?" spat the crone. "Were you here? Did you witness the soldiers sealing the city gates? Did you hear the screams of horror as the fire arrows rained down? Did you see bodies crushed by the stampede? Did you see the flesh blacken and crackle like roasting meat?" She jutted out her jaw. "The priests thought they could destroy the True, but they are eternal."

"You're wrong," said Megan, confused. "It wasn't the priests who did this. Brother Brogan would have said something. My grandfather would have said something."

"Even the priests know shame." The crone snorted. "I witnessed the glory of Ahebban and Jolecia and soon the world will witness their return. They will rally the True, and this time no one will stop them."

"If you know so much, tell me what the witches want. And why they have my sister."

"Sister?" The crone's eyes lit up. The years drained away from her face. "Twin sister?"

Megan shivered. "How did you . . . ?"

The crone started to chuckle, a wet clack that sounded like a pig getting its throat cut.

"What's so funny?" demanded Megan. "What do you know about me and Gwyneth? Tell me. Tell me!"

The crone stopped. She fixed her gaze on Megan. "I was right," she said, her black eyes shredding Megan's soul. "I can finally sleep."

Moonlight flashed on glass as the old woman whipped something out from under her rags. Eleanor yelled a warning. Megan instinctively froze, then realized the crone had a vial in her hand and was tipping its contents down her own throat. She lunged, tried to grab it from her. Too late. The crone was already convulsing on the floor of the temple, foam bubbling from her lips.

A few seconds later, she was the city's final victim.

# nine

Megan stared at the crone's body, nothing more than a heap of rag and bones. "How did she know Gwyneth was my twin?"

"Lucky guess," said Eleanor.

"Why guess at all? And what was she right about?"

"The mutterings of a crazy woman. Don't obsess over them."

"Crazy?"

"You think *you'd* keep your sanity living in this city?"

Megan shook her head. She already felt as if she was losing her mind. Nothing made sense anymore. It was as if the universe was conspiring against her, buffeting her this way and that, taunting her with hints of dark secrets. Wasn't that a sign of madness, a conviction everything was about you? But why would the witches want her and Gwyneth?

"When you've done talking people to death," said Damon, his voice thick with phlegm, "could I have a hand?"

Eleanor looked down at him. "Your voice would be the first thing that came back."

Glad of something practical she could do, Megan helped Damon to his feet. "How do you feel?" she asked him.

Damon wobbled and slumped against her. "Like I've been mugged by a wine vat."

Megan glanced back at the crone. "We can't stay here."

"The furnishings do leave a little to be desired."

"There were some buildings nearby," said Eleanor. She turned to Damon. "You think you can move?"

"With the love of two strong women, there is nothing I cannot accomplish."

"Love?"

"Mild like?"

"I'd settle for not-actively-killing, if I were you."

Megan and Eleanor each took one of Damon's arms. His legs had the coordination of a drunk fawn's, so they had to drag him out of the temple step by laborious step, occasionally stopping to massage away the pins and needles that wracked his body and made him howl.

They reached the street. It felt good to be away from the desecration, even if it was into the graveyard of the city's main square. Eleanor pointed at the buildings she had mentioned and they started across to them.

"Do you think the witches need Gwyneth for something to do with Ahebban and Jolecia's return?" Megan asked.

"I don't know," said Eleanor.

"Do you think they're going to . . . ?" *Sacrifice her? Sacrifice us?*

"I don't know."

"If we rescue her, will that stop the demons?"

"Why do you keep asking me questions I can't answer?"

"'And as Edwyn froze in the Kartik Mountains,'" said Damon, "'Rax and Oveen did come to him and promise warmth and food and all the luxuries of Werlavia if he forsook God, but Edwyn drew strength from the teachings of the Saviors and defeated the demons.' The Book of Faith. Chapter four, verse eighteen."

"And you brought that up because . . . ?" said Eleanor.

"You wanted to know if you could stop a demon."

"I could've done with a few more details," muttered Megan.

"Of course, some believe Ahebban and Jolecia are actually Rax and Oveen," said Damon. "The etymology of the names is all wrong though."

"Etymology?" said Eleanor.

"How words form and change their meaning."

"I knew that," said Eleanor in a tone that indicated she didn't.

"Not that it matters," said Damon. "The universe has given birth to many diabolical things. They are jealous of God's creation and wish to destroy it and claim the ashes for themselves."

"The Book of Faith again?" said Megan, not recognizing the passage.

"My old teacher. He could be pretty diabolical himself when he'd been drinking." He looked away. "Not a good time to be a small, defenseless boy."

The buildings turned out to be nothing more than charred walls open to the sky. Eleanor located a few scraps of unburned wood and got a small fire going while Megan divvied up the last of their food. They ate largely in silence, listening to the crackle of the flames. Megan wondered if they were mocking those who had once burned here.

Damon finished eating and dragged himself around the fire in Eleanor's direction. "So," he said, "you're what? Trafford Endalay's . . . ?"

"Granddaughter."

"Heir to the Endalay fortune?"

"There is no fortune," said Eleanor. "The witches stole it from us and the priests stole it from them to pay for their army. Or rather, their army stole it to pay themselves because they knew the priests expected them to do it for the glory of God."

"No gold or diamonds stashed in a booby-trapped hideaway?"

"No."

Eleanor made a show of sharpening her knife. Damon backed away a little. There was an awkward silence punctuated only by the snapping of burning wood.

Megan finished eating and pulled her cloak around her to block the chill wind that whipped around the exposed interior. Her stomach churned, the little food she'd had sitting uneasily on it.

Damon offered her a crooked smile. "You all right?"

Megan nodded. *Just morning sickness. It'll pass.* "You came down here looking for work," she said. "What is it you do?"

"I'm guessing thief," said Eleanor. "Or conman."

"Priest," said Damon.

"Or both."

"A priest?" said Megan. "Really?"

"An acolyte anyway. I never took my final vows. Theological differences."

"Such as . . . ?"

"They wanted to geld me; I preferred they didn't."

"Gelding?" said Megan. "Isn't that what they do to horses?"

"Yes."

"Where they . . . ?" Megan mimed snipping.

"Yes."

"Must hurt."

"I'm happy never to have found out."

The fire flickered as the wind picked up pace. Megan huddled further into her cloak. Damon wet his lips. "When my father died, he split his estate between me and my older brother. My brother didn't think that was right. He was there doing all the hard work, and I was lazing around all day."

"Sounds about right," said Eleanor.

"I was four at the time. My darling brother, for the good of my education, had me sequestered in a seminary and I trained to be a priest for ten god-awful years. And I mean that literally. Comes time to take my final vows, and someone digs up the old rule about castration. Demonstrate to God you've extinguished all impure thoughts. These days He's a little less demanding. A vow of celibacy will suffice in place of the ritual castration. And an offering of gold, of course. Only I didn't have any, and my brother certainly wasn't going to cough it up. The prospect of a nephew, even a bastard one, with a claim on 'his' estate didn't appeal to him."

"What happened then?" said Megan.

"I had a conference with Bill and Ben," said Damon. "We decided to stick together."

"Bill and Ben?" said Eleanor.

Damon pointed downward.

"You named them?"

"Doesn't everyone? Haven't you done the same with your . . . ?" he gestured to her chest.

"Nothing beyond 'left' and 'right.'"

"What happened with you and the priests?" asked Megan.

"I . . ."

"Scarpered?" finished Eleanor.

"Why are you always so disapproving of my desire to save myself?"

Eleanor shook her head. "You were right to get out of there. Some battles you can't win." She looked across to Megan. "Best to live to fight another day."

They left Trafford's Haven at dawn. The coastal road was even more overgrown than its inland cousin, but at least it was quiet. After the war against the witches, those remaining had moved inland or north, to East-port. With nothing to plunder, the Sandstrider pirates no longer bothered to raid. The road was safe but redundant.

Despite the ache in her muscles and the blisters on her feet that burst and reformed with painful regularity, Megan found peace in the journey. She listened to the gulls squawk and the waves break on the rocks, knowing the only demand on her was the simple placement of one foot in front of the other. For the first time in days she wasn't scared. When she realized this, guilt twinged within her. She should be mourning her grandfather, Wade, the rest of the villagers. She should be thinking about how she was going to provide for her baby. She should be planning how to rescue Gwyneth, how to rally the priests to her cause. There was no way Gwyneth wouldn't be scared. Was she still at sea? Megan hoped not. Gwyneth hated boats.

Five days out of Trafford's Haven they came across their first sign of civilization: a fishing village huddled at the mouth of a narrow river like a mouse cowering from a bird of prey. Megan counted twenty buildings or so, low one- and two-story dwellings with thatched roofs of dirty straw. Smoke rose from chimneys and bent to the right, pushed inland by the sea breeze. A trio of boats was tied up to a wooden jetty, bobbing on the outgoing tide. Another boat drifted out on the water, its sail furled, stick figures moving on its deck.

Suspicious eyes and the smell of fish greeted them as they entered. Nets went unmended; decks went unswabbed; a squid kept its guts for a few seconds longer. Megan offered up a nervous smile; the villagers replied with scowls. Megan's skin prickled. Even though the witches weren't expecting them here, that didn't mean one of the villagers wasn't helping them, wasn't looking out for a young girl on the run.

Damon strode up to a fishmonger whose apron and beard were spattered with blood and specks of entrails. "Inn," said Damon, miming drinking. "Food." He mimed eating. "Sleep." He pressed his palms together and rested his head upon them.

"They're not foreigners," said Megan. "They'll speak Stathian like the rest of us."

The fishmonger held up his knife. "Stab," he said thrusting the air. "Dead."

Eleanor stepped forward. "What my friend was trying to ask was if there's an establishment where three weary travelers could get something to eat and a bed for the night."

"Travelers?"

Damon walked his fingers along the air. Eleanor rolled her eyes. "If you do want to stab him, I won't object."

"Keep going the way you were," said the fishmonger. "You'll come across the Headless Fish soon enough."

Eleanor smiled and squeezed the fishmonger's arm. A faint blush passed over his cheeks.

They set off for the inn. "Do you think it's wise, staying here?" Megan said in a low voice to Eleanor. "What if one of them is one of *them*?"

"You can't communicate solely in pronouns and emphasis, you know."

"What if one these people is a witch?"

Eleanor looked around. Everyone had gone back to their previous tasks, the excitement of the newcomers' arrival proving short-lived. "We'll deal with that if we need to," she said. "Right now, we need rest and a decent meal."

Megan couldn't object to that. After a week on the road, her flesh existed as merely something to connect all the bruises together and the food they'd manage to scavenge was hardly enough to nourish her, never mind the baby beginning to grow inside her. Eleanor had been hunting using her throwing knife, which meant the ground and trees had been well killed, if not her prey.

The landlady of the Headless Fish was as broad as she was wide, with a stern demeanor that softened when Megan slipped a shilling on to the counter. "What brings you to Laxton?" she asked.

"This is Laxton?" said Eleanor.

Megan turned to her. "Aren't you Baroness of—"

"Don't," said Eleanor. To the landlady, "We're just passing through."

"I thought a baronetcy would be, you know, bigger."

"It's not just the village, it's the surrounding lands."

"Do you get given your weight in fish heads every year?"

The landlady endured this conversation with the patience of one well-versed in ignoring other people's prattlings. "Just the two of you?" she said.

"Him as well," said Eleanor, jerking her thumb at Damon. He was hanging back, watching a game of darts in progress between two of the locals.

Hearing himself mentioned, Damon came over. "And who might you be?" the landlady asked.

"My . . . son," said Eleanor.

"Her lover," said Damon at the same time.

"They're northerners," said Megan. "You know what it's like up there."

"Aye, well, we'll have no funny business here. This is a good clean establishment."

An old man clattered down the stairs, naked apart from the long johns clutched to his waist. Cheers went up as a semi-dressed buxom girl appeared at the top of the stairs, hurling clothes as she descended. The old man ducked, grabbed a shirt, then dove outside.

The landlady shrugged. "He'll have paid with clipped coins again."

The girl adjusted her dress so it made at least a nominal effort at containing her breasts. "What're you staring at?" she said to Damon.

He pointed to the boots in her hand. "Do you think he's coming back for those? I'm a bit . . ." He pointed at his bare feet, blackened and calloused by their journey.

The girl lobbed the shoes at him and stormed back upstairs.

Their shilling bought them food and a room and provisions for their journey. Another shilling promised them a bath and a change of clothes. They'd paid too much, but they didn't have much choice. Megan didn't think she could go another day using somebody's old underpants for socks.

The landlady slopped fish stew into bowls. They took their food to a dark corner, where generations of bottoms had smoothed the benches and the wood was ingrained with the smell of the sea.

"You'll never guess where we are," Megan said to Damon.

He shrugged. "Another shithole in the back end of nowhere."

"Laxton."

"Aren't you Baroness of—"

"We've already done this," Eleanor said through gritted teeth.

"I can see why you're so proud of the title," said Damon, grinning. "Where's Herth? It's not that bog we had to skip around a couple of days ago, is it?"

More customers trickled into the inn. Each of them paused to examine the grimy newcomers—not hostile but not friendly either—like they were pondering how much to offer for a catch. "I think we should change the subject," said Eleanor.

Damon leaned over the table and nudged Megan. "Lend me half a shilling."

"I'm not paying for you to . . ." Megan pointed upstairs.

"No," whispered Damon. "I can double it for you, triple it even. The dart players, they're useless. I can take them."

"We don't need to draw attention to ourselves," said Eleanor.

"Who's drawing attention? It's only a game with a little wager."

"Which'll end in accusations and fisticuffs and daggers thrust in soft tissue."

"You're a cheery one."

Damon turned back to Megan. "Once we start playing, we'll start talking. I'll pick up the local gossip. Maybe one of the fishermen spotted the witches' ship."

"It's worth a try," Megan said to Eleanor. The countess answered with a shrug.

Megan pressed a coin into Damon's hand. "Be discreet."

"I'll be so discreet they won't even realize they're talking to me."

"Why can't you be like that with us?" said Eleanor.

Damon made to rise. A meaty paw slapped him back down. "Stay there, lad."

It was a fat priest—not that Megan had ever met a thin one—his once white robes now a dull gray and spattered with food stains. Broken veins reddened his nose and his smooth chin. The only hair he had formed a greasy black band around his temples, which at least saved him from having to shave it into a tonsure. There was power behind the indulgence though. Megan could tell by the way he carried himself.

He sat down next to Damon. "I'm Brother Irwyn. You're the strangers I've been hearing about." There was silence at the table. "Aren't you going to introduce yourselves?"

"I'm Damon, brother. This is Megan and this is Eleanor." He slid the half-shilling Megan had given him across the table. "We meant to come pay our respects, brother. Something to aid the Faithful." He made the sign of the circle. Megan copied him. After a glance from Brother Irwyn, so did Eleanor.

The priest pocketed the coin and called for a flagon of ale. Megan suspected it was going to end up on her tab. "Where do you hail from?" he asked.

Megan hesitated. Brother Irwyn didn't look like much, but he was a priest. He had a sworn duty to protect the Faithful. If she couldn't tell him what had happened, who could she tell?

"Soldiers came to my village, brother," she said in a low voice. "They killed everyone and kidnapped my sister."

The priest patted her hand. "How awful for you, my child. Find comfort in the Faith. God will protect you from these brigands."

"These weren't brigands," said Megan. "The witches have returned." She looked around. No one seemed to be eavesdropping. That was good. The fewer people knew the witches were after Megan, the fewer could betray her to them.

"Witches?" said Brother Irwyn. "From the grave?"

"These soldiers bore the star-broken circle."

The priest made the sign of the circle over his heart. "Don't talk of such things."

"What, the star—?" started Eleanor.

Megan kicked her ankle. "We're sorry, brother," she said, "but they are here. We have to raise a fleet and an army and we have to go after them and get Gwyneth back before they can—"

"You won't find much of an army here," said the priest. "As for our fleet . . ."

"They have men and ships in Eastport. You can take us there, get us in to see the High Priest."

"Father Galan will want more than words. He'll need hard evidence."

"There's a novelty," muttered Eleanor.

"If you want evidence, go to Thicketford and Halliwell and count the corpses," said Megan.

Brother Irwyn helped himself to the last of the ale. "I don't doubt the tale of your tragedy, but it hardly proves the abomination has risen again. It'll be thieves, cut-throats, Sandstriders, even . . ."

"Not all the corpses are of the innocent."

The priest's cup halted midway to his lips. "I didn't think the witches left their dead behind."

"They didn't have a choice."

Brother Irwyn savored his drink. His eyes flicked between Megan, who did her best to look meek and pious, and Eleanor, who looked like she was ready to avenge the usurpation of her family one priest at a time. Damon remained subdued, shrunk into himself. Megan wondered what had happened to him during those years at the seminary.

"I'll tell you what," said the priest. "The post horse arrives the day after tomorrow. I'll send a letter to the High Priest."

"You don't have something faster?" said Megan. "A carrier pigeon? A boat?"

"The post horse is bringing our birds back. And the local boats are built for endurance, not speed." Brother Irwyn rubbed Megan's arm in a manner that was just a little too familiar. "Don't worry. I'll recommend he set up a committee to explore these allegations."

"A recommendation?" said Megan, pulling her arm back.

"Yes."

"To set up a committee?"

"Of the finest minds south of the Speed."

"The day after tomorrow?"

Brother Irwyn beamed. "It's the least I can do."

Megan's blood boiled. Gwyneth was in danger, the witches had returned, and the Realm was facing the fate of Trafford's Haven, and this stupid man was treating it as a bureaucratic exercise. "You're not wrong there," she spat, not caring for the consequences for disrespecting a priest. "We have to do something *now*. We don't have time for you to take minutes and elect vice-chairmen."

"There's no virtue in rushing."

"Screw virtue."

Brother Irwyn raised his eyebrows. He turned to Damon. "Is she always like this?"

"This is one of her good days."

"I can arrange for a special messenger to leave tonight," Brother Irwyn said, "but there are certain . . . considerations to take into account."

Megan slammed a shilling on to the table. "That kind of consideration?"

The priest examined the coin in the candlelight. "Interesting. A king's coin. Fine silver. Don't see many of these. Where did you get it?"

"It was my grandfather's. My *dead* grandfather's."

"I grieve for your loss. May God guide him home."

"He was home when they murdered him."

The landlady waddled over and bent into Brother Irwyn. "Juliana's free if you want her, brother."

"Not tonight."

The landlady sucked the remnants of her teeth. "You've gone right off your whores, haven't you? Sickening for something, brother?"

"Only the love of God." Brother Irwyn slapped his hands together. "I've some business to take care of, but once that is finished I shall go sharpen my pen. Good evening, ladies and—" he turned to Damon —"whatever."

Eleanor watched him leave. "That was a mistake," she said, brooding into her cup.

"The messenger will get there before we do," said Megan. "His words might help our cause."

"He's an old drunk exiled to the middle of nowhere," said Eleanor. "What influence do you think he has? You've wasted a shilling, and now one more person knows our business."

The steam rising from the copper tub was more the product of the cellar's iciness than the water's heat. Megan peeled off her stinking clothes and sank into the bath. The warm water calmed her. The ache in her muscles eased. The worries seeped from her body. They would find Gwyneth. They would defeat the witches. She would have a family again: her, her sister, her child.

The serenity didn't last. Memories of her grandfather and the rest of the villagers crowded in. They wouldn't see any more children born. They wouldn't laugh again, fight, love. Megan sank deeper into the water, so it lapped over her face. If the witches only wanted her and Gwyneth, why did they have to kill everyone? She would have given herself up to save the rest. *But could she have allowed Gwyneth to give herself up?*

Footsteps and a shimmer against her eyelids warned her of another's entrance. Her eyes snapped open.

"Stop hogging," said Eleanor. "My turn." She was getting undressed, her torso and limbs all muscled curves—the product of years of archery—and notched with scars, white against the pale, including a six-inch one that pinched her left side.

"Sorry," said Megan, getting out of the tub. She did her best to turn away from Eleanor so she wouldn't see her stomach. It would be a month or two before she would really started showing, but she didn't want to risk Eleanor guessing. "Used to going last and taking my time. Gwyneth always insisted on bathing first. She claimed it was her right as the oldest."

Eleanor handed her a towel. "I thought you were twins?"

"She came out first. So we think, anyway. Who knows with babies? We could have gotten mixed up dozens of times. I could be her and she could be me." If only Megan could swap places with her sister. Gwyneth wouldn't have let her languish in captivity while she wandered around half of Ainsworth.

Gwyneth's absence hit her like a punch to the stomach. "I miss her. I miss her so much. There's a piece of me missing and I don't know if I'm ever going to get it back. I wish we'd spent more time together instead of mooning over boys. At least then I . . . then I . . ."

Sobs racked Megan's body. Eleanor wrapped her arms around Megan's shoulders. Megan clung on, wishing it were her sister who was comforting her as she had done so many times, before they could even express their misery in words.

The tears subsided. Megan washed her face. "You'd better get in before the water goes cold."

After Eleanor had finished, they scampered up a freezing back staircase to their room and huddled in front of the fire that had been prepared there. The clothes they had bought were strewn on their bed. They were cast-offs, repaired too many times and smelling faintly of fish, but the fabric was thick and sturdy, designed to withstand life at sea. Megan and Eleanor sorted through them, picking those that fit best, leaving the rest for Damon, who had taken their place bathing in the cellar.

The fire was making the room hot and stuffy. Megan battled with one of the windows. Constant exposure to moisture had bloated the frame, and it took a couple of punches with the heel of her hand to force it open. Sea air wafted in, bringing with it the scent of brine and ozone. The sun was a golden sliver resting on the horizon. The village was deserted, hunkered down for the night.

The clop of hoofs drew Megan's attention. A solitary horseman was milling around on the street below. A large man emerged from the shadows and went up to him, his robes making him appear to glide rather than walk. He handed something to the horseman, who tucked it into his saddlebag. There was a glint as a coin was exchanged and the priest backed off to let the horse move out. Spurs dug in and the horse broke into a gallop.

Megan began dashing around the room, gathering their things. "We have to get out of here right now."

"What? Why?"

"That priest, Brother Irwyn. He's betrayed us."

"How can you—"

"He's dispatched his messenger."

"And?"

"South."

Eleanor's eyes narrowed. "Eastport's . . ."

"To the north, yes."

"Maybe the messenger's trying to avoid the traffic?"

"He *is* the traffic," said Megan. "Who're the only people we've seen south of here?"

"The witches sailed away."

"Maybe they sailed back?"

Eleanor needed no further convincing. They collected their belongings and snuck downstairs. Damon was soaking, his eyes closed as he rested his head on the lip of the tub. He'd shaven, and his clean features reminded Megan how young he was—barely a year or two older than her. With his golden skin and his fine blond hair, there was a touch of the angel about him, though the kink in his nose warned her he might have fallen.

He opened his eyes and gave them a lazy smile. "Come to scrub my back, girls?"

"We're going," said Megan, flinging clothes at him.

Water splashed as Damon stretched out for the bundle. "A little privacy, huh?"

"We don't have time to worry about your modesty."

"It's not that modest!"

Megan held out a towel. "Brother Irwyn's working for the witches."

"He can't be," said Damon, sinking back into his filthy bath. "He's a priest."

"Fine. You can stay here and admonish him for breaking his vows. We're leaving."

"Bastard. Could you . . . ?" Damon circled his index finger.

Megan and Eleanor turned their backs while Damon dried and dressed, or rather dried and complained about the clothes they had brought down for him.

"It's not really my color . . ."

"Just put the damn thing on," said Eleanor.

Footsteps smacked against the stairs. Megan and Eleanor flew for the door and slammed it shut just as the bottom half of Brother Irwyn descended into view. The heavy oak shuddered beneath them as he hammered on it.

"I need to speak to you," Brother Irwyn called from the other side.

"Give us a moment, brother," said Megan. The door juddered in reply. "Why don't you wait for us in the bar, get yourself some wine? You can put it on our tab."

"I'll wait here."

"The bastard really is a witch," hissed Damon. "No priest would ever turn down a free drink."

"We need another way out of here," Eleanor hissed back.

Megan glanced round. There was an archway at the far end. "There's another cellar out back," she said.

The other two hurried after her, Damon hopping as he pulled his boots on. They found themselves in a storeroom piled high with barrels that smelled vaguely of sulfur. God knew what they were putting in the beer around here. While Brother Irwyn continued to hammer against the door and demand entry, they maneuvered a barrel underneath the drop. Eleanor, the tallest of the three, climbed on it and inched open the trapdoor in the ceiling.

"All clear."

One after the other, they hauled themselves out of the cellar into the yard at the back of the inn. It was dark and still, the only light coming from candles that flickered behind the smoky glass windows. They scurried round to the road. A muffled roar went up in the inn. It reminded Megan of the cheer that went up when hunters sighted their prey.

"We should steal a boat," whispered Damon.

"How many of us do you think know how to handle a boat?" asked Eleanor.

"None?"

"And how many of the men in a fishing village do you think know how to handle one?"

Damon thought for a moment. "All of 'em?"

"I'll leave it as an exercise to imagine how long we'd survive."

"We should find horses," said Megan.

"See?" Eleanor said to Damon. "A practical idea."

He looked petulant. "How many of us do you think know how to handle a horse?" Eleanor and Megan put their hands up. After a moment, so did Damon. "All right, all right. Where d'you think they keep them?"

Angry voices followed them. They ducked into the shadows as Brother Irwyn strode from the inn, followed closely by the landlady.

". . . they mustn't be allowed to escape," Brother Irwyn was saying.

"They seemed such nice people," said the landlady. "Well, apart from *her.*"

"She means you," Megan and Eleanor mouthed at each other.

"They're dangerous, but they must not be harmed."

"I don't understand, brother. Harming is what you do to dangerous people. We got pitchforks in especially."

"You don't have to understand. Get the word out to all the men in the village."

"Shouldn't be a problem. They're all in my place getting drunk."

The landlady returned to her inn. Brother Irwyn looked around. Megan held her breath, fearing he had seen them, but he spun away and glided in the opposite direction.

"Horses," hissed Megan. "Now."

They scurried up the road, then down an alley that led to the back of the buildings. "Here, horsey, horsey, horsey," said Damon.

"Oh, for Saviors' sake," muttered Eleanor. "The stable's this way."

"How do you know?"

"I can smell it."

They upped their pace. "What do we do if there's only one horse?" said Damon.

"We take a vote on who we leave behind," said Eleanor. She and Megan looked at him.

"Oh, come on!"

The glow of a lantern and the sound of its chain creaking in the wind guided them to the stables, where they found half a dozen horses of varying quality, from poor to lucky-not-to-be-glue. Saddles were piled up in a corner. Eleanor grabbed one and led a mare out into the yard.

"Don't stand there," she urged the others. "Choose a horse and get it ready."

Approaching hollers kicked them into action. They hurriedly prepared the horses for travel: tightening straps, fastening buckles, forcing bits between teeth.

As Damon was helping Megan to mount, a voice cut through the stable yard.

"Going somewhere?" said Brother Irwyn from the other side of the fence. The smoky glow from the lantern licked across his face, giving him a demonic appearance. "But you paid for the night."

Megan drew her blade, swaying in the saddle as she struggled to keep her balance. She advanced on Brother Irwyn. "You bastard," she said. "Not only do you sell us out, you charge us for the privilege."

"You have to admire the cheek if nothing else," said Damon.

"I've sold no one out," Brother Irwyn said to Megan. "I'm following the righteous path, the path of the True. As will you. You can't escape it. Your destiny was written long ago."

"Destiny?" said Megan. "What are you talking about?"

"Joanne saw it. She knew."

"Who knew wh—"

Megan had to jerk out of the way as Eleanor's horse bolted out of the yard. Eleanor swung at Brother Irwyn, who ducked under her sword. Hoofs clicked and skidded as she yanked her horse around for another charge. Brother Irwyn vaulted the fence into the stable and rolled in the straw. Eleanor swiped the air in vain with her sword.

Megan kicked her horse forward, advancing on Brother Irwyn. He easily swayed out of the way of her clumsy sword thrust and scurried past her, into the interior of the stables. Megan began to dismount. Damon stayed her.

"I think we should use these horses as nature intended," he said. "And I don't mean as a low-cost alternative to beef."

The sounds of the approaching crowd were getting louder. Megan could see the flicker of torchlight reflected from sharpened instruments. Damon was right. They couldn't afford to stick around. She kicked her horse forward.

"It's no good," Brother Irwyn called out from the stables. "We'll find you. We'll hunt you down."

"Oh, yeah?"

Megan swiped at the lantern hanging by the stable door. It dropped to the ground and shattered, coating the straw with oil its spark fed on hungrily. Within seconds the whole stable was carpeted in flames.

The remaining horses shrieked and bolted. Megan yelled and swung her sword, aiming them at the approaching mob, which scattered in panic. She and the others turned their horses in the opposite direction. As they galloped away, Megan spared a last glance behind them and saw Brother Irwyn striding out of the burning stables, his robes smoldering. As if he had just stepped out of hell.

# ten

They pushed the horses for as long and as hard as they could. Only when they tired to a crawl did they swap the speed of the road for the sanctuary of the woods. It meant another night under the stars instead of in a real bed, but at least it was better than a bed in which they might find themselves murdered.

"Do you think they're coming after us?" Megan asked, warming her hands on the small fire they had risked.

"Possibly," said Eleanor. "If they can get the other horses back and Brother Irwyn can persuade the villagers. But it'll be dawn before they can think about picking up our trail."

"What do you think he told them about us?" asked Damon.

"Not the truth, I'm guessing," said Megan.

"If they were all working for the witches, they could have got to us anytime," said Eleanor. "And they'd still be after us." Megan and Damon looked south, in the direction of the village. "I don't think they were waiting for a cue to ambush us."

"No," said Damon. "I did sense a certain lack of dramatic timing to their actions."

"From now on," said Eleanor, "we keep to ourselves. We don't tell anyone our business, not until we've spoken to Father Galan."

"What if he's a witch too?" said Megan.

"The High Priest of Eastport is not a witch. If he was, he could have ordered the whole garrison down to Thicketford to get you. The witches wouldn't have had to reveal themselves."

"There's *one* person we can trust in Eastport then?"

"More than that. There's still a few friends of my family in the city. Well, I say friends, I mean servants."

"You woman of the people you," said Damon.

"I forgot priests were one with the oppressed masses."

"I was forced into that."

"And I was forced into my role too," snapped Eleanor. "No one chooses the part they play. We can but tackle what the world throws at us and try to make it a better place." She looked up to the night sky. "My father told me that. Not that he followed his own rules."

"Do any of us?" said Megan.

"Parents always expect the impossible of their offspring."

Talk of parents wrenched Megan's thoughts in a new direction. What kind of mother would she be? She'd hardly even considered it. "Have you ever had children?" she asked Eleanor.

The fire picked out the countess's exquisite features as she gazed at Megan. "I'm not married," she said, her voice cold.

"The two aren't exactly connected."

"I don't have any bastards lying around, if that's what you're getting at." Eleanor glanced over at Damon. "Not until recently anyway." Her eyes narrowed. "Why do you ask?"

"Oh, no reason," said Megan. If Eleanor knew about her child, there was no way she'd let her go after Gwyneth, and Megan was afraid she wouldn't be able to resist the countess. "It's just that . . . I mean . . . you're very beautiful . . . there must have been men who wanted to . . . you know . . ."

"Shag you," said Damon.

"Marry you," said Megan, shooting Damon a dirty look.

"The priests would never allow me to marry and perpetuate the dynasty."

"So you're the last of the Endalays?"

"Perhaps," said Eleanor.

"What will the priests do once they find out who you are?" Megan asked her.

"Lock me up? Execute me? Hold a celebration in my honor?"

"Not all at the same time, I assume," said Damon. "Though I've been to worse parties."

"Execute you?" said Megan.

"It's unlikely," said Eleanor. "It's a long time since my family was a threat to their position, but . . ."

". . . priests can be a bit paranoid," finished Damon.

"Whatever. It doesn't matter. We have to convince them the witches have returned, that they have your sister and that we have to get her back."


In the days that followed they avoided any settlements, and even the road unless they could be sure there was no one around. It was a hard slog through forests and undergrowth, scavenging for food and water, sleeping in the open while the rain plastered their clothes to their skin and the wind robbed every last scrap of heat from their bodies. Megan swallowed any complaints, coped with the soreness and the paranoia that enveloped her every time they heard another traveler on the road. Gwyneth was going through far worse.

They descended into the Speed valley. Eastport spread out before them. It lay a couple of miles inland from the mouth of the Speed, the great river that sliced Ainsworth off from the rest of the Realm. Locals claimed the city was so named because it lay to the east of the Harris Sea; outsiders sniggered and claimed Eastport's founders couldn't read a compass.

The city was composed of two parts: the walled inner section, where the rich had their mansions and the city's rulers their palaces, and a sprawling outer part, where the poor built their shacks and their hovels without regard for the rules or regulations or basic engineering principles. The port that formed the northern boundary of the inner city saw most of the trade that passed through the county, though some traders wishing to avoid the priests' custom duties landed their ships illegally downriver.

Megan could just make out the river, across which ferries darted back and forth, transporting men and supplies to the garrison encamped on the north bank. Would the priests order them to help her? They had to, surely, otherwise what else were the soldiers for—marching and drilling and showing off to impressionable girls?

She remembered the first time she had been to Eastport: when she and Gwyneth had started school. The city seemed to stretch for an eternity, its buildings to touch the sky. The post horse had dropped them by the school, leaving them to huddle in the noisy streets, unsure what to do. Eventually Megan worked up the courage to knock on a door and ask for Brother Brogan. The servant who answered slammed the door in her face, but a little while later a priest with food stains streaking his graying robes waddled up to them.

"I'm Brother Brogan." His finger alternated between the sisters before settling on Megan. "You. You're with me."

The sisters exchanged worried glances. "What about Gwyneth, brother?" Megan asked.

"She's going to the temple to work for the librarian there. Brother Attor."

No, they couldn't be separated. The thought of being on her own in the hostile city, so far away from home, terrified Megan. She took Gwyneth's hand in hers. Their fingers locked together in a familiar action.

"I'm sorry, brother. We have to stay together."

"There isn't a position for both of you at the palace."

"We're here to go to school, not work," said Gwyneth sullenly.

"And how are you going to pay for school?"

"Why do we need to pay? Priests don't need money."

"And your food and your lodgings?" said Brother Brogan, chuckling.

"I told you we should have gotten the treasure, Gwyn," Megan hissed.

Brother Brogan offered them an avuncular smile. "Don't worry, girls, you won't be working all the time. And you'll still see each other at school and at night."

"But . . ."

A little cough interrupted them. It came from another priest. The robes of this one were spotless; his tonsure clipped to a neat half-inch; his figure, unusually for a priest, slim and athletic.

"Which one's mine?" he asked.

Brother Brogan pointed at Gwyneth. "That one, Brother Attor."

"Excellent. And you are . . . ?"

"Gwyneth, brother."

"With me, Gwyneth."

Gwyneth stepped toward Brother Attor. Her fingers were still entwined with Megan's. Their arms stretched for a moment, bridging the ever-widening gap between them, until they broke apart. Gwyneth gave Megan a final look. Tears pricked Megan's eyes but she forced herself not to cry.

Now she was back, not to lose Gwyneth but to find her. As they failed to make their way through the crowded Eastport streets, it became obvious the horses were a hindrance. They sold them on to a dealer who expressed a deep disinterest in the provenance of the mounts; in turn Megan expressed a deep disinterest in the low amount of cash they were offered in return.

"Before we go any further," Eleanor said to Damon, "is there anything you need to warn us about?"

"Like?"

"Oh, I don't know. Merchants with empty cash boxes? Tradesmen waiting for payment? Rich widows who noticed their jewelry went missing at the same time as that pretty boy they were simpering over?"

"You think I'm pretty?" said Damon.

"To a certain type of middle-aged woman."

"You're a middle-aged woman."

"I am not," protested Eleanor. "Well, not that type. Look, if we're going to get hassled by the city guards, we need to be able to deal with it."

"Deal with it?" said Damon. "How?"

"There's a nice deep river nearby."

"You want to throw the guards in the river?"

"Not the guards, no."

They pushed through the heart of the outer city. Some merchants, driven out of the inner city by high prices, had erected stuccoed houses along the road, which at least gave the graffiti artists blank canvases on which to practice their craft. A thousand smells assaulted Megan's nostrils—frying spices, baking bread, the piss from tanners' buckets. Everyone was selling something and anything could be bought, whether in open markets that had been makeshift for hundreds of years or in back rooms safe from the eyes of the taxman and the prohibitionist. When they had first arrived in Eastport, Megan and Gwyneth would come down to watch the street performers and pool their pocket money on a cake or piece of fruit pie. Gwyneth had soon grown tired of it, preferring to shut herself in the library, but Megan had continued to come down whenever she had time off from her studies and chores, reveling in life in all its myriad varieties.

They passed people from all over the Realm: farmers from the fertile plains north of the Speed hawking their crops; snooty New Stathians who viewed the city as a hovel compared to their home metropolis; Percadians from out west looking to make a quick sovereign. They passed foreigners too: burly miners from the Snow Cities north of the Kartik Mountains, burned red by the hostile southern sun; Sandstriders in robes battered by the desert, their reputation for ferocity belied by the ease with which they joked; even a family from the Diannon Empire beyond the Savage Ocean. The daughter caught Megan's attention. She was a graceful girl coming into womanhood, with skin like polished jet, black hair hanging in a braid down her back, and a sword in a lacquered scabbard hanging from her hip. Was there sadness in her eyes, a knowledge that home was a long and impossible journey away, or was Megan seeing her own reflection?

They reached the gates leading into the inner city, which hadn't been closed once during Megan's stay in Eastport. The city guards loitered around, leaning on their pikes. They wore jerkins dyed a blotchy crimson and dirty white surcoats embroidered with the sign of the circle, less a symbol of piety and more a bullseye. The older, more experienced ones wore mail vests under their surcoats; the younger ones preferred to avoid the weight and expense, but if they survived their first encounter with a drunken knife-wielder down a dark back alley they changed their minds.

One of the guards hailed them. "You three! Stop!"

He began to amble over. "Act innocent," Damon whispered.

"We *are* innocent," said Megan.

"Oh, yeah. Still finding the concept a novelty."

"Where're you going?" asked the guard.

Megan pointed through the gates into the inner city. "Um . . ."

"What's with the sword?"

"It's ceremonial," said Eleanor. Her own weapons were concealed beneath her robes.

"Ceremonial? That whacking great big thing?"

"Big ceremony."

The guard folded his arms and sucked his teeth. "Weapon that large, I'll have to tax it."

"I often have that problem," said Damon.

"How much?" said Megan. Damon started to stretch his hands apart. "I was talking to the guard."

"Shilling should do it."

They had no choice. Megan didn't want to enter the city unarmed.

After sorting out the paperwork, they made their way through the inner city. Gaderian Square—the traditional meeting place for friends, lovers, and pickpockets—was its usual packed self. Megan used to meet Gwyneth by the fountain here, either to people-watch or as a starting point for exploring the city. Habit made her look around now, a tiny part of her expecting Gwyneth to come squeezing through the crowd. The forlornness of the hope made her heart sit heavy in her chest.

They jostled their way down the avenue that led to Gaderian Square's more genteel twin—Endalay Square, these days just referred to as the main square. The palace, from which the Endalays and then the priests had ruled the county, dominated the north side. Its front was a marble colonnade topped by statues of the Counts of Ainsworth, which the weather and a second-rate sculptor had reduced to homogenous blobs.

There was a look on Eleanor's face that was half wistful, half annoyed. "Guess I'm home," she said.

"Which one's your father?" Megan asked, pointing at the statues.

"You don't get one until you're dead, and somehow the priests never got around to commissioning one for him."

A line snaked out of the main doors, down the steps and onto the square itself. "That us?" asked Damon, handing Megan a bread roll of uncertain provenance.

Megan didn't have time to wait in line. Provoking glares and catcalls, she led Damon and Eleanor straight to the doors, where a quartet of guards stood sentry outside. Megan went up to the one with the least-rusted armor.

"I want to see the High Priest."

"That's nice for you, love."

"Please," said Megan. "It's urgent."

"It's always urgent."

Eleanor stepped forward. "We need to see him *now*, you good-for-nothing piece of scum."

The guard gave her a shove. "Get to the back." The line assented to this command with varying levels of politeness.

They sloped to the end of the queue. "You shouldn't have talked to him like that," Megan said to Eleanor.

"My father told me you had to treat guards with a sense of disdain, otherwise they won't respect you."

"Your own, not other people's."

"If my father were here now . . ."

"We'd have the undead to worry about as well," said Damon.

They waited and, when that was over, they waited some more. There was a moment of excitement when the queue shuffled along, but it was only someone leaving for a piss. When he returned, they shuffled back down. Damon shouted a halfhearted "Jumper!" up the line, but no one paid him any notice.

He bounced on his heels and looked around. "We should have brought some cards, set up a game. Money to be made here."

"In view of the priests?" said Eleanor. "Gambling's a sin."

"*Untaxed* gambling's a sin."

The temple bells tolled the sixth hour, marking the end of the working day. In the cloisters behind the pillars, priests folded up their desks. There they offered legal and clerical services for a fee—notarizing contracts, advising on lawsuits, arranging tax affairs. Officially they were meant to cooperate for the greater good, but they hawked their services incessantly, boasting about their level of access and the size of their kickbacks.

The priests emerged between the gaps in the pillars like bees leaving the hive. Wooden sandals beat a rhythm on the stone steps as they descended to the square and crossed to the temple on the south side for the evening service. As the priests filed past, Megan searched their number for Brother Brogan. He didn't have much influence—he was only a tutor to poor kids from the provinces—but he had more pull than she did. There was no sign of him. One of the priests, his black hair and skin greasy as if he had been fried, caught her looking and stared back. His piggy eyes bore into Megan. She shuffled on the spot and cast her gaze down.

"Maybe we should go worship," she said.

"If you're bringing religion into this, I'm off for a drink," said Damon.

"I thought you were studying to be a priest."

"I spent ten years praying—look where it got me. I'll be in the Dropped Handkerchief if you want me."

He sloped off. "Do you think we should follow him?" Megan said. They'd had nothing to eat or drink apart from Damon's filched roll since they'd arrived in East-port, and her throat and stomach were starting to make their displeasure known.

"There's still time yet," said Eleanor. There was a boom as the doors to the palace shut. "Or not."

"What?" said Megan. "No!"

She pushed her way through the dispersing queue up to the palace. The officer in charge there rolled his eyes. "Not you again, love."

"I really need to see Father Galan."

"Come back tomorrow."

"You don't understand," said Megan. "The wi—"

"The what?"

Megan looked around. The commotion had attracted the attention of the crowd. Most no doubt were waiting for someone to get hit, but there could be someone with more sinister purposes whose interest might be piqued by a teenage girl claiming the witches had returned. There could be people in the city looking for her.

"Nothing," she said.

They hurried away before anyone could start asking questions. "We should find somewhere for the night," said Eleanor. "I know a couple of people who . . ."

Megan shook her head. She hadn't come all this way to hang around. "If I can find Brother Brogan, he can get me in to see the High Priest tonight."

"You don't know that."

"I won't until I try," said Megan.

She started to march across the square. Eleanor sighed and hurried after her.

Carrier pigeons flapped from the towers of the temple as they rounded its vast circle. Megan's old school huddled in its shadows. The crumbling brickwork, the stepped roof and the curved nature of its walls indicated its origins as a segment of the old temple that had survived demolition. It was drafty in winter, baked in summer, and the windows let in so little light the priests often had to take their pupils outside to teach, but Megan had been happy there, sucking in knowledge and glimpsing the nature of the universe. If she closed her eyes, it could be a year ago and her in that class, reciting passages from the Book of Faith for Brother Brogan or answering questions on Werlavia's history for Brother Shult. Maybe she still was, maybe all this was nothing but the result of a fever brought on by the summer heat and her dream self had finally found its way back to her body.

Megan stepped into the building. The air was stuffy inside and smelled of ink and chalk dust. An inscription was chiseled into the stonework over the archway that led to the classrooms. The first Pledge of Faith in old Werlay: PRANA SALAT SUCTAMO PROCTERO— I pledge obedience to God and His priests.

"Can I help you?"

Megan started and turned. The questioner was a middle-aged priest with a tonsure composed of tight graying curls and a chin shaped like a ramp. "I was looking for Brother Brogan, brother."

"Brother Brogan? Oh, I see. The Sisters will need your mother's permission, of course—" he nodded at Eleanor —"but given the circumstances, I don't think that's going to be a problem."

"I'm not . . ." said Eleanor. "She's not . . ."

"His usual type? Yes, I know, but she does have a certain rustic charm."

Megan resisted the urge to caress her stomach. Surely she wasn't showing yet? "I am not having Brother Brogan's baby," she said, hoping no one would question the specificity of her denial, "but I do need to speak to him. It's urgent."

"He can't marry you, no matter what he said. The vows are for life." The priest patted her arm. "Don't worry, the Sisters of the Faith will take care of you."

It was hard to dislodge an idea from a priest's head once it got there. "Are you saying you don't know where he is, brother?"

"God knows where he is, and that's what matters."

"How long has he been missing?" said Megan.

"Let's see," said the priest. "We had to dig Brother Bray out of retirement when Brother Brogan didn't show up for his classes and that would be . . ." He counted on his fingers. "About two weeks ago."

Two weeks? Around the time Thicketford was attacked. The stultifying air became hard to breathe.

Megan looked to Eleanor, who kept her face neutral. "You didn't think to look for him?"

"Oh, he'll be in the bottom of some barrel somewhere. I've no doubt he'll turn up. They always do. He'll do penance for his sin." The priest's eyes narrowed. "As should you."

Megan reckoned she'd done enough penance to last a couple of lifetimes. She donated a half-shilling to help with the upkeep of the school and stepped outside. She leaned against the wall and gulped in fresh air.

"I know what you're thinking," said Eleanor. "It's a coincidence, nothing more."

"My old tutor goes missing at the same time my friends and family are killed and kidnapped?"

"Not everything's about you. He's probably got his own reasons for disappearing."

Megan hoped that was true, wished it was. They already had one example of a priest working for the witches; she didn't need to be paranoid to suspect another. She remembered his avuncular smile, the praise at work well done. Had he been planning the slaughter all this time? Shouldn't she have known? She felt both useless and used.

If Megan were to find Brother Brogan, or find out what had happened to him, it'd be in a pub somewhere. Only trouble was, there were so many of them around the temple, as she recalled from her days trying to find and drag him back to the palace before curfew. Where he ended up depended on where his tab hadn't reached eye-watering proportions.

Megan settled into a familiar pattern, traversing a route honed to take in the maximum number of drinking establishments in the least amount of time: from the dives that were nothing more than a guy with a roof and a barrel of ale, to converted mansions that once belonged to petty lords and now catered to the rich and connected. Coins prompted memories, but they were old memories, of sorrows being drowned weeks ago. No one who remembered him had seen him recently. The consensus was he'd slipped—or someone had pushed him—into the river. It was the usual fate of drunks in Eastport. One wench hoped his pickled insides wouldn't give the vultures too much of a hangover. Maybe Megan *was* being paranoid; maybe Brother Brogan's drinking had finally killed him.

They ended up at the Dropped Handkerchief. It could be considered upmarket in that it averaged less than one homicide a night, a statistic aided by the low ceiling that made it hard to get a good brawl going. Damon was drinking and playing dice with a local who was all scar tissue and pornographic tattoos. Damon was winning. From the murderous look in his opponent's eyes, Megan didn't think this was a good idea.

She peered over his shoulder. Damon's dice showed two threes and a four; the Eastporter's a five, a four, and a two. The Eastporter was looking to claw his way back into the game unless Damon paid to roll again.

"What do you think?" he asked before taking a slug of wine. The redness of his eyes and the slackness of his face suggested his imbibing had reached priestly levels.

A one, a two, or a three would leave him still short of the Eastporter's score; a four would roll the pot over to the next round; a six and he would bust. Only a five would give him the perfect twelve he needed.

"Give up the round," said Megan. "You won't win."

"You're probably right," said Damon. He winked and dropped an extra shilling into the pot, to go with the two already there, and picked up one of the dice showing a three.

He held his fist up to Megan's mouth. "Blow for luck?" Megan sighed and did as asked. As she did, she noticed Damon's free hand dip surreptitiously into his pocket.

Damon brought his hands together and gave his fist a loose shake. A die tumbled out of it and shivered to a halt on the table. Five pips showed on its upturned face. Murmurs went around the table.

"What do you know?" said Damon. He raked the pot toward him and gathered the dice. "Another round?"

The Eastporter scowled at him. "I don't think so."

"Your loss." Damon pocketed his winnings and the dice, then took Megan by the hand. "Shall we?"

"Oi! Dice!"

"Oh, right, sorry." Damon tossed the dice at the Eastporter.

A pair of priests drained their cups and vacated their alcove table at the other end of the inn. Damon pulled Megan and Eleanor toward it and called for wine.

"Did you get to see the High Priest?" he said.

"We'll try again tomorrow," said Megan.

"And if they won't help you?"

"I'll go to the Supreme Priest in New Statham if I have to. I'll go to God if I have to."

"God?" said Damon. "How're you going to manage that?"

"We'll send you as her personal messenger," said Eleanor.

"Sometimes I get the feeling you don't like me."

"Only sometimes?"

A barmaid slapped a carafe of wine and three cups on their table. Damon looked to Megan. She rolled her eyes and passed a coin to the barmaid, who made a show of testing its authenticity before moving to the next customer.

"I've been talking to a guy who knows some guys who might be able to help us," said Damon.

"What kind of guys?" asked Eleanor.

"Mercenaries."

"You're suggesting we put our trust in people who kill for money?"

"Better than people who do it for a hobby."

Megan tried the wine. It cauterized her taste buds, which at least made the second sip more endurable. "We can't afford to pay for soldiers," she said. "And certainly not in the numbers it'll take to confront the witches."

Eleanor slid out of the booth and pulled up her hood. "I'm going to organize somewhere to stay," she said. "I won't be long. Try not to drink too much."

Megan peered into her cup. "Not much chance of that." She was convinced the wine was dissolving the glaze.

Damon cocked his head as he watched Eleanor swish out of the inn. "Is she really a countess?" he asked.

Megan frowned. She hadn't considered Eleanor might not be whom she claimed. Why wouldn't she be? It wasn't as if the aristocracy was popular. "I think so. Yes. Yes, of course she is."

"One guy I knew at the seminary claimed he was the incarnation of one of the Saviors, come to renew the Faith and smite the non-followers."

"How do you know he wasn't?"

"The autopsy confirmed it," said Damon.

Megan picked up her cup, remembered what it contained and put it back down again. "Why the sudden suspicions?"

"I was asking around," said Damon. "No one's heard of her."

"Why would they? She was a baby when the Endalays were last in power."

"I suppose." He rolled a die across the table, scooped it up, and repeated the action. Both times it landed on five.

"Why do you have a die loaded to roll a five?" asked Megan.

"It's cheaper than one loaded to roll a six." He shrugged. "Weird, I know." He pocketed the die and leaned across the table. "Countess or not, do you think she likes me?"

"I'm the last person who should be giving advice on love," said Megan.

"There's someone . . . ?" Damon's face dropped. "Oh. I guess he's . . ."

"It wasn't serious." Megan swirled the wine in her cup. She couldn't bring herself to drink any more. It couldn't be doing her insides or the baby any good. She pushed it over to Damon. "I don't know."

"She hasn't talked about me?"

"Not in a strictly positive sense . . ."

"But she's not dismissed the idea?"

"Not really come up," said Megan. "What with us being hunted down the length of the county and my sister in the hands of . . . you know . . ."

"I suppose we have been a bit distracted."

"Try being more considerate. Listen to her. Stop making jokes in inappropriate situations."

"Not be myself, you mean?" said Damon.

"I didn't mean that." Megan considered. "Well, possibly I did . . ."

"You were right. You *are* the last person I should be asking for advice on love."

Eleanor returned a couple hours later. "I've found us somewhere to stay," she said. "Or I think I have anyway."

"Not another inn," said Megan.

Eleanor shook her head. "An old family servant. Wasn't sure if he was still alive."

"Ooh, servant," said Damon, slurring the *s*. "Aren't we classy?"

"You let him get drunk?" Eleanor said to Megan.

"I seem to have that effect on people."

Twilight had calmed the city streets. What people were around didn't loiter or talk about their business but flitted from point A to point B, occasionally dashing to point C chased by anguished cries. Damon started up a song that was quickly shot down by Eleanor once its rhymes took on a family-unfriendly flavor.

They were heading for the corner of the inner city tucked between the Speed and the west wall, where the main sewer drained into the river. On good days, there was a vaguely unpleasant smell; on bad days, it was gut-wrenchingly nauseating. That night, with the river high and fast, the odor was bearable; certainly no worse than Damon.

They reached the waterfront, quiet now after the business of the day. A war galley skulked on the other side of the Speed, reduced to a silhouette by the setting sun. Its sisters would be out at sea on patrol. Megan wondered if they had already run into the witches' ship. Gwyneth could be getting rescued at this very moment. She imagined Gwyneth waving at her from a docking ship, watching as her sister picked her way down the gangplank, flinging herself into waiting arms in the knowledge it was all over. Then Damon barged into her as he staggered about looking for a gutter to throw up in, and reality came crashing back.

Eleanor led them to the last house in a row of crumbling buildings that looked one storm away from being reduced to rubble. She banged on the door. The Speed churned as they waited. Eleanor banged again.

"Silas!"

Through thin curtains, a light could be seen making its way through the building, brightening and fading, skipping behind walls and popping up in unexpected windows. Metal scraped as bolts were drawn back and the door opened with a rheumatic creak.

An old man greeted them, hunched over a candle. He wore a nightgown that stretched to his knees, leaving his gnarled shins and feet exposed. The odd rat's tail of gray hair sprouted from his spotted pate, and one eye was obscured by a milky film. He didn't spare Megan or Damon a glance, instead fixing his attention on Eleanor. He looked rapt for a moment, as if contemplating the mysteries of the Faith, then his face hardened.

"You look like your mother," he said. "There's a marriage that never should have happened."

Eleanor slapped him—a sharp, contemptuous blow with the back of her hand. Silas crumpled to the floor of the hallway. The candle fell from his grip, spluttered and died.

"Insult my mother again, and my hand will have a blade in it."

"You have your father's fire, though. That's good. We'll need it."

"We need to stay here, Silas."

"Lynette tell you to sod off?"

"There would have been . . . political difficulties."

Eleanor strode past Silas, making no effort to help him off the floor. Megan held out a hand. "I'm sorry," she said, pulling the old man to his feet. "Eleanor's a bit . . . well, I suppose we're all a bit . . ."

Damon stumbled past. "We're trying to work on her man-management skills. You don't have anything to drink, have you?"

"That's Lady Endalay to you," Silas said to Megan. To Damon he said, "We have water."

"Nothing more exciting?"

"I can piss in it, if you like."

They found Eleanor prowling the living room. Silas relit his candle and used its flame to light the stub of another that was set upon the fireplace. The twin flames revealed whitewashed walls streaked with black mold, a wooden chair with one of its legs propped up by a wedge of cloth, and a rickety table upon which a book had been laid. A constant drip sounded underfoot: the cellar must have flooded.

"We'll need warmth, food, and bedding," said Eleanor.

Silas scuttled to the fireplace and began preparing it. "Of course, my lady."

"Hot water too, if you can manage it."

"I will."

"And do something about the smell."

"You brought him, my lady."

Silas got the fire going and retreated from the room. Megan got the impression he was avoiding turning his back on Eleanor; whether it was out of respect or fear she might stick a knife in it, it was hard to tell.

"Why did you treat him like that?" Megan asked, warming her hands.

"He's a servant."

"So was I."

"A year or two in the priests' kitchens," said Eleanor. She brought the chair close to the fire and sat. "Silas's family has served the Endalays for ten generations. He expects a firm hand."

"A thank-you wouldn't go amiss."

Eleanor raised an eyebrow. "You're scolding me?"

"Someone has to," said Damon. He was slumped against the wall, contemplating the space between his knees.

"Do you know who you're talking to?" Eleanor said to him. "My ancestors ruled this city, this county, for centuries. They helped Edwyn the Unifier conquer the Realm, they beat back the Sandstriders when they swarmed over the Endalayan Mountains—hell, they even *named* the Endalayan Mountains. My father led the first battle against the witches. My—"

"But what did you do?" said Damon.

"I . . ."

"You're bragging about the deeds of some random blokes who happened to shag your mother or your grandmother or whoever. What did you do yourself? Apart from follow a sixteen-year-old girl around like a bewildered puppy."

"You don't know what—"

Eleanor's protest was interrupted by Silas's return. He cleared the table of the book and placed upon it bread, cheese, and water. "Good," said Eleanor. Megan caught her eye. "Thank you, Silas."

Silas looked bewildered for a moment, then bowed. "It is an honor to once more serve the house of Endalay."

"It's not much of a house these days," said Eleanor.

"No . . ." said Silas. He turned to Damon. "Go down to the docks, see if the fishermen have any catch left. If it pleases my lady."

"I don't mind," said Damon. "I'll do the booze run while I'm at it."

He held out his hand. Silas looked at it, then at Eleanor. She in turn looked at Megan, who reached for her purse. "Other people are allowed to pay for things," she said. "I won't feel offended."

Silas pointed at her. "May I have the services of your serving girl?" he said to Eleanor.

"I'm not her servant."

"More the other way round," muttered Damon.

Eleanor glared daggers at Damon. Megan feared they'd turn into the real thing. "But I'll be happy to help."

Megan followed Silas to the kitchen at the back of the house. He dropped a couple more logs on the remains of the fire, which added a little life to the dingy room, and filled a pot with water.

"Keep an eye on that," he said, hanging the pot over the fire. "When it's ready, call my lady. There's soap there," he added, pointing to a sliver resting on a deformed clay dish.

"Can I eat first?"

Silas pressed in close and lowered his voice. "She's getting old. She should have returned sooner. Is she still fertile?"

"What?"

"Can she have babies?"

"I know what fertile means."

"How long have you been with her?"

"A couple of weeks."

"And in that time has she proved herself worthy of the name of Endalay? Or is she a cowardly fool like the rest of her mother's family?"

"You don't like them, do you?"

"The Kalverts were good-for-nothing scoundrels whose only talent was producing pretty daughters. They even sold one poor girl to the barbarians in the Snow Cities. We can thank the witches for getting rid of *them* at least." Silas gripped Megan's wrists. "Will men follow her? Will men die for her?"

"She's brave and loyal and I wouldn't be alive without her, and why—are you planning a war?"

"Isn't that why she's here? To reclaim her birthright from the priests?"

"We're here to enlist the help of the priests, not fight them."

Silas's brow creased, emphasizing his deep wrinkles. "I don't understand."

"The witches took my sister. I have to get her back. I need ships, soldiers. Only the priests have those."

Silas made the sign of the circle at the mention of the witches. "They've returned?"

"You don't believe me?"

"The priests said they'd defeated them. Should've known it was another of their half-truths." He shook his head. "If the witches have your sister, you need the priests to pray for her soul, not to fight for you."

"Don't say that!"

"I'm sorry, lass. I really am." Silas patted her arm and shook his head. He sat down at the table, an operation that involved much painful folding of limbs. "There's some wine in that cupboard there."

"I thought you didn't have any."

"Reckon you deserve it. Pour me a glass too. I don't deserve it, but if the witches are back I'll be dead before it can do me much harm."

Megan poured two cups, heavily diluting her own. "You fought in the war?"

"I wouldn't say I fought. I was Lord Endalay's squire, which meant I fetched and carried and wiped his ass 'cause he couldn't reach his own backside in that stupid armor of his."

"So you saw what the witches did to their prisoners?"

"Don't think about it, lass."

"How can I not think about it?" said Megan.

"Drink enough of this stuff, and it'll be easy."

"They could be doing anything to her. What did you see? What did they do?"

"You're torturing yourself."

"That's nothing compared to what I'll do to anyone who's hurt my sister."

# eleven

They ate and went to sleep early: Megan and Eleanor so they could try to see the High Priest first thing in the morning; Damon because he had drunk himself into a coma. The two women shared Silas's bed, which was better than the weeks they'd spent sleeping on the hard ground, but only in the way dysentery was better than cholera. It was like sleeping on rocks, and every time Megan turned, some fresh lump ground into her flesh.

She woke to find Eleanor gone from the bed. Elsewhere in the house, the snores of Silas and Damon competed for the honor of which would incite homicide first. Out in the city, a bell was completing its toll. She counted at least three. Moonlight peeked in through the thin curtains. Eastport was as quiet as it ever got. The Speed continued its eternal roar. The odd yell or bark penetrated the darkness. There were thousands of people out there. She was as ignorant of them as they were of her, yet she needed their help. She was desperate for it. If only she had something to offer in return other than gratitude.

Megan swung out of bed. She stubbed her toe on something that skidded across the floorboards and thudded against the skirting board. She rubbed away the smarting and examined the object she had kicked. Eleanor's throwing knife, its blade almost liquid in the silvery night. Megan slipped it into her pocket and frowned, wondering how it had fallen from its sheath.

The countess was down in the living room, drinking the last of the wine Damon had fetched along with the fish. She was staring through the open window at the black waters of the Speed. The moon bleached her pale skin, making her look like a ghost, a spirit pining for a lost love.

The book Silas had removed from the table still lay on the floor. Megan picked it up and angled it to the light to read the title. *A History of the Noble House of Endalay.*

"My father commissioned it when he married my mother," said Eleanor. "I wouldn't recommend it. Its dullness is only matched by the atrociousness of its grammar. A long list of my forbears fighting and procreating, occasionally at the same time."

"Are you in it?"

"The last sentence is the announcement of my birth. That's it, that's all I ever achieved in life. I existed."

"I thought you were a happy drunk."

"I'm not drunk," said Eleanor. The reek of her breath suggested otherwise. "Silas expects me to reclaim my inheritance."

"I heard."

"My father tried it once, after the war. He and the few lords that had survived. They expected the people to rise to support them. The people had other ideas. What had my father done for them? The priests had saved them from the witches. My father . . . hadn't." She grabbed a second cup, threw its dregs out of the window, and filled it afresh. "Here, have a drink."

Megan accepted, if only to stop Eleanor finishing off all the wine herself. "You saved my life," she said. "Damon's too. That's got to be worth something."

"I think the two only balance out."

"You shouldn't be so hard on him."

"Girl needs a hobby."

"He likes you."

"He's—what?—twenty, twenty-five years younger than me," said Eleanor. "I'm not interested in boys. You have him."

"I'm not interested in boys either." Not after the mess Wade had got her into. Megan put her pregnancy out of mind. When she had Gwyneth back, then she'd be ready to face it.

She remembered the knife and handed it to Eleanor. "You dropped this."

"Yes, I did, didn't I?" She weighed the blade in her palm, then slipped it back in its sheath. A serious look came over her face. She seized Megan's hand. "I swear I'll protect you, Megan. I won't let any harm come to you. I won't let you down again. We'll find your sister. I'll make sure you get the life you deserve. Do you believe me?"

The vehemence of the declaration threw Megan off-balance. "How much have you had to drink?"

"This isn't the drink. Do you believe me?"

Megan swallowed and nodded. "Yes. I believe you."

But was belief enough?


Megan and Eleanor started queuing at dawn—they left Damon at Silas's nursing a hangover—and crossed the threshold of the palace a little after the temple bells struck ten. They got no farther than the atrium, a vast open space constructed of marble and populated with exotic plants from all over the Realm. To provide the right environment for these plants, the once-open ceiling had been roofed with glass panes, which magnified the sun and baked the milling petitioners. Only burning incense prevented the stench of sweat from becoming overpowering, and that made Megan light-headed. She gave in to necessity and bought a cup of cold water from one of the serving girls who weaved through the crowd.

Tucked away in the shade of the cloisters that circumscribed the room, priests sat at their desks, listening to petitioners' complaints with all the enthusiasm of schoolboys facing a geography lesson on a summer day. Megan and Eleanor moved to a free one. The receptionist there looked up at them, quill poised over parchment. The bags under his eyes aged him, but the light olive skin was smooth and blemish-free. Instead of the traditional tonsure, he had opted to shave his head completely; a couple of nicks specked with dried blood suggested he'd done it that morning.

He gave them the dead-eyed smile of the bureaucrat. "I'm Brother Alwyn and I'll be your facilitator today."

"Our what?" said Eleanor.

"Your facilitator." Brother Alwyn caught their blank looks. "I facilitate things. Honestly, you try to drag things into the fourth century . . ." He sighed. "Name?"

"Megan of Thicketford."

The priest wrote it down. "And your companion?"

"I am Eleanor of the house of Endalay, Countess of Ainsworth, Baroness of Laxton and Herth, First Lady of Kirkland, Overlord of the Spice Isles, and Defender of the Southern Lands."

The priest blinked, unimpressed. "Sure you are. I'll have to shorten it a little."

He scratched away at the parchment. Eleanor craned her neck. "That's not how you shorten—"

"What is the nature of your visit?"

"We need to see the High Priest, brother," said Megan.

Brother Alwyn sucked his teeth. "There's a bit of a waiting list, I'm afraid. However for certain . . . considerations, the process can be expedited. We have a number of packages to suit all size of purse. For ten shillings, our Silver Package will—"

"You expect us to pay a bribe?" said Eleanor.

"It's not a bribe," said the priest. "More of a . . . consideration."

"What's the difference?"

"You get a receipt."

Megan leaned over the desk. "Men came to my village. They kidnapped my sister and killed everyone else."

"I'm sorry for your loss," said Brother Alwyn in a manner that suggested his only sorrow arose from hearing about it.

"You have to do something about it!"

"I'll make a note. In the records."

"You'll what?"

"The official records. For a donation of half a shilling, an acolyte will say a prayer for the soul of your loved ones." He looked down at his parchment and murmured, "For a full shilling he might even mean it."

Megan slammed the desk. Ink splashed out of the priest's pot and spattered his parchment. "My sister is suffering God knows what and your response is to scribble something down?"

"Not anymore," said Brother Alwyn, mopping up the spilled ink with a handkerchief. "Guard!"

A pot-bellied guard lumbered over and rested on his pike. "Brother?" His surcoat was a little cleaner than the norm, but his crimson jerkin was stained with sweat. He had the bored expression of someone who was counting down the hours until he could go to the pub.

"Remove these women."

The guard made a lazy grab for Megan. She slipped out his way and reached for her purse.

"How fast does that get us in?" she asked, slamming a sovereign down on Brother Alwyn's desk.

The priest examined the coin. He waved the guard away, then he checked his parchments. "Let's see. There's some old fool complaining brigands burned down his inn—he can wait. Will this afternoon do for you?"


Everyone was staring at Megan. She looked into their faces and saw them wondering who this nobody was and preparing to jeer: the guards who lined the walls of the great hall, supporting themselves on their pikes; the priests and acolytes who sprawled on the benches of the galleries, their robes varying in color from pristine white to dirty gray; the hook-nosed Sister of the Faith who hovered in an alcove like a vulture waiting for the scraps; the city council who sat at the back of the stage muttering to themselves; and, at the head of it all, Father Galan, High Priest of Eastport and governor of Ainsworth, who occupied his throne resplendent in blue silk that shimmered in the light streaming down from the clerestory windows.

Megan forced herself to approach the stage. Her back felt naked without the sword hanging there—the guards had confiscated it before ushering them in—increasing her sense of vulnerability. The fried fish they'd bought down at the docks for lunch shifted in her stomach and threatened to end up as a greasy splat on the polished floor.

She looked to her side. Eleanor was gazing at the giant gold circle attached to the wall above the High Priest's head. The plaster in the middle of the ring was discolored by a shield-shaped patch. The emblem of the county's ruling family would once have hung there. Eleanor's family. Megan knew what it was like to have your home defiled.

Father Galan gripped the arms of his throne and bent forward. Rings set with glittering stones decorated each of his plump fingers like the world's most expensive knuckleduster. "Who is this?"

Megan shuffled forward. Unsure what to do, she curtsied. A titter went around the hall. "I . . ."

Belatedly, Megan realized Father Galan wasn't talking to her but to the trim priest at his shoulder.

There was something familiar about him. It was Brother Attor, the priest Gwyneth had worked for in the temple library. More than worked, possibly. She recalled throwing herself on Gwyneth's bed, beside her sister. Gwyneth had snapped shut the copy of the Book of Faith she was reading, but not before Megan caught scribbling on the page where the Pledges were written.

She gasped. "You *wrote* in the Book of Faith?"

Gwyneth shook her head. "Not me. Brother Attor. It's his."

"Why've you got it?"

"We've got that test, remember? He lent it to me so I could study."

Megan, along with the rest of the class, had to make do with copying the verses they needed to learn onto scraps of paper and parchment. "And what does he get in return?"

"Nothing," said Gwyneth, drawing up her knees. "Brother Attor's just being nice."

"Ooh, *nice*. Does he have nice eyes, Gwyn? A nice smile? A nice—"

"You don't know what you're talking about, Meg," snapped Gwyneth. "You're just a little girl."

"What does that make you then?"

Gwyneth sighed and affected a superior pose that suggested the answer to Megan's question was too obvious to make.

"Are you going to let him . . . ?" Megan made a gesture she'd picked up down at the docks. Gwyneth shook her head. "Does he not want to?"

Gwyneth looked as if she was about to say something when their dorm mates piled in, jabbering away to themselves. She clammed up. Megan never found out what had happened. She could only assume Gwyneth had a crush on the only priest in Ainsworth with a set of morals.

Now it seemed Brother Attor had been promoted to be the High Priest's secretary. He leafed through the documents he held. "We have one Megan of Thicketford, father," he said to the High Priest, "and one Eleanor—we really must stop Brother Alwyn making personal comments on official documentation."

"Thicketford?" said Father Galan. "Never heard of it."

"It's a small village, on the road between Cheetham and Trafford's Haven."

"People still live down there?"

Brother Attor checked his records. "Not anymore, if this girl's to be believed."

"Why am I being bothered about this?"

"Why don't you ask me?" Megan blurted out. A whisper shot round the room. "I'm sorry, father."

Priests nudged their neighbors. One or two of the guards pushed off the walls and readied their pikes. Megan resisted the urge to scurry away to the nearest dark hole.

"Speak when you're spoken to," said Brother Attor.

Father Galan waved him back. He smiled indulgently at Megan. "Tell us what troubles you, my child."

Megan licked dry lips. "The witches have kidnapped my sister."

The murmurs around the hall silenced. Priests looked at their neighbors. Guards took a firmer grip on their pikes. Something clattered on the marble tiles. Everyone jumped. A priest mumbled, "Sorry," and retrieved his dropped cup.

Father Galan gathered himself. "We struck down the witches forty years ago," he said. "Them and their demon overlords."

"Then who slaughtered everyone in my village? Who murdered my grandfather? Who kidnapped my sister? Who is hunting me . . . and *why*?"

Megan was shaking. Eleanor put an arm around her shoulder and drew her close. Megan squeezed her hand, then stepped out of the countess's embrace. She had to do this by herself.

"They were men in black armor, father," she said. "They bore the star-broken circle. They took my sister. They tried to take me. You have to help. The fifth Pledge of—"

"You think to lecture *me* on the Pledges?"

"I'm sorry, father."

The High Priest beckoned to a servant hovering in the corner. He took a long swig on the wine brought to him and was about to say something when one of the priests behind him, a hunched old man with white hair sprouting from the sides of his head, spoke up.

"I was at Trafford's Haven, girl. Ten thousand of the bastards there were, eight foot tall and armed with hellfire."

"Nine," said his neighbor. He retained more of his hair than the first priest, but fewer teeth.

"What?"

"Nine foot tall, they were. With horns and red eyes and rows of sharp yellow teeth."

"I don't remember horns."

"One of them skewered Brother Horton in the gut."

"I thought he fell drunk on a rock."

"Brother Horton? Drunk? He never touched a drop."

"Brother 'Mine's a Double' Horton?"

Megan clenched her fists, forcing herself not to shout at the babbling old men. Father Galan cleared his throat. "Brothers, if we could . . . ?"

"Is it lunchtime already, father?"

"We have matters of state to attend to."

"Don't let me stop you."

"Are we going to listen to senile buggers all day?" said Eleanor.

"Show some respect, woman," snapped Father Galan. "The wisdom of my brothers has earned them indulgence. You, on the other hand, who are you, exactly?"

"Eleanor of the house of Endalay, Countess of Ainsworth, Baroness of Laxton and Herth, First Lady of

Kirkland, Overlord of the Spice Isles, and Defender of the Southern Lands."

The reaction to Eleanor's pronouncement wasn't as severe as when Megan had announced the return of the witches, but it wasn't far off. One of the two guards took a step forward. Did they intend to arrest Eleanor? It might not have been such a good idea to announce herself in front of everybody who had a reason for getting her out of the way.

Father Galan waved the guards back. He curled his lip and slouched on his throne. "We have no need for lords anymore. God delivered us from their tyranny."

"The witches did that," said Eleanor. "Careful they don't exterminate another ruling class."

"And what do you mean by that?"

"I was merely reminding you, *father*, of what happened during the first war against the witches. If you don't act quickly, there might be a second."

"Eleanor," Megan said through gritted teeth, "this is not helping."

"Is this some pathetic plan to regain power?" said Father Galan. "Panic the people into believing the witches have returned and claim you're the only one who can save them?"

Brother Attor nudged him and handed over a piece of parchment. Father Galan read it, then looked at Megan. "When did this . . . incident occur?"

"About two weeks ago, father."

"You know a Brother Rennie?"

"He's the village priest."

"And he perished too?"

"They killed everyone, father."

"Then why do we have a letter from him dated a week ago?" said Father Galan.

Megan was stunned. "You . . . ? You can't. That's . . . that's impossible."

"And yet here it is, in my hands. God provides the righteous dead with eternal life, but I didn't think He stretched to a postal service."

Laughter went around the hall. Faces contorted into mockery at her expense. Megan cringed. "It's a fake," she protested, aware of the pathetic whine in her voice.

Father Galan looked to his secretary. Brother Attor shook his head. "The handwriting matches his previous communications. He also provided the year's tithe."

"How much?"

The secretary cast his eyes down to his records. "An ounce of gold."

"I'm being bothered with this nonsense for a solitary ounce?" Father Galan waved dismissively. "Who's next?"

"You have to listen!" shouted Megan.

She attempted to get to the High Priest, but a wall of crimson and white was already surrounding her, the sign of the circle on the surcoats a mockery of the faith it represented. The Faithful were meant to be one people, where everyone fought for everyone else, but it looked as if Megan had been condemned to fight this battle alone.

The guards marched Megan and Eleanor through the palace and threw them out into a trash-strewn yard. Their swords followed moments later, blades clanging together as they landed in the dirt. Megan grabbed hers and swiped as hard as she could. Her blow bothered nothing but empty air.

"Why won't they listen?" she said. "Don't they understand? Don't they care?"

Eleanor brushed moldy peelings from her cloak. "They're scared, and when people are scared they'll rewrite the evidence to make it less frightening, something they can handle. Would you want to go up against demons and witches and the armies of hell?"

"You think they forged that letter themselves?"

"No. The soldiers would have forced your priest to write and postdate it before killing him. Including the tithe was a nice touch."

"We have to tell them!" Megan banged on the side door that led back into the palace. "Let us in! We've got more information!" Servants watched through murky windows, but none moved to comply with Megan's demands.

Eleanor pulled her away. "Save your efforts."

"For what?" said Megan. "If they won't help, who will?"

"There're always alternatives."

"I don't need platitudes. I need . . ." What did she need? She needed someone to believe her. Someone on her side. Someone with power. "What if we bypass the priests and go to the garrison directly?"

"Appeal to the soldiers' sense of chivalry?"

"I suppose."

"Good luck with that."

Megan and Eleanor sheathed their swords and made their way out of the yard, into the network of alleys winding their way around the perimeter of the palace. Around here, there was always a smell of rotting vegetables and a slimy coating on the cobblestones. It was a good idea to move through fast and wear quality footwear.

"What do you suggest we do?" Megan asked.

"I don't know. Keep our heads down and our ears open."

"In case the ground has any good ideas?"

"It's better to do nothing than to do something stupid," said Eleanor. "We don't know where they are, what their numbers are, or what their intentions are. We'll hear some gossip eventually. Gossip always finds its way here."

Megan rounded on the countess. "You want us to do nothing while they're doing God knows what to her?"

"We're running out of options."

"Don't say that." Thoughts tumbled over themselves in Megan's mind. "Brother Irwyn, the crone in Trafford's Haven, that witch we killed, they all knew about me and Gwyneth. If we knew what they knew, why the witches want us, we might be able to figure out where they've taken Gwyneth."

"And how're you going to do that?"

"There must be writings on the witches."

"They'll be in the Forbidden Collection," said Eleanor with a weary shake of her head. "You'll never get access."

The Forbidden Collection was where the priests stored all the books they deemed unfit for public consumption. It was located on the top floor of the temple library and was guarded around the clock. Unless you were a senior priest, you had to have a warrant signed by the High Priest to get access. No chance of Megan getting one of those. But there were alternatives.

"We can sneak in," she said.

"How?"

"Gwyneth worked there."

"They gave a peasant girl access?"

Megan wished the countess had pronounced "peasant" with less disdain. "She fetched drinks, cleaned, that kind of thing. There's a back entrance, used by the servants."

Eleanor pulled Megan into a doorway. A dog barked on the other side of the gate. "You want to sneak into the Forbidden Collection?" she hissed. "You can't be serious. If you're caught in there, the priests will gouge your eyes out."

"They'll have to catch me first," said Megan. "If we can find some information, we can find out where they're holding Gwyneth, go there and get her out."

"I feel this is the point where I make an offering to the God of Sarcasm."

Anger flared inside Megan. She grabbed Eleanor and shoved her across the alley against the wall opposite. "This is my sister we're talking about," she spat into the countess's face. "You wouldn't be so glib if it was your mother."

Megan yelped as Eleanor swept her legs out from under her and knocked her flat on her back. The countess pounced on her like a bird of prey—the whirling cloak her wings, the knife that flicked into her hand her talon. The point rested on Megan's throat, her artery pricking against it as it pulsed. There was a look on Eleanor's face, like she was trying to make herself do something. Ram the knife home or pull it away?

The knife disappeared back into Eleanor's sleeve and she helped Megan to her feet. Megan withdrew a couple of paces, not knowing what to say, her attention fixed on Eleanor. Her heart was fluttering, trying to find a rhythm and failing. She took a few deep breaths.

"Stay out of the Forbidden Collection," said Eleanor. "We don't need to antagonize the priests. Saviors know, we have enough enemies."

Megan's gaze drifted to Eleanor's forearm and the knife she had stashed under there. Was the countess really that touchy about her mother, or had Megan done something else to anger her? Whichever, Megan would have to be on her guard around her from now on. Sometimes you had more enemies than you thought.

# twelve

They returned to Silas's. After eating early in a strained silence, Eleanor announced she was going out on business and told Megan and Damon to stay put. As Silas had gotten more wine, Damon was happy to comply, but Megan continued to brood. The more she thought about the Forbidden Collection, the more convinced she was the answers were there. Eleanor's warnings were well founded, but didn't Megan owe it to Gwyneth to take the risk?

"I'm going out," she said to Damon.

He frowned. "You heard what Eleanor said."

"Is she the boss of me?"

"Interesting sociopolitical question," said Damon, waving his cup. "Does the authority of the priests, who derive their authority from the Saviors, override that of the aristocracy, who derive theirs from the Unifier? If one accepts the latter, then one has to accept the illegality of the priests' usurpation and the Endalays' primacy in this part of the Realm, and why are you looking at me like that?"

"I didn't ask for an essay," said Megan. "I need to get into the Forbidden Collection, find some information on the witches."

"Evil. Demon worshippers. Kill a lot. What more is there to know?"

"I need to find out why they took Gwyneth. And why they want me too."

She headed for the door. Damon scurried around her and blocked her way. "Leave it—"

"You're not going to stop me."

"Let me finish. Leave it another hour. The priests'll be at dinner. The library'll be deserted for hours. All night, if it's a feast day." He cocked his head. "What day is it? Sixth day after . . . it's the feast of Jonas the Unreliable."

"What did he do?" asked Megan.

"God came to him in a dream and told him to do something or other."

"Something or other? Is that an exact quote?"

"They didn't call him the Unreliable for nothing."

"Why does he warrant a feast?"

"There was a gap in the calendar."

Damon led Megan back to the table and poured them both another drink. "How are we going to do this?" he asked.

"We?" said Megan.

"I hear the priests have some . . . interesting wood-cuts in the Forbidden Collection."

"You any good at picking locks?"


He wasn't. A bead of wax dribbled down the candle Megan was holding and solidified on the leather of her glove. Damon was crouched beside her, poking away at a door lock with a set of picks they'd acquired in some shady dockside inn.

"Come on," said Megan, glancing up and down the corridor. She expected priests to appear at any moment. "Even a squirrel with a bit of bent wire would have had it opened by now."

There was a crash. Megan cringed. The light from her candle juddered across the wall. Just a dropped cup in the temple dining hall at the end of the corridor. She exhaled in relief.

"Hold that still," said Damon. He withdrew his picks and stared into the keyhole. "This is a good lock, this is. Who knew the priests'd protect their porn so well?"

"We are *not* doing this to obtain pornography."

"Maybe *you're* not . . ."

Megan bounced on her heels and rubbed her arms. The gloomy temple corridor was freezing, its stone walls seeming to radiate cold. Portraits of holy men glared down at her with the thunderous looks of someone who had spotted another having a good time. The last time she had been here, she'd been waiting for Gwyneth. She shouldn't have been there then either, but if anyone asked she would have claimed she'd been sent over from the palace to help with some chore or other. No one had though. She had been just a little girl, insignificant when one had the mysteries of God, the universe and the night's dinner menu to contemplate.

Gwyneth had eventually appeared. Her eyes were red; her hair, normally brushed into submission, wild. Megan rushed to her. "What's up, Gwyn? What's happened?"

Gwyneth looked at Megan if trying to place her. "Meg? What are you doing here?"

"I've hardly seen you for weeks," said Megan. "I was worried." Gwyneth had been coming back to their dorm late and leaving early. Long shifts at the temple library, she claimed.

"I have to get some wine for Brother Attor."

"Did he make you cry?"

"Because I have to get wine?" said Gwyneth. "We're serving girls, Meg. It's what we do."

"You'd tell me if something was wrong?"

"Nothing's wrong." Gwyneth wiped her eyes on her sleeve. "Everything's more right than it could ever be."

"You sure?"

Gwyneth nodded. "Absolutely."

Megan wasn't convinced. She pointed up the steps that led up to the Forbidden Collection. "Can I have a look?" *See if Brother Attor is hurriedly getting dressed.*

"You know you're not allowed."

"Is it true they have pictures of people doing—"

"You're never to go up there, Meg!" snapped Gwyneth.

"All right, I was only—"

"You don't want to know what'll happen to you if you do."

Now Megan had to go into the Forbidden Collection. She noticed Damon tense. "What is it?"

"Someone's coming."

Megan looked around. "I don't see—" The door swung inward. Damon lost his balance and toppled into the stairwell beyond. "Oh."

A mouse of a serving girl gawked at them, an empty tray clutched to her chest like a shield. She could have been no older than twelve or thirteen. Damon looked up from the floor and waved. "Hi."

"You're not allowed to be here."

"That's why we're having to break in."

"I don't think this is the best time for honesty," said Megan.

"You want me to lie in a temple?"

The serving girl shrank against the wall and edged along. "Please don't hurt me," she said, eyes shiny with tears.

A year ago, the girl could have been Gwyneth. Megan pressed a two-shilling piece into her palm. "Forget we were here."

"If the priests find out, they'll beat me."

"No one will find out," said Megan, placing a hand on the girl's shoulder. "We're not here to steal. We just want to look at something."

The girl looked at the coin, then at Megan, then fled.

"Do you think she's gone to tattle on us?" said Damon.

"We'll have to assume she hasn't," said Megan.

"Nothing can go wrong with that assumption."

Megan led Damon up a spiral staircase, to the top-most floor where the Forbidden Collection was located. She eased the door open and peeked inside. It was deserted. The priests were all at the feast.

They snuck into the library, a twilight forest of shelves and bookcases and deserted desks on which sat extinguished candles in skirts of wax. The curve of the temple walls made it seem as if the knowledge was warping space. There was a musty smell of parchment and old leather. If you held your breath, you could make out the whispers of books exchanging secrets.

"Where're we looking?" asked Damon. "Under 'p'?"

"Don't start that again."

"You said your sister worked here."

"As a servant. They didn't make her memorize the catalog." Megan racked her brain. "There was a book. We found it at this inn outside Thicketford. *The True History of the Witches* by . . . what was his name . . . ? Brother Deegul?"

"Deogol?" said Damon.

"You know him?"

Damon snorted. "He was a crank. He thought there were secret codes hidden in the Book of Faith. Apparently, if you take every nineteenth letter from the second chapter, you get a half-decent recipe for chicken soup. Well, chicken 'sop.' I wouldn't take any notice of anything he wrote."

Megan felt a little better that Eleanor had condemned the book to the flames. "All right then," she said. "We look for any other books about the witches we can find."

They crept across the deserted library, the floorboards creaking under their feet, examining the treasures on the shelves. The tomes seemed innocuous enough. Megan came across volumes on philosophy, theology, history, biography, and even a book of fairy tales, a few of which her grandfather had told her when she was younger. Some were written in unfamiliar scripts: both flowing letters that whirled around in a hyperactive scrawl and boxy shapes that rained down the page in columns. She hoped they weren't the books they were looking for.

Her brain registered the presence of a third candle but was unable to get the message to her legs in time. Megan rounded a corner and bumped into the back of an old priest, making him splutter wine over the parchment laid out on the desk in front of him. She panicked, muttered an apology and tried to mop the wine up with her sleeve.

"What?" demanded the priest, batting her away. "Who are you? What are you doing here?"

Megan's mind raced, trying to think of an excuse. "We're . . ."

The priest cupped a hand to his ear. "What? Speak up."

"We're . . ."

"What?"

"Cleaners," said Damon.

"You're not allowed in the Forbidden Collection," said the priest.

"Is it forbidden?" asked Megan, affecting innocence.

"We're cleaners," Damon said again, raising his voice. He mimed sweeping. "Cleaners."

"I don't want you to polish my rhubarb," said the priest. "I don't even *like* rhubarb."

"Huh?" Damon looked to Megan, who shrugged. "I was sweeping, right? I mean, it was obvious."

A hand bell, of the type used to summon servants, sat next to the priest's goblet. The priest reached for it. Megan tried to grab it first, but he beat her back with a claw of a hand that possessed more power than it appeared to. The priest smirked in triumph and reached to ring the bell. A pale hand wrapped round his scrawny wrist. Megan swallowed a yelp as she realized it was Eleanor.

"I don't think you want to do that," Eleanor said to the priest.

"Let me go!"

Eleanor bent forward and whispered in his ear. The priest's eyebrows shot to the top of his head. Eleanor patted his arm, gave Megan a disapproving look and sashayed away. The priest watched her retreat, then scurried after her.

"She didn't look at all pleased," said Damon. "What's she doing here anyway?"

"I mentioned it to her earlier," said Megan. "She must have found we weren't at Silas's and come looking for us."

"See, she can't bear to be without me."

"I don't think it's you she was worried about."

Damon took up the priest's former position at the desk. He helped himself to the wine and also to the food the priest had there: bread, cheese, and a spiced sausage, one end of which was gnawed and glistening with saliva. He put his feet up and looked over the priest's manuscript.

"Aren't you going to help me look?" asked Megan.

"Man's allowed a break," said Damon. "It's guaranteed in the Book of Faith."

"No, it's not."

"Oh, you laypeople and your over-literal interpretations of scripture. Sausage?"

Megan dismissed him with a wave and resumed her search. Some of the shelf labels caught her eye. Their ink was fresher than the rest, the handwriting awfully familiar. "I think Gwyneth wrote these," she said.

"In the past hour?" asked Damon.

"No."

"Doesn't mean much then."

"Thanks for your support," said Megan.

"Just trying to be realistic." Damon swallowed and turned a page. "Which is more than I can say for that particular illustration."

Megan went through each of the labels in turn, fingering the writing as if touching Gwyneth's words could bring her closer to her. She could imagine her sister grumbling as she copied them for Brother Attor—Gwyneth had always hated writing.

She paused at the last one. Ran her finger over it again. "What does 'Occ' stand for?"

"Occult, I guess," said Damon.

"Occult?"

"Paganism, alchemy, magic . . ."

"Witches?"

Damon threw the manuscript he was reading back on the desk. He hurried over to Megan. They ransacked the shelves, pulling out each book, discarding it as soon as they determined it wasn't what they were looking for.

It was awkward having to examine the books one-handed, so Megan dribbled a little wax onto the floorboards and stood her candle in it. She glanced to the side and saw a slim volume bound in black leather jammed flat under the bottom shelf. It had the star-broken circle inscribed on its spine.

"I think . . ." The words lodged in her throat. "I think I've found something."

"It's only words," said Damon. "It can't hurt you."

"You say that . . ."

Damon stretched out his hand. "All right, I'll—"

"No," said Megan. "I'll do it."

She pulled the book out, surprised it didn't burn her fingers. A larger version of the star-broken circle was etched on the cover—carved might be a better description—and below it the title: the Book of the True. She steeled herself and opened it. A scrap of parchment fluttered out. Megan put the book aside and picked up the scrap. It was covered in a script written in a reddish-brown ink, faded with age. No, not ink.

"Is that . . . ?"

"Blood," said Damon. "Writing material of choice for psychopaths everywhere."

Megan read the title on the parchment. "'The Final Prophecy of Joanne.' It's dated forty years ago. From the time of the witches."

"Joanne?" said Damon. "Where've I heard that name before?"

"Brother Irwyn, the priest in Laxton. He mentioned her. He said she . . ."

"... knew."

This was what Megan had been looking for, but she was too scared to read it. She wanted to hide in ignorance. Gwyneth didn't have that choice though. She brought the parchment closer to the flame so she could make out the words.

Fear not, O True

God will watch over you

When the world has gone

Four score times around the sun

My sisters will be born again

To clean the world of its stain

And in their sixteenth year

A Savior each will bear

A daughter and a son

Jolecia and Ahebban

Born to a dead father

The True they will gather

To save them from the scourge

The false will be purged

No more the liar, the priest

Only His eternal peace

Megan read it again, then handed the parchment to Damon. "What do you think?" she asked.

"Well, I wouldn't have rhymed 'gone' with 'sun.'" He attempted a grin. It quickly faded.

"We've heard this before," said Megan. "That crone in Trafford's Haven. She predicted the return of Ahebban and Jolecia."

"I think the crone and Joanne may be one and the same."

"How do you figure that one out?"

"What did she say?" said Damon. "'I was right?'"

*Before she killed herself.*

Megan noticed scrawled lines on the back of the parchment. She indicated to Damon to turn it over. The ink on the reverse was younger and a lot less bloody.

"Looks like a family tree," said Damon. "We've got Joanne and a couple of older sisters. Joanne had no issue, but her sisters Cearo and Darel each had a child . . . oh . . ." He licked his lips and swallowed. "Ahebban and Jolecia."

This was their family tree? Megan took the parchment from Damon and examined it. "They had the same father," she said. "And went on to marry each other. Which'd make Ahebban and Jolecia—" she counted on her fingers —"half-siblings, cousins, and spouses."

"There's a spirit of economy in that family, if nothing else," said Damon. "They do things different in demon land, huh?"

Megan's gaze traveled back up the tree from the incestuous Ahebban and Jolecia to their mothers. The sisters' date of birth caught her eye. It was the same for each of them.

"Cearo and Darel weren't just sisters," she said, "they were twins. Their birthday's the sixth day of midsummer."

"Uh-huh."

"That's my birthday too. Mine and Gwyneth's."

The glow of the candle cast long shadows on Damon's worried expression. "If you're sixteen, then . . ." He checked the family tree and counted off on his fingers. "You were born eighty years after Cearo and Darel."

"To the day."

Damon's voice dropped to a whisper, but it was as loud as a scream in the silent library. "'When the world has gone four score times around the sun . . .'"

"'My sisters will be born again,'" Megan whispered back.

The air tasted dead. The mustiness of decaying parchment and paper was suffocating. The walls threatened to cave in and bury her. She was misinterpreting the prophecy, twisting it so it was all about her. The witches hadn't returned for her; they'd returned because of her. They wanted her to bring back the demons. No, it couldn't be true. Please, God, it couldn't be true.

A figure shimmered through the darkness: Eleanor. "What've you got there?" she asked.

Damon handed the parchment over. She read it, her features still and white as if chiseled from marble. "Where did you find this?"

"It's just a coincidence," said Damon. "Nothing to worry about, right? You can't put faith in something whose primary concern is whether the words scan. I mean, it's not as if Megan's pregnant, is it?"

Megan let out an involuntary groan. Damon and Eleanor turned to her in unison. She bowed her head, unable to look them in the eye, wishing the floors of the temple library would disappear and she could plummet to her death.

"No," said Eleanor.

Megan managed the smallest of nods.

"Oh God," said Damon.

Eleanor poured herself some wine, her shaking hand clinking the flagon against the rim of the goblet. The horror etched on her features was nothing compared to that gripping Megan. She couldn't move. A great weight was pressing on her, numbing her limbs, draining the life from her.

"How did this happen?" asked Eleanor.

She glanced across to Damon, who spread his palms in innocence. "Don't look at me!"

"Why don't you take a walk?" said Eleanor.

Damon pointed down the corridor formed between the shelves. "I'll just go and . . . I'll go see if there're any racy philosophy texts knocking about."

Eleanor knelt beside Megan and took her hands in her own. Her sapphire eyes locked onto Megan's. They were pure, noble, beautiful, and Megan felt anything but. She looked away, unworthy to hold the countess's gaze.

"Are you sure about this?" said Eleanor. "You do know what's involved, don't you? It's not just kissing. You have to—"

"I know!" snapped Megan, jerking her hands out of Eleanor's. "I was an idiot. There was this boy, Wade, and I let him . . ."

"What happened to him?"

"The witches killed him along with everyone else." *Born to a dead father.*

Megan stared into the candle flickering away on the floor, wishing its flame could burn the knowledge from her mind. "Wade," she said, her voice trembling. "He was one of them, one of the witches. He was the only one who knew about the baby. That's why the witches knew to come to Thicketford. He deliberately got me pregnant. And Holt. Oh my God. He did the same with Gwyneth. She's . . . she's . . ."

Megan thought back to Wade's brief courtship. Every word was a lie, every look a betrayal, every gift poison—and all for a bastard cause they were prepared to die for. How could she have not seen what was going on, how could Gwyneth not have? Two silly girls impressed by flattery.

Megan felt stupid, used, dirty. She clawed at herself, wanting to flay off the skin Wade had touched, wanting to rip out the abomination festering within her.

"What am I carrying?" she cried out to Eleanor. "What the hell is growing inside me?"

# thirteen

Everything she had been suppressing burst out of Megan like a dam breaking. Sobs racked her body and tears flooded her eyes, their blurring of the physical world only sharpening the one inside her head. She fell into Eleanor's arms, burying herself in the other woman's embrace as if she could hide there from the memory of the attack replaying itself again and again in her mind.

"They did all that because of me. They killed . . ."

Eleanor shushed her and stroked her hair. "It's not your fault."

"I know, but . . . that prophecy. It's not true. It can't be true. I can't be . . . because we share a birthday? There must be other twins born on that day, somewhere in the world."

"Possibly . . . probably."

"Then why did this not happen to *them*?"

"I'm sorry. I'm so sorry. I should have been . . ."

Megan curled into a ball on the floor of the library as the sobs took over again. Eleanor held on tight, as if trying to keep her in this world, but it wasn't enough. Megan wanted her own mother, her father. But if they had been there, the witches would have cut them down as easily as they had her grandfather, obstacles easily dealt with by an arrowhead or an ax blade. Only Megan and Gwyneth were important. Everyone else was an offering to the demons growing inside them.

There was a slap of footsteps. "Someone's coming," said Damon, panting as he ran back to them. "And I don't think they're bringing tea."

Eleanor shook Megan. "We have to go."

"What does it matter? Let them take me."

"You say that now," said Damon, "but you'll change your mind once the molten eyeballs are running down your cheeks."

Eleanor held out her hand. Megan didn't have the will to flee, but she didn't have the will to resist either. She let the countess haul her to her feet.

Damon scooped up the parchment and the book they had found it in. Eleanor tugged Megan along. They abandoned the candles and scurried for the back entrance, hoping to lose themselves in the shadows.

There was an ominous creak as the main doors of the Forbidden Collection were shouldered open. The priest they had disturbed had returned, this time flanked by a pair of guards. There was an ugly gash on his forehead.

"Seize them!"

"I knew I should have hit him harder," muttered Eleanor.

They clattered down the back staircase, adrenalin guiding them in the blackness. Heavy boots thudded behind them. Megan's heart pounded, threatening to rupture her ribcage. Why was she scared? What could they do to her that she didn't want to do to herself? But still she ran, unwilling to surrender.

She stumbled as the steps gave way to level ground and slammed into Damon, who in turn slammed into the door that blocked access to the corridor beyond. She pushed him aside and groped for the knob, slapping against the solid oak until her palm brushed cold iron. Megan twisted and yanked. The door refused to budge.

Eleanor ran into them, knocking the breath from Megan's body. "What? Why? Go, go!"

"The little servant bitch locked the door on us," said Damon.

"Um . . ."

"It was you?"

"You left it open," said Eleanor. "Anyone could have seen it. Can you unlock it?"

"No problem. Apart from the lack of light and the lack of time and the lack of . . ."

"Ability?"

The approaching footsteps had slowed with the need for caution on the dark staircase, but approach they did, leather scuffing on stone, ponderous breathing getting louder and louder.

"Maybe they're just passing through," said Eleanor.

"He yelled, 'Seize them,'" said Damon. "You don't do that unless you're serious. You'd sound silly."

"Guards!" shouted Eleanor. "Hurry and get this door open! I have urgent business with the High Priest."

"That *never* works," hissed Damon.

Shapes descended into view, their silhouettes more absence than presence in the gloom. "He's right," said one of the guards.

"Do you think we're stupid?" said the other.

"No," said Damon. "I'm sure you had to pass exams and everything for this job."

Even in the dark, Megan had no trouble finding her sword. She drew it and gripped it with both hands, feeling the rough metal lattice of the handle grip into her palms. There was a *ching* as she rapped the blade against the stone flags at her feet. She didn't feel so helpless anymore.

"All I want to do now is hit something and keep on hitting, whether it's an enemy or a friend or myself, so I advise you to let us go before I let my temper go. Otherwise I won't stop until someone kills me."

Ragged breaths filled the stairwell as both sides weighed their options. The guards hadn't had the time or space to bring their pikes to bear in the narrow stairwell. Megan jabbed her sword forward. Something soft yielded to the gentle pressure. A little more and she'd pierce flesh. So easy to hurt someone.

"You'll be wanting a key."


As soon as the door was opened, Megan dashed into the corridor. Ignoring Eleanor's exhortations, she ran away from the library as fast as she could, as if by distancing herself from the place of revelation she could distance herself from the consequences. She burst out of the temple, almost knocking over two Sisters of the Faith, and kept going, across the main square, through the dark streets, her course as panicked and erratic as her thoughts.

She found herself at the docks and sprinting down a jetty, momentum carrying her toward the black waters of the Speed. They offered oblivion, escape from the pain, the knowledge of what had been done to her. All she had to do was fling herself off the pier, let the river fill her lungs.

Her foot caught on a loose plank and she went sprawling. Wood smacked against her face and palms, expelling her determination. She lay there panting as the dampness from the timbers seeped into her clothes and chilled her skin. Only a few feet to the river, but she could find neither the will nor the energy to make it. She couldn't even cry. All she could do was stare out and wonder what she had done to bring this upon herself and Gwyneth.

Planks vibrated as someone approached. "There you are," said Eleanor. She tucked her cloak underneath her and sat beside Megan. "We've been searching all over the city for you."

"Where's Damon?"

"He had a theory you might be hiding in a pub. He's gone to check it out."

"Which one?"

"All of them, knowing him."

Megan pushed herself into a sitting position and watched her breath condense in the night air. It wasn't just her breath now: she shared it with another. The thing was small, but it would grow, devouring as it did so. It would be born in blood and would hunger for that blood for the rest of its life. The first coming of the witches had seen the deaths of tens of thousands; how many would curse their second? And she would be responsible.

"At least you know your sister's alive," said Eleanor.

"She never said anything about being pregnant," said Megan. "Why didn't she tell me?"

"Maybe she wasn't." Eleanor left the next sentence unsaid—*But maybe she is now.*

Megan shook her head. "I know she and Holt were . . . you know. She was letting me tell Grandfather first, let him vent all his anger on me."

A loose nail was hanging out of the plank next to her. She pulled it out and threw it into the Speed. The river swallowed it like a dog accepting scraps. "You must think we're a right pair of sluts."

"Of course not."

"A countess wouldn't let herself get pregnant."

"Considering the only man I saw for the best part of forty years was my father, I should think not." Eleanor sighed. "None of this is your fault. Do *not* blame yourself. *They* did this to you."

"I let them. If I'd followed what the Book of Faith teaches . . ."

"You'd be the only person who's done so since the Unifier. You were doing what comes naturally. The witches perverted it."

Megan cradled her stomach and pinched the flesh there. "Do you believe it? What this Joanne wrote?"

"It doesn't matter what I believe," said Eleanor, "it's what *they* believe. And they're trying their best to make it come true."

"Maybe we're reading too much into this," said Megan. "Maybe we're scaring ourselves with some crazy ramblings. Maybe the witches attacked Thicketford because that's what they do and the birthdays are a coincidence and they have no idea I'm pregnant and . . . and . . ."

Each clause uttered told her the opposite of what she hoped for, whittled away what remained of her hope. "I'm not important, am I? I'm just a peasant girl who wanted to be left alone." She wiped away the tears with the back of her hand, smearing the dirt there. Strange, she didn't remember getting dirty.

Eleanor rubbed her back. "You are important."

"Not as important as a countess, huh?"

"It's a dead title. Meaningless."

"Why do you keep using it?"

"My father convinced me it was worth something."

Men wheeled barrels along the jetty opposite and hauled them into a boat tied up there. Ale for the garrison on the other side of the Speed. Laughter and indecipherable jokes drifted the short distance downriver. One of the men beckoned Megan and Eleanor over, seeking entertainment for the soldiers. They pretended they hadn't seen him.

"How did they find me?"

"The temple birth records, I guess."

"But you have to be a priest to . . . Brother Brogan."

"He's dead."

"He's *rumored* to be dead." Megan bowed her head and clawed the planks of the jetty so hard splinters came away under her nails. "He set all this up." The bastard had turned out to be responsible for her pregnancy after all.

"You're jumping to—"

"He knew Gwyneth and I were twins. About the right age. He checks the records and . . . and . . ."

Eleanor placed a calming hand on her shoulder. "This isn't helping," she said. "We can do something about your . . . condition though. There are herbs. They can make . . . they can make your problem go away."

The priests forbade it, but it was Megan's body. She was the one who had to carry this thing, she was the one who would have to give birth, she had to be the one to get rid of it. If not for herself, for the good of the Realm. *I pledge to uphold the Faith and destroy its enemies*, went the second Pledge of Faith. What was the demon inside her if not an enemy of the Faith?

"Where do we get these herbs?" she asked.

"City like this?" said Eleanor. "There's bound to be somewhere."


They found the place on the outskirts of the outer city, crammed between a brothel and a butcher's shop. Hundreds of conflicting smells greeted them as they entered: sweet and bitter, pungent and aromatic. Megan didn't know whether to salivate or throw up. Jars lined the shelves, filled with leaves and dried flowers, coagulating powders, liquids of every color, and animal parts floating in alcohol. A heap of copper filings sat in a scale pan, waiting to be mixed into some potion or other.

The owner greeted them with the kind of smile that made you want to check your purse. He was in his midtwenties and short enough even Megan towered over him. He wore frayed silk robes that had been made fifty years earlier for someone two feet taller. A polished disk of glass jammed in his right eye magnified the pupil, giving him the mismatched face of a gargoyle.

"I'm Pierce," he said. "Herbalist and alchemist."

"Alchemist?" said Eleanor. "Turning lead into gold?"

"Turning lead into gold is for idiots. *Copper* into gold, that's the real alchemy."

"How's that working for you?"

Pierce stuck his finger in the mound of copper filings and dabbed the result on his tongue. "Getting there." He brushed his hands clean.

Megan was skulking in a corner. This wasn't the time for idiotic small talk. She wanted to get the herbs and get out of here, get rid of the thing inside her, get back to finding Gwyneth. She jerked her head at Eleanor.

Pierce picked up on the gesture. "Now, ladies, what can I do for you?" He bent backward and cast a none-too-subtle glance at Megan's stomach. "A little addition we'd like to subtract?"

"You think I'm that kind of girl?"

"Everyone's that kind of girl. Otherwise none of us would be here," said Pierce. "How long since . . . ?"

"A few weeks," said Megan.

"A little irregularity isn't unheard of."

"I'm sure."

Megan and Eleanor cringed as a scream reverberated outside the herbalist's. Pierce affected indifference. It was hard to tell whether it came from the left or right, from the butcher's or the brothel. Megan hoped it was the former.

"You can help us?" said Megan.

"It won't be cheap."

"How much?" said Megan. Pierce spread the fingers of one hand. "Five pence?"

"Shillings."

"*Shillings?*" said Eleanor.

"If you want it done cheap, I know an old woman with a—"

"I've got the money," interrupted Megan, not needing to hear the alternatives.

She counted the silver from her purse and handed it to Pierce. He in turn lifted the lid of a cedarwood box and plucked out a tiny leather pouch from the dozen stored there. "Best take it with wine. The stronger the better."

"Is it safe?" asked Megan.

"Probably."

"*Probably?*"

"What kind of poison are you selling us?" said Eleanor.

"The kind of poison you came in here to buy," said the herbalist. "You thought you were getting rose-water?" He shrugged. "You can have your money back, if you like. It's not as if another girl in your predicament won't turn up tomorrow."

Megan shook her head. "No, we'll take it."

"Are you sure?" asked Eleanor.

"What choice do I have?"

Pierce tapped his chin a moment, then handed Eleanor a vial filled with a bluish liquid. "On the house," he said. "If things go wrong, you might want to give her that."

"Is it an antidote?"

"No. It'll make sure she dies quickly."

# fourteen

The leather pouch sat open next to the cup Eleanor had poured for her hours earlier before retreating to the kitchen. The contents looked innocuous, dried flakes sprinkled with fine powder; they might be nothing more than a collection of spices intended to make the wine more palatable. They promised life or death, salvation or retribution; either way her problems would be over. Megan just had to tip the mixture into her drink and let it slide down her throat. And yet she couldn't.

The seer's parchment lay on the floor. Occasionally one of its corners lifted as a draft caught it. Megan had tried to throw it in the fire, but the ball she had made of it unraveled midarc and it had fluttered unharmed to the floorboards as if saved by the power inherent in its prophecy. Burning it would have done no good anyway: Megan couldn't help but memorize its words.

There was a gentle knock. Damon poked his head around the door. He pointed at the herbs. "I see you've not . . ."

"I don't know if I can," said Megan. "We don't even know if they'll work on a demon."

"No . . ."

He flashed a book at her. "Before you do, you might want to listen to this."

"I don't need a lecture, especially from a man. No offense."

"You know me," said Damon, offering a sympathetic smile. "When it comes to offense, I'm a giver, not a taker. But, seriously, listen."

He was serious too. His mouth was almost in a frown, the almost-permanent look of amusement was absent from his eyes. "Go on," said Megan.

Damon sat down, cross-legged. There was a pitter-patter of pages as he flicked through his book.

"'God, born of the eternal universe, sought solace from His solitude and willed the Planets, the Stars, and the World into being. To share in the wonders of His creation, He brought man into the World and, so that man might know Love, bestowed upon him Free Will.'"

That was it? "Don't quote the Book of Faith to me," said Megan. Things were hard enough as they were, without scripture's absolutes.

"This isn't the Book of Faith," said Damon. He showed Megan the cover, with its star-broken circle etched in flaking gilt: the Book of the True. The witches' book.

"I've been reading it all day," continued Damon. "Or rather, rereading. The words are awfully familiar. 'And man angered God by his Vice and Wantonness. The seas boiled and ash filled the skies and the sinners were turned to Stone. For twenty-one days the people wailed and begged for Forgiveness and promised to keep the Faith. Their Humility touched God and He calmed the seas and banished the clouds and Islands rose at the site of His Anger, filled with Bounty and signs of His Beneficence.'"

"The creation of the Spice Islands," said Eleanor from the doorway. "What have you got there?"

"It's the witches' version of the Book of Faith," said Damon. "Only it's the actual Book of Faith, word for word. Well, almost, anyway."

"Are you sure?"

"I trained to be a priest," said Damon. "Do you know how many times I've had to copy it? God help you if you get the capitalizations wrong." He thought for a moment. "Well, maybe not. He was the bastard who insisted on them in the first place."

"You said it was almost the Book of Faith," said Megan. "What's the difference?"

"Listen to the Pledges of Faith," said Damon. "I pledge obedience to God and His Saviors."

Megan's brow creased as childhood lessons reasserted themselves. "That's not right," she said. "It should be . . ."

". . . God and His priests," finished Eleanor.

"Interesting, huh?" said Damon. "In the original Werlay, the word for Saviors—heavenly messengers— is *procterō*. The word for priests—earthly messengers— is *proctero*."

"They're the same," said Megan.

"There's an accent on the first."

"I didn't hear it."

"It's a silent accent," said Damon. "Werlay's a weird language. Why do you think no one speaks it anymore?"

"Are you saying the witches' book is the same as ours apart from one mistranslation?" said Eleanor.

"Mistranslation, or merely translation? The priests' whole authority rests on the first Pledge. If it doesn't mention them . . ."

". . . there's no justification for their existence," said Megan.

"You can see why the priests went to war."

"The king went to war," said Eleanor. "My father went to war."

"And my grandfather," said Megan.

"The priests told them they had to," said Damon. "They had to destroy the True before their beliefs became widespread, before the general populace began questioning whether the priests deserved their obedience.

So the priests demonize the True—literally, in this case. Make up all kind of stories about them being witches, Ahebban and Jolecia being demons demanding human sacrifice, that kind of thing. The king rallies his forces in response and there's a big war. I wonder if the priests expected the witches to annihilate the aristocracy or if they just got lucky." Eleanor glared at him. He turned to Megan. "See what I mean about offense?"

"Did you know about this," Megan asked him, "or are you just guessing?"

"I heard rumors at the seminary. Nothing solid. Not the kind of thing you want to get caught investigating."

"What about that priest? Brother Irwyn? Why would he follow the witches when they want to abolish him?"

"He's actually religious," said Damon. "Unusual in a priest, I know."

Megan stalked round the room. "No," she said. "They're not just us without priests. Not after what they did."

"Think about it. Is there any real evidence to suggest we're up against black magic or demons or the forces of hell?"

Megan looked to Eleanor, who was slumped against the wall, lost in deep thought. She shook her head. "Not directly . . ." said Megan.

"They're men. Evil bastards, sure, but just men."

Megan couldn't grasp what Damon was saying. It went against everything she had been taught. *Everything she had been taught by the priests.*

"This whole thing is based on a lie?" she said. "The witches? The war?"

"Yes."

"So the priests could maintain privilege, power?"

"All fighting's about power," said Damon. "Even if it's to stop someone having power over you."

Anger seared within Megan. She thought of the thousands who had risked their lives, the thousands who had paid with their lives. She didn't know a single person who hadn't been scarred by the war, a family who didn't mourn a lost loved one. The priests really had burned Trafford's Haven. They wanted to bury their deceit in its ashes.

"If it was a lie, it was a necessary one," said Eleanor. "Do you think the world would be a better one if the witches ruled, the dead fewer?"

Megan remembered home and shook her head. "But why maintain the lie?"

"Who knows what the truth is?" said Damon. "Who dares to speak it? It's lost in decades of myth and propaganda."

"It does leave one question," said Eleanor. "If Ahebban and Jolecia aren't the witches' demon overlords, then what they hell are they?"

"Isn't it obvious?" said Damon. "'To save them from the scourge . . . a Savior each will bear.'"

\* \* \*

The room spun. A wave of nausea hit Megan. She stumbled while the world shook on its axis. Hands caught her before she hit the floor and guided her to the chair.

"Are you all right?" asked Eleanor. Megan hardly heard the words. "Are you all right?"

"Yes. Just morning sickness."

"Have a drink."

Megan accepted the cup and drank a little wine, clenching her fists as she willed herself to keep it down. "This is . . ." she said. "Gwyneth and I . . . we're not going to give birth to the Saviors. That's . . . They're . . . We can't . . . I mean, how?"

"The Book of Faith is a bit vague on what the Saviors actually are," said Damon. "Human or divine? Did God send them to preach the Faith to the Unifier or were they the product of Edwyn's delirious imagination?" He grimaced. "Incidentally, don't write the latter in your theology exams. Can lead to repercussions."

"You don't believe this, do you? That I'm . . . ?"

"Of course not," said Eleanor.

"Insane idea," said Damon.

Which meant it was no creature of heaven growing within Megan, no spawn of hell, but an innocent babe. It was no more guilty of the sin of its conception than any other child. Preventing its birth might be the best thing for it—what kind of life could Megan offer?—or it could be an attempt to spite the seer's prediction.

She scrunched up the pouch and took it over to the fire. The flames crackled as they snatched at the air, sensing an offering. She held the poisonous herbs above the curtain of heat, hoping for some sign of what she should do.

"Megan," said Eleanor, "do you think that's such a good idea? The witches are going to come for this baby. Best it never exists."

"Are you saying if it goes away, the witches go away?"

"I don't know."

"Will they return Gwyneth?"

Eleanor didn't answer that question.

Megan pulled her hand back. The fire was beginning to burn; that's what she told herself anyway. "It's just a baby. It can't do anything."

"It doesn't have to. The witches will rally to it. It doesn't matter whether they follow demons or some distorted version of the Faith. The child will have power because they're desperate to give it power. They'll use it, corrupt it. Do you want to see that happen?"

The room fell quiet until all they could hear was the water lapping under their feet in the flooded cellar and the distant cries of the city going about its business. Damon flicked through the Book of the True without settling on any particular page. Eleanor wandered over to the window and stared out of its dirty panes. Megan crushed the pouch of herbs between her palms, torn over what to do.

"What happens if I do it?" she asked. "Do the witches magically vanish?"

"I think we've established they're not magic," said Damon.

"You know what I mean."

"I don't know what they'll do," said Eleanor. "They might come for you and try again. They might take it as a sign you're not the ones and look for another set of twins."

"And in that case, what will they do with Gwyneth? Set her free?"

"It's possible . . ." said Damon.

"You know as well as anyone what the witches or the True or whatever they're called do to people they no longer have a use for."

"Are you really going to be able to rescue your sister and carry a child?" asked Eleanor.

"I'll be pregnant, not paralyzed," said Megan. "If I take these," she held up the pouch, "I might be dead."

"And childbirth's renowned for its safety."

Damon nodded. "You don't know how many dead mothers and babies I've had to say the funeral prayers for. Sometimes one survived. Often as not . . ."

"I thought you were only an acolyte," said Eleanor.

"*Poor* dead mothers and babies."

"You think I should get rid of it?" Megan said to Damon.

"I never said that." Damon shuffled uncomfortably. "I think . . . I think . . ." He poured himself some wine, threw it down his throat so fast he could hardly have tasted it. "Do you want to be a mother?"

Megan thought about the pain of childbirth, the stigma of being an unmarried mother, the fear the witches would take her child from her. She thought about holding her baby for the first time, how the loss of her family made her ache, how she could imagine no greater joy than to see them again.

"Yes."

"You know what to do then," said Damon. "And remember, you'll always have us. Me and Eleanor."

Megan cast the herbs into the fire. She would fight to avenge those the witches had killed. She would fight for her sister. She would fight for her unborn child.

# fifteen

Silas shuffled in with a plate of cold beef, though from his exaggerated stoop you'd think he was lugging in the whole cow. He proffered the plate to Megan. "Eat up. You need meat in your condition."

"You know?" said Megan. "You were eavesdropping?"

"It's in the job description for a servant," said Damon.

"Do you think I'm doing the right thing?" Megan asked Silas, not that she knew why. Maybe he reminded her of her grandfather, maybe she was desperate for any kind of validation.

"No."

"I'm not sure it's your place to—" started Eleanor.

"Were any of you there?" said Silas, cutting her off. He looked grim. "Did any of you fight the witches? Did any of you wade through the blood, pick your way through the body parts? You don't give the bastards nothing. Nothing."

"I don't intend to," said Megan.

"Aye, well . . ." Silas looked across to Eleanor. "I'll fetch you some wine, my lady."

Megan picked up a slice of beef. She hesitated before putting it in her mouth. "He wouldn't put anything on this, would he?"

Eleanor shook her head. "He might disagree with you, but he'll be loyal to his last breath."

Megan nibbled at the meat. There was no bitter taste: no poisons. "Do you think we can do this? Defeat the witches and get Gwyneth back?"

"With my brains, Eleanor's beauty, and your sheer pigheadedness, what can stop us?"

"If you're the brains of the outfit, an awful lot," said Eleanor.

"Fine," said Damon. "I'll be the beauty, you be the brains."

"I knew I should never have intimated you were attractive."

Damon winked at her. Eleanor tried to look stern, but a ghost of a smile haunted her lips.

"We need to figure out where they took Gwyneth," said Megan. "Do we have a map?"

"There's one in my family history," said Eleanor.

She retrieved the book, opened it to the center pages and unfolded the map stitched into the spine. The bottom part of the Realm and the top of the Andaluvian peninsula lay before them. The area between the River Speed to the north and the Endalayan Mountains to the south—Ainsworth—was colored pink, to mark the territory Eleanor's family had once controlled. Megan could trace the whole of her journey, one that had taken her the length of the county, in a few inches. Thicketford was so small it didn't even warrant its full name, just a tiny "T'ford."

Silas returned with the wine. He poured two cups and was about to pour a third when Damon stayed his hand. "Megan's already had enough," he said. "It's bad for the baby."

"Since when?" said Megan.

"Since I realized we only had enough for me and Lady Lush here."

"I am *not* a lush," said Eleanor.

"Fine," said Damon. "Megan can have yours."

"Perhaps you should stick with water, Megan."

Megan didn't care. She tapped the black spot that marked Trafford's Haven. "Here's where the witches left. Where would you go after that?"

"Anywhere," said Damon. "After that place, you could see the good points of hell. Maybe they're still at sea."

"They wouldn't want to risk getting caught up in a storm," said Megan. "Not with Gwyneth on board." She followed the line of the mountains into the Harris Sea with her finger until she reached the Spice Islands. "How about here?"

Eleanor shook her head. "We'd have heard if someone had disrupted the spice trade. There's way too much money involved for it to be ignored."

Megan pushed her finger up the map. There was nothing there save for the expanse of sea, and if the witches had landed, they would have run into them on their journey up to Eastport. That left down, south to Andaluvia.

"You think the witches are with the Sandstriders?" asked Damon.

"Why not?" said Megan. "We've never heard of them fighting each other, have we?"

Eleanor shook her head. "And they were retreating that way at the end of the war."

The first city south of the Endalayans was the port of Dustor. The Sandstrider settlements in the north of Andaluvia were sparsely populated, especially now their pirates no longer sailed from them. Few Sandstrider merchants drove their caravans that far from their capital on the south of the continent. The perfect place to hide a ship.

"That's where they are," said Megan. "Out of the priests' reach but close enough to the Realm to . . ." *Come for me.*

She looked to Damon and Eleanor for confirmation of her hypothesis. Damon shrugged and nodded. Eleanor tapped her cup against her bottom lip.

"You disagree?" said Megan.

"I don't know," said Eleanor. "It's a lot of wild speculation on what the witches are, what their plans are, where they're hiding . . ."

". . . where they're holding my sister. But it's obvious the priests aren't going to help us. I have to rescue Gwyneth myself."

"On your own?"

"Not necessarily," said Megan. She turned to Damon. "How do we hire these mercenaries you mentioned?"

"You really think mercenaries can take on the witches?" asked Eleanor.

"Why not?" asked Megan. "They're just men, right? And not too many of them, otherwise they wouldn't be so desperate to hide themselves from the priests. Anyway, they don't have to take on the witches and *win*. They just have to get me to Gwyneth. I'll do the rest."

"Oh, what a surprise," said Eleanor. "We're meeting in a pub."

"It's not a pub," said Damon. "It's a drinking den."

"Is that better or worse?"

Two men burst out of the dive and fell to the ground grappling each other. "Guess that answers that question."

The man on top groped for a dagger he had stuck in the back of his belt. He raised his arm to strike. Eleanor caught his wrist and twisted. The man shrieked as bones cracked. He dropped the knife.

"We don't have to do this," Eleanor said to Megan, shoving her victim into the street. "My father still has supporters in the city. They might come to our aid."

"Because they have a great record so far."

Inside, the den stank of sweat and stale beer. Although it was barely after noon, numerous men were dead drunk, snoring facedown in puddles of ale and vomit. Others, Megan suspected, were just dead, their forms still and oblivious to the world.

She kept her hood up as they pushed through the crowd, one arm across her stomach, the other ready to draw her sword. "These are the men you expect to help us?"

Damon stepped over a prostrate man who had taken offense to the floorboards and was repeatedly punching them with a bloodied fist. "We're meeting the captain in a suite upstairs. Well, I say suite; I mean closet you can rent by the half-hour."

"It's all class, this place," muttered Eleanor.

Megan flinched when she heard the word "captain." That's what the witch who had ordered the assault on her village had been called. Did it make him feel better to think his killing was in some honorable cause, a noble war?

A serving girl led them to a dingy chamber. A few beams of light shone through the slats in the blinds, illuminating a backless couch slashed like a murder victim. Stools were arranged round a wooden table littered with half-empty cups, the dregs of wine decaying to vinegar. A bloody piece of gristle floated in one of them. The top of an ear.

Damon plopped on the couch and stretched himself out. Eleanor huddled in a corner, hand on her sword. Megan slipped the serving girl a coin and told her on no account to bring them anything to drink.

"Where's this captain of yours?" she asked Damon.

"He'll be here."

"Before or after someone robs and murders us?"

"It's not that bad. Reminds me of my student days."

"An immoral den of drunken debauchery with an ever-present threat of violence?" said Eleanor. "Weren't you at a seminary?"

"And?"

The mercenary captain arrived a couple of minutes later. He was a cautionary tale on the perils of a lifetime hitting and being hit, held together by spit and scar tissue. The smoke from the pipe jammed in his mouth smelled sweet at first, but there was an underlying rottenness to it, like decaying fruit.

"I'm Captain Landon," he said, sitting down. "The boy here says you can pay well. Let's see it."

Megan took the seat across the table from Landon and slid one of the sovereigns across to him. "That's a king's sovereign," Eleanor said from the corner. "Three of those will buy you seven of the priests.'"

"Indeed."

"Even the moneychangers in the palace will exchange them one for two."

"There's more," said Megan. She drew her sword and laid it across the table. It was the last thing she had of her grandfather's. She hoped he'd understand why she had to give it away.

Landon ran his finger down the length of the sword, then he tipped it toward himself to examine the topaz in the hilt. The inscription on the blade, which Megan hadn't taken note of since that day in the cave, flashed in the dim light: KALVERT. Kalvert? Eleanor's mother's family?

"Very nice," said Landon. "Very nice indeed. Don't get workmanship like this much anymore."

"The steel's from the Snow Cities," said Eleanor. "Best there is."

The mercenary leaned into Megan. His breath counted as an offensive weapon in its own right. "How many d'you want killing?"

"None, as such," said Eleanor. "Though we're not averse to . . . accidents."

"If you want sneaky stuff, go elsewhere. My men are strictly bash-them-on-the-head-in-the-open-street kind of guys."

"We—" started Eleanor.

Megan cut her off. It was her sister they had to rescue. She had to be the one to negotiate. She couldn't hand off responsibility to Eleanor. "How many men have you got?" she asked Landon.

"Enough."

"And a ship?"

"Ship? What do you want a ship for?" The captain indicated the sword and sovereign. "This ain't going to buy you a ship."

"There's more of it," said Damon. "A *lot* more."

"Define 'a lot.'"

"You heard of the Endalay fortune?"

"Who hasn't?" said Landon. "The witches stole it."

"And my grandfather stole it from them," said Megan.

"I would have heard about someone having that much money," said Landon. "If nothing else, I would have tried to rob him."

"So would the priests. He kept it hidden, spending a little at a time so he wouldn't arouse attention. It didn't work. Someone . . ."

"Claimed it from him?" said the captain.

"And we'd like to claim it back," said Eleanor.

"A treasure hunt, eh?"

Megan saw the gleam in the mercenary's eye. No one was bothered about going after a defenseless girl, but dangle a large pile of cash in front of them and they became very interested. She wished she'd tried this with the priests.

Landon gave Megan's sword an experimental swing. "What kind of cut we talking?"

"Fifty–fifty," said Damon.

The captain snorted. "Ninety–ten."

"Sixty–forty."

"Ninety–ten."

"Seventy–thirty."

"Ninety–ten."

"You're not taking this haggling seriously, are you?" said Damon.

"I'm taking it very damn seriously, boy. You wander in here looking for men and ships, promising a fortune. Something tells me there's a whacking great big catch to all this." He looked to Megan. "What is it?"

"The Sandstriders took it. We have to sail to Dustor."

Megan jumped as Landon slammed the sword back down on the table. "I'm not going there. I'd rather buy a vacation home in Trafford's Haven."

"I think he's scared the Sandstriders might fight back," said Eleanor.

"Of course I'm scared. They're damn animals."

"I've always found them to be most civilized."

"Until you piss them off, which I think sailing into one of their cities and stealing off 'em might just do."

They had thought it best not to mention it was the witches they wanted to fight, but hadn't taken into account the fact the Sandstriders' reputation was almost as bad as the witches'. It wasn't just the desert and the mountains that protected them.

"Dustor's a ghost town these days," said Megan. "Fifty men, a hundred at the most, should get us what we want with virtually no trouble."

"It's that 'virtually' that worries me," said Landon. "How many of that hundred are going to make it back?"

"As few as possible," said Megan. "Dead men get no share." Ideally none of Landon's men would make it back. She didn't know what their reaction would be once they found there was no treasure, but she doubted they'd laugh it off. It was something she'd deal with once she had Gwyneth.

"You're a coldhearted little bitch, aren't you?"

"Your men will know what they're fighting for. If they aren't skilled enough to stay alive . . ."

"I'll have to recruit outsiders to make up the numbers," said Landon. "Soldiers from the garrison perhaps. It gets boring marching around all day. I'm sure they wouldn't mind some action. Especially some well-paying action."

"Even better. You won't have any sense of misplaced loyalty to outsiders."

"Of course, to you I'm an outsider."

"What can you fear from me?" said Megan. "We have a deal?"

"What's to stop me sailing without you?"

If the mercenary was already planning on double-crossing her, he'd already taken the bait. Megan suppressed a smile. She was one step closer to finding Gwyneth.

"We know exactly who and what we're looking for," she said. "Besides, is ten percent worth the cost of betrayal?"

Landon leaned back and played with the blistered paint on the wall behind him. "I'll have to talk to my lieutenants, see what they think. We have a system of democracy in our company."

"See who's for and against you?" said Megan.

"It helps with tactical decisions. Who leads the attack against a horde of ferocious Sandstriders . . ."

". . . and who stands behind them with a knife at the ready in case they survive?"

Landon grinned. "You have command experience?" He banged the ash out of his pipe and started to refill it. "Give it a day or two. We'll be in touch."

"How do you . . . ?"

"You're staying by the docks with an old geezer who, rumor has it, used to work for the Endalay household."

Eleanor turned to Damon. "You let them follow you?" Damon's face was a picture of wounded innocence. Eleanor's expression indicated she would prefer it wounded in the traditional way.

"I like to know who I'm dealing with," said Landon, "my lady. Not much gets past me."

Especially when Damon had deliberately let them follow him. People trusted information more if they thought you didn't want them to know it. Having the last Endalay secretly trying to regain the Endalay fortune lent credibility to its existence.

"It's best you forget who I am," said Eleanor.

"Whatever," said Landon. "You ceased to be important a long time ago."

Eleanor raised her sword a couple of inches out of her scabbard. Landon pulled a knife out of his belt and held it at the ready. Megan tensed and prepared to make a grab for her sword, which Landon had left on the table.

"Please, please," said Damon. "No decapitations or dismemberments. We'll only have to pay extra for the cleaning."

Eleanor let her blade slide back. "They clean this place?"

"Only when there's a decapitation or dismemberment."

"That regularly?"

Landon turned his knife to picking the dirt out from under his nails. Megan rose. "We'll expect your answer by sundown tomorrow at the latest," she said, casting one last look at her sword. "Otherwise we'll find someone else."

"There is no one else."

Megan feared he was right.

*  *  *

As soon as they left the drinking den, Megan turned on Eleanor. "You were going to kill him? How was that going to help us get back Gwyneth?"

"If I didn't react to the insult, he'd think I wasn't an Endalay," said Eleanor.

"Why? Does your family have a history of stupid overreaction?" asked Damon.

"Try me and find out."

There was a sly look on Damon's face that suggested he was considering it. Megan thought it best to change the subject. "That sword belonged to your family, didn't it?" she said to Eleanor.

"It was part of my mother's dowry."

"Why did you let me give it away?"

"Same reason you were prepared to. Best Captain Landon has it," said Eleanor. "Shows we're serious. You couldn't handle the thing anyway. You weren't built for it. Sooner or later, it would have gotten you killed."

Still, it seemed so fickle to throw it away like that, on what was nothing more than a gamble. "I could have learned."

"Provided you doubled your body weight and grew an extra foot." Eleanor saw the smirk forming on Damon's lips. "Of *height*." She took Megan by the arm and led her away from the den. "I've heard of a place where we can get you some weapons you can cope with."

Megan nodded. "What do you suggest?"

"Innocent girl like you?" said Damon, scurrying to keep up with them. "All sweetness and light and butter wouldn't melt? Knives. Concealed knives."

They made their way through the outer city, hoods up and alert for danger. They were in the rough end of the rough end of town, where the widest streets were no more than alleys, and the actual alleys had to be squeezed through single file and sideways. People around here built wherever they could seize a scrap of land and with whatever materials they could find—often bricks and timbers cannibalized from a neighbor's property. Upper stories slumped against each other like weary travelers, forming archways over the streets and casting the world into shadow.

The way opened out a little. Paving slabs provided stepping-stones through the muddy streets. Ground-floor windows became shop fronts for items whose chain of ownership wasn't exactly uncontested. Faces broke into the kind of smiles only a fresh mark could bring.

Damon drew level with Megan. "I've been thinking," he said.

"I thought we'd agreed you weren't the brains," Eleanor said from behind them.

"About when this is all over."

"Over?" Megan couldn't contemplate such a thing. She feared she'd be chasing Gwyneth forever. "What of it?"

"It's going to be hard, being an unmarried mother. If you need help bringing up the kid, someone to, you know, stop everyone talking, I'd be happy to . . . well . . ."

"Are you *proposing*?" said Megan.

"Sort of," said Damon.

"Rather you than me," muttered Eleanor.

"It'd be a friendship thing," said Damon. "You wouldn't have to, you know . . . I don't want you to be on your own."

"I'll have Gwyneth."

"You're not allowed to marry your own sister," said Damon. "Well, except in certain parts of Andaluvia. Mind you, there you can marry a camel."

"You don't want a proper wife?"

"I'd only end up cheating on her. This way it'd be with someone who wouldn't mind."

Was Damon serious, or was it some spur-of-the-moment offer prompted by pity and never intended to be accepted? Maybe he did care. Why else had he stuck around after they had reached the safety of Eastport, continued to put himself into danger?

She kissed him on the cheek. "It's very sweet of you, but after everything I've been through I'm sure I'll be able to cope."

"You don't want me in your child's life?"

"You can be an uncle."

"The type who shows up on Saviors' Day to drink all the booze and make a pass at the servant," said Eleanor.

"I can manage that," said Damon. "As long as you don't hire Silas," he added to Megan.

"I'm not really a servant-employing kind of girl."

The clang of metal upon metal suggested they were headed for a smithy; the heat and smoke confirmed it. The blacksmith was hammering away at his anvil, the sweat making his naked back gleam as if it had been oiled. He took the glowing horseshoe he had been battering into shape and plunged it into a bucket of water. Steam billowed out.

"We're looking to trade," said Eleanor.

The blacksmith wiped his hands on his apron. "I'll have the girl off you, but the lad looks like a waste of space."

Eleanor shook her head. "We're after . . ." She leaned forward. "We're after your more specialized items."

"How specialized?"

"Pointy specialized."

"Don't know what you're talking about."

"Items with points. For . . ." Eleanor mimed stabbing.

"Yeah, I get that," said the blacksmith. "I don't have any. You can sod off back to the tax office."

Eleanor spread her arms. "Do I look like a customs inspector?"

"Who knows who the priests are using these days."

Megan reached for Eleanor and made a show of jingling her purse. "We'll go elsewhere," she said. "Damon, you must know someone."

"That's right," said Damon, scowling, "because I'm the kind of lowlife scum who mixes with such people."

"Do you?"

"Yeah, loads."

"Let's not be hasty," said the blacksmith. "I do have some interesting metalwork ladies such as yourself might be interested in."

"Sounds . . . interesting."

"Out back."

Leaving Damon to keep watch, Eleanor and Megan followed the blacksmith to the rear of his shop. They entered a cramped storeroom, filled with old tools and scraps of rusting metal. The blacksmith heaved a crate aside, revealing a hidden trapdoor. He lit a lamp and led them down to a cellar.

A small arsenal lined the walls: bladed and blunt, swords and maces, axes and war hammers; crude compared to the sword Megan had just given up, but no less deadly. There was armor too: mail, plate, and leather.

The blacksmith pulled a cloth bundle out of a drawer and unrolled it. Knives gleamed in the lamplight like shark teeth. "We'll need scabbards," said Eleanor. The blacksmith opened another drawer and deposited a heap of leatherwork in front of her.

Megan sorted through the knives, selecting two short ones for slashing she could strap to her forearms, stilettos to be stashed in her boots and a pair of heavy daggers to go in the belt around her tunic. Eleanor, meanwhile, tested the weight of a throwing knife before slipping it into the empty wrist scabbard on her right arm.

"You ladies expecting trouble?"

"Nothing laceration won't solve," said Eleanor.

Megan paid the blacksmith and they returned to ground level. A crowd had gathered around Damon. Men were lining up to toss horseshoes at a spike that had been driven into the ground fifteen paces away. Damon beckoned Megan and Eleanor forward. Copper coins clinked in his hands.

"Want to play?" he said. "Penny a shoe, tuppence if you get it around the spike."

"No," said Eleanor.

"In that case, do you fancy handing some drinks around, talk the game up? You know, encourage the punters."

There was a *clang* and a *thud*. A cheer went up as a horseshoe wrapped itself around the spike. "Well done, sir!" cried Damon, tossing the successful pitcher a two-penny coin. He leaned into Megan and Eleanor. "I'm sure the fool's cheating."

"Those are my shoes, boy," said the blacksmith.

"And fine work they are too," said Damon. "It'd be an honor for them to be nailed to my feet."

The blacksmith reached for his hammer. "We can soon sort that out."

"Tell you what," said Damon. "Why don't we let you take over this little operation in return for a small cut?"

The blacksmith grabbed a handful of nails and jammed them between his lips. "And when I say small, I'm kind of thinking zero."

The blacksmith flashed him a mouthful of iron.

Another cheer went up. Again a horseshoe had settled around the spike. Damon pointed to the blacksmith. "See my friend here."

He went to move off, but not before the winning gambler clutched his shoulder. "It was you I paid, and you who'll give me my . . ."

Damon squirmed out of the man's grip. The man made a second grab for him, but this time only caught his tunic. Both pulled away from each other. The tunic paid the price and tore, exposing Damon's bare shoulder.

Except it wasn't bare. He had a tattoo there. A circle broken by two five-pointed stars.

# sixteen

Megan's heart stopped. Damon tugged the torn flap back over his shoulder, but it was too late. The knowledge of what was inscribed there had already shot through the crowd. The mob contracted around him; someone pulled the target spike out of the ground.

"What the hell is that?" said Megan, pointing at his shoulder.

"What?" said Damon, his voice cracking. "I asked for a butterfly!"

A workman, all muscles and facial hair, pulled Damon's hand off his shoulder and spun him around, showing the offending mark for all the crowd to see. There was a collective gasp. Many made the sign of the circle. Some of the children ran off.

"This isn't what it looks like," said Damon. His eyes darted from side to side as he looked for an escape route. The crowd blocked them on all sides. "It's a prank gone wrong, that's all. There was lots of wine and these strange mushrooms and dares and one thing led to another and before I know it I'm branded with the mark of eternal evil and—"

A stone skimmed out of the mob and struck Damon on the cheek. He yelped and touched his face. Blood smeared his fingers.

"Look, you can't think I'm a witch, can you?"

There was a collective hiss. The workman forced the struggling Damon to his knees. "We need to get rid of this abomination." He held his hand out. "Knife." Someone in the crowd volunteered a serrated dagger. Rust stained its teeth like plaque.

"I'm not sure that's hygienic," said Damon, trying to wrench himself free of his captor.

The workman pressed the knife against Damon's tattoo, preparing to carve it off. Droplets of blood welled up. Damon squirmed in the man's grip. Another stepped forward to hold him down. Blood lust misted their eyes. They weren't going to stop at slicing off the tattoo.

Without thinking, Megan whipped a knife from her belt and slashed at the workman's arm. Blood sprayed out. Her target dropped to his knees, cradling his wounded arm.

Megan brandished her knife at the man holding Damon. "Let him go."

"Or?"

Eleanor drew her sword and twirled it, letting everyone know she knew how to use it. There was uncertainty

in the crowd's faces. They had the numbers and the
brute strength, but the women had the blades. They
backed off a step, leaving Damon's restrainer isolated
and outnumbered in the circle they had cleared.

The man shoved Damon toward Megan and Eleanor. Megan tucked Damon behind her and Eleanor, but
then she remembered the crowd surrounded them on
all sides. Her head flicked from side to side. One man
swung a horseshoe in his fist, working up the courage
to hurl it.

"I think we should . . ."

"Run?"


They pelted through the city, weaving through alleys
and back streets, barging into astonished traders and
skipping across the paths of laden wagons plodding to
market. The muscles in Megan's legs burned, her lungs
couldn't suck in enough air, her side felt as if a wolf had
torn a chunk out of it. Eleanor slapped the rump of a
horse as they careered past. It reared, throwing its rider,
and stampeded into the mob.

The startled animal was enough to throw off the
last of their pursuers, whose appetite for the chase had
dwindled as fear and physical ineptitude had reduced
their number. Panting, the three stumbled into a courtyard across which washing had been strung up to dry.

Megan collapsed on the step of someone's back door and battled to keep the contents of her stomach down.

"We're never short of opportunities for exercise, are we?" gasped Damon.

His smirk made Megan snap. He was reducing this, of all things, to one of his stupid jokes? She charged into him, sending him flying. He became entangled in the washing and crumpled onto the flagstones. Megan kicked out. Red petals bloomed against the white linen.

Damon struggled free of the damp shirt. He crumpled it into a ball and wiped his bleeding nose with it. "What the hell, Megan?"

"You're one of *them*?"

"What?" He saw the knife in her hand. "Hey! No, no! You don't understand."

"I think you'd better make us understand," said Eleanor. Her voice was cold as she slipped her own blade from its arm scabbard.

"You saved me from that mob so you could kill me yourself?"

Why had they saved him? Why didn't he deserve to be torn apart? Because Megan wanted to believe the star-broken circle meant nothing? It did mean something though, something she didn't want to contemplate.

"Explain," she said.

Damon swallowed. "Like I said—"

"Bollocks," said Megan. "No tattooist would ink *that*."

An old woman appeared on a balcony a couple of stories up. She tutted at the sight of the disturbed washing, but the sharpened steel kept her disapproval at bay.

Damon held his hands up in surrender. His eyes glistened with tears. Real or forced? "I was on a ship out of Eastport a month or so back. There were . . . things I needed to get away from. You don't need to know what. We were taken. Pirates, I thought. Wish they had been. They were witches looking for recruits, especially anybody who knew the area around Thicketford."

"And you were eager to sign up?" said Eleanor.

"They weren't exactly tolerant of religious differences. It was either swear yourself to their god or be thrown overboard. And I'm a terrible swimmer."

"You led them to me," said Megan.

"Oh, come on," said Damon. "Thicketford's on the Cheetham Road. Any idiot could have found it."

Megan's skin crawled. "You were with the witches when they attacked. When they killed my grandfather. When they took Gwyneth. How many of my friends did you murder?"

"No one!" protested Damon. "They wouldn't let me join in." He grimaced as he realized his choice of words. "I was a lookout. They were paranoid the priests had found out what they were doing and were lying in wait for them."

"No wonder you knew who the witches really were," said Megan. "You're one of them."

"No, no. I had suspicions, that's all. It wasn't until we found the Book of the—"

Eleanor grabbed him from behind. "We should kill him now. We don't want him reporting back."

"Reporting back?" said Damon. "To who?" His head jerked back and forth between Eleanor and Megan. "You can't think . . . They tried to kill me!"

"How high does the tide reach near Trafford's Haven?" said Eleanor. "Were you really under threat? Maybe you were a plant, a spy to worm your way into our confidence."

"A *what*? Can you hear yourself? They didn't even know you were down there."

"You're not denying it?"

"No, I'm not a spy or a plant or a damn unicorn, come to think of it." He reached out to Megan, eyes imploring. "I would never do anything to hurt you."

"But you did."

"I was a look—"

"You never did anything to stop it."

"What could I have done?"

"You could have tried." Softer, Megan repeated, "You could have tried."

"I was just trying to stay alive. I didn't know what they had planned. I didn't expect them to roll into villages and start slaughtering everyone."

"They're witches! What did you expect them to do?"

"Not that," said Damon.

Eleanor held her knife to his throat. "We should do it now before someone disturbs us." She leaned over Damon's shoulder. "Though once they see what you are, I don't think anyone'll object."

He had been there. He had helped them to destroy her life. He deserved to die for that alone. Didn't Thicketford deserve justice? Didn't her grandfather?

"Do it," said Megan.

Eleanor yanked Damon's head back. He squirmed in her grasp, but her archer's strength locked him into place. His skin whitened around the knife that pressed into his throat.

"You don't want to do this, Megan," said Damon, babbling now.

"I have to."

Eleanor's arm tensed. Megan looked away. Did it have to come to this? If they'd gotten to the beach by Trafford's Haven a few minutes later, the water would have done her work for her. She would have never known him; never come to regard him as a friend; never had to imagine that friendship was false.

"Wait! Wait!" cried Damon. "I saved you. Outside Thicketford. In the fields."

"What?"

"That was you hiding in the wheat, wasn't it? Whatshisname . . . he was coming for you. He hadn't seen you, the blind bastard, but I had. I persuaded him to stop looking for you. We had to get to that mill."

"That mill was my home!"

Damon winced. Eleanor's blade was digging in now, tasting his blood. "I thought I could at least help one person get out of there."

Megan thought back. Had she told either Eleanor or Damon what had happened in Thicketford, how she had escaped Wade's execution only to witness her grandfather's? The soldier who had ordered the ax man away had spoken with an accent similar to Damon's, but when she tried to recall it she could only hear Damon's voice.

She turned her back on them both and stared up into the blue sky, looking to God for answers. As ever, He was keeping His own counsel. Any decision would have to be her own.

"Are we going to execute him by old age?" asked Eleanor.

*Execute*—did they have the right to execute someone? That was the priests' job. Could Megan honestly say she wouldn't have done the same thing in Damon's position, sacrificed people she didn't know to keep herself alive? She wanted to say no, never, but she knew deep down that wasn't true.

"Let him go," she said.

"Are you sure?" said Eleanor.

"No, but do it anyway."

Eleanor slackened, allowing Damon to slip out of her embrace. "Thank you," he said. "Thank you."

He touched Megan's shoulder. She jerked away. "Go," she said. "Just go. I never want to see you again."

"But I can help you. You need me."

"I said *go!*"

Footsteps retreated, reluctant at first, then picking up pace. A tear trickled down Megan's cheek. She wiped it away and forced herself not to turn and watch Damon's retreat.

Megan needed time alone. Eleanor was exuding smugness, an air of told-you-so—even though she hadn't— she needed to escape. As soon as they passed through the gates that led into the inner city, she told the countess she'd meet her back at Silas's, then lost herself. She wandered the streets, brooding over what had transpired. Banishing Damon might have been the worse decision possible: she had either driven away an ally or left one of the witches' agents free to report to his masters.

It didn't matter, she told herself. Damon had revealed the true—or True—nature of the witches; he'd put them in touch with Landon. There was nothing more he could do for her now. She'd soon have the mercenaries on her side and they'd be sailing for Dustor, but did she want to be someone who valued people solely on their usefulness, whose loyalty she had to buy? She had no choice if she was to get Gwyneth back.

Droplets of the workman's blood stained her face and arms. She stopped by the fountain in Gaderian Square and washed herself in its chilly waters. One or two passers-by cast her pitying looks, assuming the blood was her own. Young girls didn't inflict violence, they had it inflicted upon them.

Megan pulled her hood up so she wouldn't have to make eye contact with anyone and scurried across the city, checking her back every minute or so until she realized she was only drawing attention to herself. She slowed to a normal pace and kept her eyes down, only scanning for pursuers when she crossed the street or when she found a trader's wares to hide her actions.

She entered Silas's house by the back entrance, which pleased the old servant as he had yet to accept she was anything more than Eleanor's chattel. He was kneading dough and singing a song about some knight who had committed many brave deeds, most of them involving slaughtering people less well armed than him.

"Where is she?" asked Megan.

"My lady is not to be disturbed."

"The living room?"

"I said my—"

Megan ignored him and strode out of the kitchen, through the hallway and into the living room. Eleanor was sat beside the blazing fire. She had changed into an emerald gown of shimmering satin that dropped heavy hints about the curves it covered. Her hair was down and shone like the setting sun. She was even wearing makeup: kohl around the eyes; a little blush to highlight her cheekbones; lips painted red.

Megan assumed it was for the benefit of her visitor. Despite the heat of the flames, he was swathed in heavy robes and thick leather gauntlets protected his hands. A half-mask was pulled across his nose and mouth, but he couldn't disguise the skin around his eyes. Darker even than Megan's, bronze burnished by the desert sun.

"... once more with the noble house of Endalay," the Sandstrider was saying.

"The pleasure is all mine, Excellency." Eleanor held out her hand and the Sandstrider kissed it through the silk of his mask. "Show the ambassador out, Megan."

Megan held her tongue and led the Sandstrider to the front door. Once he had left, she hurried back to Eleanor.

"Does he know something about Gwyneth? Are the witches in Dustor?"

Eleanor shook her head. "It's diplomacy, nothing to worry about. The Sandstriders have had yet another drought and they need to buy food. They want to open official trade routes with the Realm."

"And what can you do about that?"

"Some of my father's supporters have influence with the priests, or rather their purses do. The Sandstriders want me to talk to them."

"Why don't they go direct to the priests?"

"They did," said Eleanor. "They didn't like the price they demanded."

"Which was?"

"Conversion to the Faith. The Sandstriders would prefer to die. Hopefully we can persuade the priests to accept their gold in lieu of their souls."

"Shouldn't be hard."

Eleanor headed for the stairs. "This dress is ridiculous. I feel practically naked."

"I think that's the idea," said Megan, trying not to stare at Eleanor's backside as she followed her up to their commandeered bedroom. "Where did you get it?"

"Silas."

"Bit low cut for him, isn't it?"

"It used to be my mother's."

Eleanor shimmied out of the gown, which rippled down her body as if made of air, and changed into her regulation outdoor wear. "You think we did the right thing?" said Megan. "With Damon?"

"Who knows?" said Eleanor. "It's hard to kill a friend, even if you think it's for the best."

It wasn't something Megan thought she'd ever had to consider. "But if they forced him . . . ?"

There was a commotion outside, followed by a heavy splash. Megan went to the window. A fellow was bobbing in the Speed, crying out to his companion, who was trying to pull him to shore with a pole half the length required. The current was too strong. It was carrying the man out into deeper waters, jerking him under then letting him go for the briefest moment, like a cat toying with its prey.

Megan was about to dash for the river when her attention flicked to the dockside. Guards in the livery of the Faith were marching toward Silas's house, the two at the end of the column pointing to the drowning man and laughing. Leading the line was a priest. He looked up for a moment, giving Megan a glimpse of his face.

"It's him," she hissed.

"Who?" said Eleanor, adjusting her sword belt.

"The priest. The fat one. Bald."

"You'll have to be more specific."

"The one from Laxton. Brother Irwyn. The witch."

# seventeen

Eleanor hurried to the window to confirm Megan's identification. "We need to get out of here."

"You think?"

Silas met them at the bottom of the stairs. "There's . . ."

"We know," Megan and Eleanor said together.

The door rattled as fists rained upon it. "Open up in the name of God and His priests!"

"Damon," muttered Eleanor. "Bastard."

"You don't know that," said Megan. "Half of East-port knows we're here."

"Quick, out the back."

Silas shook his head. "There's guards there too."

"Maybe we can fight our way through," said Eleanor, her hand going to her sword.

"There's too many of them."

The thuds became heavier. Axes had replaced fists.

Eleanor bounced on her heels, all nervous energy craving release. "We—"

"The cellar," said Silas.

"It's flooded," said Megan.

"They're unlikely to search it then."

"Open up!"

"There should be some air pockets down there."

"*Should* be?"

A splinter flew off the door and caught Megan's cheek. They had no choice.

Silas led them to the kitchen. He hauled open a trap-door. A couple of stone steps, slick with green slime, led to an inky pool whose surface rippled in time to the guards' hammering. Megan stretched out a foot. The water reached out to devour her, numbing her with its icy bite.

"Head to the front," said Silas. "The floors are higher there."

Megan filled her lungs and plunged into the flooded cellar. This was no mountain-fresh water, purified by nature: this was fetid waste, despoiled by man. It promised not life but death, a million invisible creatures eager to eat her from the inside out.

She kicked blind, pushing herself through the water, and bumped into something solid. A wall. It must separate the rear cellar from the front. There had to be a way through. She searched, kicking and slapping. Had she lost her bearings, headed for the back by mistake? No, there was the archway. She dove and shot through it.

Megan broke the surface, or the top of her head did anyway. There was a gap of only eight inches or so before the floor of the living room cut it off. She had to lean back to breathe, clinging on to a beam to keep the water from reclaiming her, bathing in the meager light that snuck in between the floorboards.

There was a splash as Eleanor surfaced. Her hair was plastered to her head and her kohl had run, blackening her eye sockets. This, coupled with her skin, which the cold had bleached a deathly white, made her look like a skeletal monster risen from the dead.

"What was that?" asked a rough voice. One of the guards.

"Just rats," said Silas. "You're not scared of—"

A third voice cut in: silky, educated. Brother Irwyn. "Where's the girl?"

"What girl?" There was a smack and Silas cried out in pain. "I don't know about no girl."

"That's not what I've been led to believe."

"You're a priest, you'll believe anything. That's your job."

Another cry of pain. The floorboards rattled as something heavy hit them. Boots thundered through the house.

"Where's the girl?"

"I can't tell you what I don't know."

"Take one of his hands off."

"No!"

The scream echoed through the house. Megan gripped the beam so tightly she thought she was going to rip it out. Eleanor closed her eyes and muttered something. A prayer?

"Where's the girl?"

Silas's reply came through sobs. "I don't know about any girl. Oh God. God help me."

"If you want God to help you, you must help Him. Tell me where she is, and He'll let you keep the other hand."

"I don't—"

This time Megan ducked under the water to muffle the shriek.

She surfaced to the clatter of feet and a new voice. "This dump's empty, brother. We did find this."

"Whose gown is this?" demanded Brother Irwyn. "Is it hers? The Endalay bitch?" If Silas made a reply, it was indecipherable among his wailing.

"We're not going to get anything out of him, brother. We could take him with us, let Trymian have a word."

"And where would we fit the manacles? Oh, shut him up, someone. He's getting tedious."

There was a squelch, a grunt, and then silence. Something plinked into the water. Blood, dripping through the gaps in the floorboard, dissolving into a hundred tiny threads. Megan choked back a sob. Not another death.

"What now, brother?"

"They must be skulking elsewhere in the city. Some sympathizer of the Endalays. We'll find them; there's no hurry."

Boots clomped above their heads. Shadows flitted between the gaps. Had they all gone? Megan fought the compulsion to run, fearful of attracting attention. Beside her, Eleanor continued to float in the stagnant water, her face still as the corpse that lay above them.

Megan peeked into the hallway. Through the fragments of the front door she could see a guard patrolling in the street, specks of sun dancing across his chest plate as he paced from side to side. A hooded passer-by tried to sidle past. The guard grabbed him, prompting a yelp of alarm.

"What you got under there?" demanded the guard. He yanked down the hood, revealing a bald pate infested with oozing growths. The guard gave him a shove. "Get out of here." The man hurriedly covered himself up and scuttled away.

Water splashed on the floorboards behind her: Eleanor squeezing out her hair. "How many?" she asked.

"Just the one, I think," said Megan.

"There's another one around the back."

"What do we do? Hole up here?" Megan desperately hoped not. Her gaze drifted to the front of the house, where Silas lay. He had given his life for hers, but who said that was the better trade, that she was worth more than him? Would she have done the same for Silas? If not, didn't that prove he was more worthy? Except he hadn't done it for her. He'd done it for the woman in front of her, one he'd served for decades despite not knowing if she was worth it. Megan didn't know whether to find such devotion inspiring or sickening.

"We go around the back," said Eleanor, slipping out a blade. "It's the traditional place for knife crime. Wait here."

Megan should have said something, demanded Eleanor not hurt the guard, but she sat, shivering in sodden clothes, as snatches from the scuffle outside drifted in. Whether the guard was a witch or was merely following a lifetime's worth of conditioning by obeying Brother Irwyn, he had done nothing to save Silas, he had stood by while he'd been dismembered and then killed. Maybe he'd even been the one who had struck the blows.

Eleanor reappeared. "All clear."

Megan followed her through the back yard and into the alley that ran behind the house. "What did you do with the body?" she asked.

"Somewhere it won't be found for a while," said Eleanor. A scream echoed through the streets. "Well, I say a while . . ."

Hollers answered the cries. Boots thundered toward them. They dashed in the opposite direction. Too late, Megan registered the city wall looming above them, realized the alley was coming to a dead end.

She pointed at a pair of rickety gates. "There."

Eleanor skidded to a halt and made a stirrup with her hands. Megan boosted herself over the gates and tumbled into the yard beyond. Eleanor hauled herself over, grimacing as she hit the ground.

"Did we—?" started Megan. Eleanor put a finger to her lips. Megan dropped her voice to a whisper. "Did we lose them?"

Approaching voices answered that question. ". . . sure it was two women?"

"Yeah. Can I have my shilling now?"

There was a crack followed by a cry of pain. "Sod off."

Footsteps drew close and stopped. Megan tried to swallow her breath, will her heart to stop racing. The latch securing the gates began to lift. Megan suppressed a gasp—she hadn't thought to see if they were unlocked—and shot a hand out. She pushed down on the latch with all her weight, gritting her teeth as she forced herself to stay silent.

The force against her dissipated. Their pursuer was convinced the way was locked. There was a *thump* and a rattle as the gates were punished for their noncompliance. Megan bowed her head and risked a deep breath. Her eyes fell on a small puddle at her feet. The fetid water from the cellar was dripping from their clothes and dribbling through the gaps under the gates.

She dragged Eleanor to the ground just as a pike crashed through the gates, sending wood flying everywhere. The guard from outside Silas's marched into the yard. Eleanor curled into a ball, then suddenly straightened, sending the gate smacking back into his face. She scrambled to her feet and snatched at the outstretched pike. The guard thrust. Eleanor yanked. They both went flying. Eleanor's head cracked on the paving stones.

The guard pushed himself to his knees and scrabbled for his pike. Megan charged, knocking him back to the ground. She looked around for something to knock him out with. Pain flashed in the back of her knees as the pike shaft slammed into them. The world lurched.

A shadow fell upon her. The guard drew back his fist. Megan raised her arms to protect her face. Her hand bumped the knife strapped to her wrist. She whipped it out and lunged upward. The blade pierced the guard's throat. Blood gushed over her hands. The guard slumped, pushing his neck further down onto the blade. Megan ripped the knife out of his flesh and rolled away before he toppled on her.

There was a stifled scream. A woman stood by the house to which the yard belonged, a small child hiding behind her skirts. Megan took in the detritus, the moaning countess slowly pushing herself up, the bleeding corpse by her side. Had she really killed him? The knife in her hand and the blood dripping down her arm suggested so, but the whole sequence seemed unreal, like a briefly indulged fantasy.

She swallowed and offered the householders what she hoped was a friendly smile. "We'll pay for the gate," she said. Woman and child backed off. Megan spread her arms. "You don't have to be scared. We won't hurt you."

"There's bits of windpipe on your knife," said Eleanor, rubbing her head.

"Oh." Megan flicked her wrist. The gristle splatted against the wall next to the woman. "Sorry."

Megan and Eleanor grabbed dry clothes from the householders' laundry pile and hurried away from the area before more guards appeared. They flitted from alley to alley, keeping their heads down, ducking into doorways when men marched past. Whatever Brother Irwyn had told the city guard, they had their own reasons for hunting Megan and Eleanor now.

"We need to find Landon and get out of the city," said Megan.

"You sure we can trust someone who came with Damon's seal of approval?"

Megan tugged at her gloves. Underneath, the skin was sticky. It was disturbing that she'd needed to wash blood off her hands twice in a single day. "You think Landon's working for the witches?"

"Possibly."

"Better be careful he and Damon don't get the two of us on our own in a darkened room then," said Megan. "Oh, wait a minute . . ."

"Don't think you know everything that's going on."

"I think I know a diabolical master plan when I don't see one."

They approached the Western Gate. An extra contingent of guards was stationed there, checking everyone passing through into the outer city and causing a sizable queue to back up. Megan and Eleanor spun in unison and walked away, trying to look casual or, rather, trying not to look like people who were trying to look casual.

"What now?" asked Megan.

Eleanor stopped. Megan bent around, trying to peer under the countess's hood. Eleanor was biting her lip. "Follow me," she eventually said.

"Where're we going?" Megan asked, hurrying to catch up with her. "Another one of your old servants?"

"Something like that."

They made their way through Eastport. The sky was darkening to indigo and the first stars of the evening were putting in an appearance when they arrived in a well-to-do part of the inner city. Eleanor led Megan up to a trim house with plate-glass windows and freshly painted timbers. She rapped on the door. There was no reply. She tried again. Again nothing.

Eleanor felt for the knob. Polished brass. It turned with a click. She leaned her weight against the door, easing it open.

"What's going—?" started Megan.

Eleanor put a finger to her lips and entered the house. Megan slipped out a knife, hiding the blade against her wrist, before following her inside. A bitter smell with a hint of stale eggs filled her nostrils. It was strongest from the left, from the room where the light shone. She inched to the interior door. Floorboards creaked. So much for surprise. She kicked the door open.

The room was bare apart from a small, battered barrel squatting in one corner and a desk in another. A priest sat at it, reading by candlelight. He'd changed since Megan had last seen him. His hair seemed grayer, the wrinkles in his forehead deeper. Stubble had sprouted on his cheeks and the top of his head, but it was a forlorn growth, like weeds in a wasteland.

"You brought her here?" said Brother Brogan.


Megan's head was whirling so much it took a moment to realize her old tutor was talking not to her but to Eleanor, who looked grim. "I thought it was time."

"I don't recall asking to witness the task God gave you."

Megan looked at Eleanor, who refused to meet her eye, then at Brother Brogan. The hairs on the back of her neck rose. She found herself stepping away from both the priest and the countess.

"What's going on here?" she said.

"There's nothing to worry about, Megan," said Eleanor.

Brother Brogan's face told a different story.

"Why did you bring me here? How did you know where—"

"Sit down, child," said Brother Brogan.

And put herself in a position where she couldn't run, couldn't fight? "Did you tell the witches about me, brother? Are you one of them?"

A stack of books by Brother Brogan's side served as a table for his supper: bread, chicken, olives. He plucked an olive from the plate and rolled it between finger and thumb. "I remember when you weren't quite so harsh, when you were a sweet little thing, always willing, always eager. You were my favorite, you know. Well, one of them anyway."

He ate the olive and spat the pit out into the empty fireplace. "I thought the circumstances of your birth were an amusing coincidence, a little joke for the few of us who knew of Joanne's prophecy. Then smugglers out of the Sandstrider cities started spreading rumors of ships sailing from the Diannon Empire under the flag of the star-broken circle, and I knew it was no joke."

"So you sought them out to tell them about Gwyneth and me?"

"No," said Eleanor, "he sought me out."

"*What?*"

"The last scion of the noble house of Endalay," said Brother Brogan, "whose mother had been killed by the witches. She was the only one I could trust to have no sympathy for their teachings. And she failed." Brother Brogan turned to Eleanor. "To think I wanted to see your family restored to its previous position. You're not worth the one you occupy now."

"My horse broke a leg. I had to walk half the way."

"And there's only one horse in the county?"

"You were there to save me and Gwyneth?" Megan said to Eleanor. "Why didn't you tell me?"

"Embarrassment at her incompetence."

No, it wasn't that. "You weren't there to save us. You were there to stop the prophecy."

"Same difference," said Brother Brogan.

"There are only two ways of stopping the prophecy. I get rid of the baby. Or I die before giving birth."

The denial died on Eleanor's lips. Her eyes confirmed the truth of Megan's accusation.

Brother Brogan made a move toward Megan. She backed off even further, but a wall halted her retreat. She flipped her knife into view. He hesitated. Eleanor pulled her sword a few inches out of her scabbard, then thought better of it and let it fall back.

"You *armed* her?" Brother Brogan said to Eleanor.

"She needs to defend herself."

"From you," said Megan.

"Megan, I'd never—"

"You should have slit her throat as soon as you found her. It would have been merciful."

"I'm not a murderer," said Eleanor. "I had to know if she was . . ."

"And now you do? Why is she still walking?"

Eleanor was between Megan and the door. If she was quick enough, Megan might make it past her before she could draw her weapon, but weeks of traveling with the countess told her she couldn't outrun or outfight her, not unless she disabled her first. She had a knife though; she could do it. Slash or thrust, wound or kill. This was the woman who had watched her sleep at night, wondering whether to allow her to wake. Didn't Megan have the right to strike first, to protect herself, to protect her baby? She held off. She might have the right, but she didn't have the will.

"There was something you didn't tell me, wasn't there?" Eleanor said to Brother Brogan. "About the true nature of the witches."

"What of it?"

"It's not some demon spawn Megan's carrying. And it's not one of the Saviors either. It's a baby. An innocent human baby."

Guilt—or was it shame?—flickered across Brother Brogan's face. Whatever it was, he soon got over it. "It won't stay innocent."

"It will if I have anything to do with it."

"You would give them figureheads?" said Brother Brogan. "A pair of incestuous bastards to rally behind?

They'll swarm over the Realm like locusts, spewing their sins and blasphemies."

Megan recognized the argument: Eleanor had made a similar one the day before, trying to talk Megan into taking the drugs so she wouldn't have to kill her. Not that killing her would have been hard: Eleanor could have smothered her in her sleep, pushed her into the Speed, mixed poison in with her food. Yesterday morning, after they had seen the High Priest, when Eleanor had had a knife at her throat. Had her anger been real, or had she been working herself up to complete the mission Brother Brogan had given her? Megan shuddered. How close to death had she been?

"Blasphemies?" said Eleanor. "Like their disavowal of priests, *brother*?"

Brother Brogan twitched and turned away. He grabbed the bread and tore a chunk off it, but instead of eating he continued to tear. "God's laws are not for the picking and choosing. You can't rewrite the ones you don't like."

"But who was doing the rewriting?"

The bread had been reduced to crumbs in Brother Brogan's hands. He brushed them clean. "How did you find out?"

"It takes a lot longer than four decades to bury a secret like that," said Eleanor, "though I can see why you tried. A lot of people might agree with the witches, especially after forty years of your rule."

"You're expressing sympathy for the witches now? Have you seen what they've done?"

"Yes, I've seen what they've done. I've seen what you've done. And, yes, before you say it, I know what my father and his forefathers did too. We're all capable of the same evil."

Brother Brogan rummaged through the detritus on his desk and pulled out a short-bladed knife. Megan steadied herself, preparing to fend off the expected blow and counter strike. It didn't come. Instead Brother Brogan crouched by the barrel in the corner of the room. He jammed the blade between two of the planks near the bottom of the barrel and twisted. Coarse black power poured out and accumulated into a heap on the floor.

Brother Brogan went back to the desk and flicked through the parchments strewn there. "I should have known not to delegate God's work. He called on me to do it, and do it I must." He selected a parchment. "Ah, Joanne's prophecy. How appropriate." He rolled it up into a tube and held it to the candle. The old skin caught alight. He stared into the flame, mesmerized.

"Megan," said Eleanor. "I think we should . . ."

Brother Brogan motioned to toss the burning parchment at the heap of powder by the barrel.

"Run!"

# eighteen

Megan dove through the doorway. Eleanor pulled her behind the wall and slammed the door shut. There was a brilliant flash, an almighty bang, and the world shook. The pain that jarred Megan's bones told her she had smacked into the ground. Scorching air rushed over her like the breath of a dragon.

She looked up. The world was formless, reduced to a gray cloud that obscured everything. A single continuous shriek filled her ears. Was she dead? She breathed. Dust caked her insides. She coughed and spluttered, feeling her throat burn. Still alive then. Hard to say for how much longer.

Megan groped around in the emptiness. Her hand fell on something soft—Eleanor's leg. It kicked back, albeit feebly. It was alive, and still attached to the countess. She could see to herself then.

Finding Eleanor at least told Megan her position. She crawled over the prone woman, feeling in front of her for the front door logic told her should be there but fear insisted wasn't. She moved slowly. Her palms and knees gouged tracks in the sediment coating the stone flags beneath her. Each breath seemed to rob her body of air rather than provide it.

Her hand slapped wood, stinging her fingers. She heaved herself into a sitting position and groped until she found the door knob. Slumping against it, she was able to use her entire body weight to twist it. The door cracked open. The air shifted. A sliver of light pierced the gray, the first hint the world was anything but a uniform nothingness.

The world trembled, a sensation Megan felt in the pit of her stomach rather than heard. The building was threatening to collapse. She didn't have long to get out. Neither did Eleanor. Megan stretched her arm out behind her. She touched only dust. Let Eleanor be buried under the weight of the house. She had conspired with Brother Brogan to kill her. Why mourn her death?

Another tremble, this one shuddering through her body and jolting her numbed bones. Could she leave Eleanor like this? She had saved Megan from the witches—for her own reasons, yes—but saved her all the same. *I pledge to defend His people.* She owed it to Eleanor to at least try.

Megan crawled back into the hallway. It was like wading through sand. A coughing fit left her nearly paralyzed. Her eyes were watering so hard she could feel the tears dripping off her cheeks and onto her hands.

She bumped into Eleanor. She shook her. Eleanor gave her a disgruntled reaction, like someone objecting to being woken up early. Megan ran her hand up her body and smeared something warm and sticky across Eleanor's face: blood.

"Are you all right?" she said, or thought she said. She couldn't hear the words coming out her mouth. If Eleanor heard the question—and was capable of answering—her reply was also inaudible.

Megan slipped her hands under Eleanor's armpits and prepared to drag. She heaved. The strain almost killed her. The deadweight of the woman's body threatened to wrench her arms free of their sockets. Every breath she took filled her lungs with suffocating dust. She lost track of distance and direction. Maybe she had died and this was hell: carrying Eleanor her eternal punishment.

She reversed into the front door, knocking it shut. Megan eased Eleanor to the ground and felt for the knob. The door came open a little, then jammed. Eleanor was blocking the way. Despite the protests of her spine, Megan hauled her clear.

She yanked the door open the whole way. Light showed her the way out. She dragged Eleanor to it. The air dissipated. Dust gave way to the clear night. Amorphous blobs resolved into figures.

Then everything went black.


Megan heard a woman's voice: soft, unfamiliar. A pungent smell of burning herbs filled her nostrils. When she swallowed it was as if a hundred tiny claws were scratching at her throat. She opened her eyes. Candlelight triggered a throbbing in her forehead. She winced and narrowed her gaze. Focus gradually arrived. She was sprawled on a soft bed. An attractive middle-aged woman was tucking a blanket around her.

"There's no sign of any blood, my lady," she said.

"The baby's survived?" Eleanor's voice.

"It looks that way. I can call for a midwife if you want to be sure."

Megan had been washed, her wounds tended to, and dressed in a linen shift. "What's going on?" she croaked. "Where am I?"

She looked around for a weapon. Her gaze fell instead on Eleanor. The countess wore a simple white tunic and had braided her hair into a thick copper rope. Ointment the color of rust had been smeared over the cuts on her cheek and hands.

"You need to rest," said Eleanor.

The bed was comfortable, more comfortable than Megan had ever known. The blankets were fleecy and warm, high-quality wool. They whispered to her, seducing her to sleep. Megan resisted. "Where am I?"

"My house," said the woman. "You're safe here."

"How did we . . . ?"

"My men brought you here."

"Lynette owns the house where Brother Brogan was staying . . ."

"I think we have to say *owned* now, my lady."

". . . and the rest of the street. She used to be one of my mother's serving girls."

"A life of wiping noses and cleaning up shit," Lynette said to Megan. "See how far I've come."

She turned to Eleanor. "You'll have to be gone by morning, my lady. Once the priests have finished the mopping-up operation, they'll be looking for you."

"What happened to Brother Brogan?" asked Megan.

"He *is* the mopping-up operation. They're bringing him out in buckets."

"What was . . . ?"

"Gunpowder," said Lynette. "A novelty from the Diannon Empire. They use it to make pretty lights in the sky."

"That was more than a pretty light."

"I understand they don't normally use that much at once. It's dangerous."

"No kidding."

Megan's throat felt as if she had eaten half the city. She hawked and looked for somewhere to spit. Lynette thrust a bowl at her. Megan coughed up a mixture of grit and phlegm.

Lynette wrinkled her nose. "I'd better tell Odette to cancel the oysters."

Eleanor placed a hand on her shoulder. "Can you give us a moment, please?"

"Of course, my lady."

Megan shook her head. "She can stay."

"I won't hurt you," said Eleanor.

"Really?"

Lynette's eyes flicked between Megan and Eleanor. She gave Megan a sympathetic smile. "I'll be just outside."

"Eavesdropping?" said Megan.

"You can take the girl out of servitude, but not the servant out of the girl."

Lynette left, her soft footsteps making no noise on the rugs that covered the floorboards. Eleanor stoked the fire then took Lynette's place on the end of the bed. She examined the end of her braid, avoiding eye contact.

Megan sat up, pulling away from her. "Where are my clothes?"

"Burning. They were in no condition to be worn again. Lynette'll get you some fresh ones."

"And my knives?"

"Under the bed," said Eleanor. "Looking to stab someone?"

"Maybe."

Megan looked around the chamber. Rich tapestries lined the walls. The furniture was polished mahogany, picked out with gold leaf. The candlesticks looked like solid silver. A mirror stood on one of the cabinets, in which she could see Eleanor's back. There was a fresh cut at the base of her neck.

"We should have come here first," Megan said. "Left Silas out of it."

"The priests are always looking for an excuse to fine someone," said Eleanor, "and a rich widow conspiring with a member of the overthrown aristocracy is too tempting a target."

"Poor Silas had nothing to confiscate, huh?"

"No."

"Apart from his life."

"That was uncalled for."

Maybe it was, maybe it wasn't. Megan wasn't sure Eleanor deserved an apology.

There was a pitcher of water by her bedside. She poured herself some. "Is this the bit where you explain your quest to murder me and I go, 'It's all right, don't worry about it'?"

"You know why I thought it was necessary," said Eleanor. "It was one life versus thousands."

"Bit hard to stomach when your life is the one."

"If you feel that way, why did you drag me out of that building?"

"Same reason I didn't let you slit Damon's throat," said Megan.

"You're comparing me to *him*?"

"True. He was forced to do what he did."

Eleanor wandered over to the mirror and checked her face, scraping away dried bits of ointment with her fingernail. "I thought it was for the good of the Realm. We don't need another war. Look at the devastation it caused last time, what we lost."

"Palaces, fortunes, power . . ."

". . . my mother."

Megan rolled her eyes.

"Oh, I'm sorry," said Eleanor. "Don't other people's families count? You saw what the witches did at Thicketford and Halliwell. Do you want that to happen to every village, every town, every city in the Realm?"

"Fine. If it's that important, kill me now. There are knives under the bed and I doubt you're wandering around unarmed." Megan spread her arms wide. "It's not as if I'm in any position to fight you off."

"You know I can't."

"Because you can't look me in the eye?" said Megan. "Blindfold me if it makes it any easier."

Eleanor's braid swished as she shook her head. "I thought getting you away from Thicketford was enough, but Brother Brogan said we had to make sure. I had to make tough decisions to save the Realm, prove I was worthy of my name. But I came to realize the tough decision wasn't killing you. It was fighting for you. Dying for you. You're the only friend I've ever had, and no matter what rational reason I could come up with, I didn't want to give that up. The witches are using your sister for their own ends. I'm not prepared to do the same. I swore to protect you and Gwyneth from them, and I will do that. If you'll let me."

Could Megan let her? Could she trust her? They had all betrayed her: Wade, Damon, Brother Brogan, Eleanor. No one cared about her. They all wanted to use her and abuse her and see her dead. She was a fool for trusting in them.

Megan crossed her arms over her stomach. You could only rely on family. Blood was what counted. But she couldn't bear to lose anyone else. She wanted to hate Eleanor, but she needed to forgive her. She couldn't do this by herself. The world was too big and too scary, with everyone hunting her. The thought of facing it on her own made her want to run away and hide in the deepest, darkest hole she could find.

Tiredness seeped through her. The decisions she had to make were too hard, the implications of where they would leave her too terrifying. She wanted to lose herself to oblivion. Forget everything. Pretend for a few hours everything was all right, everyone was safe. Even if she knew it so very wasn't.

She sank back into the pillows, soft and reassuring. Her eyelids fluttered. "I need to sleep," she said, her voice thickening. "Try not to murder me."

"I promise."

Before she drifted off, Megan felt a pair of lips brush her forehead. Half of her wanted to recoil, to distance herself from any further betrayal; the other half wanted to lean in and be embraced, to reassure herself there was someone in the world who cared for her. Sleep took her before she could decide.

Dreams came in the form of memories, of when Megan had told Gwyneth she was pregnant. They had been walking back home from Thicketford after dropping the day's bread off at Freya's inn. It was one of those hot summer days when you wanted to lie in the grass and close your eyes and lose yourself to the birdsong and the drone of dragonflies. Unfortunately, there was no way Megan could relax.

"Are you sure?" Gwyneth said.

Megan nodded. "You said it couldn't happen."

"I was only telling you what Bliss told me."

"Bliss? The girl who believes in unicorns and fairies and the celibacy of priests?"

"She said everyone knew it."

They crossed the bridge and headed along the riverbank up to the mill. Megan slowed her pace, postponing the moment she would have to cross its threshold. "Grandfather's going to kill me," she said.

"Not you," said Gwyneth. "You're his favorite."

"He won't be able to live with the shame. He'll kick me out."

Gwyneth took Megan by the arms. "I'll always be here for you. I won't let any harm come to you or your baby."

Megan hugged her, but as she clutched tighter the vitality of her sister's body was replaced by the unresponsive lump of a pillow, and the reassurance she offered evaporated and left an aching void.

It was dark when Lynette woke her. She had brought Megan some clothes and a breakfast of bread and cold meat. Megan pulled on a thin shift and started eating while Lynette poured the tea. It was one of those brews formulated to evoke the scents of nature; in this case, that of a fetid swamp. Megan hoped Lynette didn't expect her to drink it.

"Don't you have someone to do that for you?" she asked. Maybe the servants refused to be in the same room as the tea.

"The fewer people who have contact with you the better," said Lynette.

"You ashamed to be associated with me?"

"Not you, no."

"Aren't you and Eleanor good friends?" said Megan.

"I've only seen her a few times since she was a baby," said Lynette. "Countesses don't have friends. Exiled countesses have even fewer."

Lynette left Megan to finish her breakfast. While she ate, Megan contemplated the knife provided to cut the meat. A good point, a sharp blade. She searched through the drawers until she found a linen pillowcase, which she tore into strips. One she wrapped around the blade of the knife, another she used to strap it to the inside of her bare thigh. Not a weapon she could access quickly in the heat of battle, but one Eleanor didn't know about.

She pulled on the rest of the clothes, good-quality garments designed for the rough winter, and slipped the rest of her knives into their usual places. Properly equipped, she went downstairs. She found Eleanor in the kitchen, drinking tea with Lynette in what Megan could only assume was penance.

"I need some way of getting hold of Landon," she said. "Silas's place won't be safe, and if I can't get out of the inner city . . ."

"Lynette's already taken care of it," said Eleanor.

"One of my servants has contacted him."

"He's coming here?" said Megan.

"Saviors, no," said Lynette. "Having that kind of character around here would lower property prices faster than Brother Brogan's gunpowder experiment."

"We're to meet him down at the docks before morning worship," said Eleanor.

"We?"

"You don't think I'm going to let you do this alone, do you?"

"Wouldn't want to be alone with someone who might kill me, would I?" But despite everything, Megan was glad Eleanor was coming with her. It was good to think she had someone. Besides, she didn't think Eleanor would take no for an answer.

"Down at the docks?" she said. "Does this mean Landon's got a ship?"

"Who knows?" said Eleanor. "Maybe he just likes sailors."

Megan turned to Lynette. "Thank you for, well, everything."

"I wish it had happened in better circumstances."

They bid Lynette good-bye and slipped out of the house. Eastport was rising from its slumber. Dockers stumbled to the waterfront, cursing that final cup of wine the night before. Servants scurried around, looking for supplies for their masters. Builders in dusty leather aprons hauled themselves up the scaffolding surrounding the latest conversion of wealth to ostentation. A wagon rattled by, the casks of milk chattering to each other on the back. The temple bells tolled the hour, calling the Faithful to the first worship of the day. One or two priests even responded.

They reached the banks of the Speed. Upriver, the light of the rising sun dappled the surface of the water. Crews prepared fishing boats and merchant vessels for journeys that might last a day or weeks. Sailors scurried over the docked war galley in preparation for patrol; the city's thieves and whores would be gearing up to fleece the crew of whichever ship it was relieving of duty.

"How long will it take to reach Dustor?" Megan asked.

"We should be there within a week, given good weather."

That "we" again. "You're coming?"

"Whether you like it or not," said Eleanor.

Megan liked it better than she should have. "Someone's got to protect me from those mercenaries."

"And them from you."

Landon leaned out of an alley and beckoned to them. Before they could say anything, he disappeared back the way he had come. Megan and Eleanor looked at each other.

"Some people have to be dramatic," said Eleanor.

They followed the mercenary into the narrow passageway. A mangy dog looked up from its snuffling in a pile of garbage and scurried off. Landon leaned against the wall and put a hand on his sword—Megan's sword.

"Let's talk," he said.

"What is there to talk about?" said Megan. "You're either going to—"

She heard the footsteps behind her too late, could do nothing about the blade pricking her back. She started to turn to Eleanor, but Landon whistled.

"Eyes on me."

"This the best you can do?" said Eleanor. "I thought you might have come up with something more original than a back-street mugging."

Landon curled his lip. "Shut up, your . . . your . . . what is the correct term for addressing a countess?" The mercenary hummed. "Ah, yes. Shut up, your whoreness. I've got a proposition for you."

"We don't negotiate with scum," said Eleanor.

"Must make dealing with your customers tricky."

"What do you want?" Megan said to Landon.

"You pay us, say, fifty sovereigns and we won't turn you over to our friends."

"Friends?"

"They're very keen to speak to you."

The blood drained from Megan's face. The breath caught in her throat. The witches. How had he known? Had the word gone out for her and Eleanor, or had Landon been approached directly by someone who knew he was working with them?

"We don't have that kind of money," she mumbled.

"But you know people who do. Supporters of the most noble house of Endalay who don't want to see its last member dead in an alley." Landon sneered at Eleanor. "You know back-street muggings never end well."

"And if we can raise the cash," said Eleanor, "what then? What will you tell your friends?"

"I'll say you went somewhere else. Maybe on a pilgrimage to Statham."

"And you'll take us to Dustor?" said Megan.

"Megan, I don't think he's—"

"'Course I'll take you to Dustor," said Landon.

He was lying. Megan had realized why he didn't want them to turn around: there was only one man behind them. If that's all Landon had been able to recruit for a simple hold-up, there was little chance he'd be able to get a company together for a raid on a Sandstrider port. He would take the money he planned to extort from them and turn them over to the witches. They needed to get away from him as soon as possible and then . . . and then what? Landon wasn't only robbing her of money, he was stealing her chance of getting Gwyneth back too.

"We'll get you the cash," she said. "Meet us here in a couple of hours."

"Think I'll tag along," said Landon. "Dangerous city, this."

"Do we have a choice?"

"No."

Landon crooked his finger at them and started down the alley, heading away from the river. The women shuffled forward a few steps. Megan faked a stumble and threw herself to the ground. Eleanor overtook her. Landon's partner drew level.

"Get up, you—"

Megan whipped a stiletto from her boot and drove it into the man's thigh. His cry of agony echoed around the alley. He slashed back at her. She rolled under the wild blow, pulled out one of the knives in her arm scabbard and hacked at his hamstrings. He crumpled into a screaming heap.

Landon was coming at them, brandishing the sword given to him for services very definitely not rendered. She hadn't realized how big it was, how sharp, until it was her turn to be on the receiving end. She scrambled to her feet. Eleanor put herself between Megan and the mercenary captain and drew her own sword. It looked as effective as a butter knife.

"I don't think the people you're working for will be very pleased if we're dead," she said, taking a step back.

"You sure about that?"

Megan hurled her knife at Landon. It shot past him.

"That was stupid," said the mercenary. Megan produced the knife's twin. Landon nodded. "Got to admire a girl who's prepared."

Megan and Eleanor retreated backward down the alley as Landon advanced. He was too big—too well armed—for them to engage in a straight fight and emerge unharmed. They were heading toward the bustling riverside, but Megan wasn't sure the crowd would save them. In this part of town, men with big swords were viewed as upstanding citizens who should on no account be interfered with.

A gust of wind on her face told Megan they had cleared the alley. Time to make a run for it. She tugged Eleanor's sleeve, turned, and froze. One enemy had turned into many. City guards were advancing on them at the double, crimson jerkins rippling in the wind, pikes at the ready. Twenty of them, at least, nearer thirty.

"Drop your weapons!"

"You first," said Eleanor.

Her swagger dissipated at the advance of two-dozen sharpened pikes. Metal clanged as she threw her sword on the ground. Megan followed, letting her knife drop from her grasp. It felt as if she was surrendering hope.

Guards rushed forward and roughly searched them. Knives rained from belts and sleeves, to the guards' increasing befuddlement.

"What the . . . ?"

"They were cheaper if you bought in bulk," said Megan, affecting what she hoped was a nonthreatening smile.

Hoofs clip-clopped on the cobblestones. The guards made way for the horse and its rider. A priest, riding side-saddle so as not to disturb his pristine robes. Brother Attor, the High Priest's secretary. He looked down at Landon, who swaggered out from the alley.

"You delivered them then?" he said.

"Good as my word," said Landon.

Megan was confused. He was working for the priests, not the witches? But what did the priests want with them? They'd shown precisely zero interest in their plight. "What's going on, brother?"

"You're under arrest," said Brother Attor.

"On what charge?" said Eleanor.

"Murder. Blasphemy. Treason." Brother Attor leaned toward them. "All three carry the death penalty."

# nineteen

Centuries ago, the city's jail had been the palace of the Counts of Ainsworth, but the cold, the damp, and the rats had forced them to build a new one further inland. What had been drawbacks for a residence were plus points for a penitentiary. Once-fine rooms had been partitioned into cells; the central courtyard that had formerly hosted chivalric tournaments now hosted the hangman's noose; and the cellars, well, Megan had never known anyone keen to discuss what happened there.

She huddled on a stone block that served as a bed, trying to warm herself. The barred window was too small to admit the warmth of the sun, but not small enough to prevent the wind from whipping in off the river and freezing the skin. She had the cell to herself: the guards had marched Eleanor off the moment they had arrived. Interrogating her, no doubt. Megan swallowed. It'd be her turn next.

She'd been there for hours, without food or water or even an explanation of the charges. Nothing kept her company apart from her own fears. Once or twice she almost dropped off, then a scream would echo through the jail and her pulse began racing as she tried to determine whether it belonged to Eleanor and, if so, what would happen once they came for her.

Footsteps approached out in the corridor—heavy slaps of leather on wet stone. Keys rattled. Eyes peered at her through the small grate set in the door. Was this it? Megan huddled on the stone block, trying to make herself smaller, insignificant, not worth torturing.

Rusty hinges squealed as the door swung open and a jailer entered. In his hands was a tin tray holding a hunk of bread, spotted with mold, and a cup of water. He dropped it on the floor, spilling half the water, and left.

A pitiful wave of gratitude swept through Megan. She hadn't quite come to licking the condensation off the sweating walls, but another couple of hours of isolation might have driven her to it. She scrambled over to the tray and wolfed down the bread, mold and all, then swallowed the water in a couple of gulps.

The jailer had failed to lock the door or even close it. Megan held off at first, fearing a trap—hacked down while trying to escape—but eventually curiosity got the better of her. She crept into the deserted corridor beyond. Other cells lined its length. She peered into a couple. The first was empty; the second contained a man reduced to skin and bone, muttering to himself and chewing the gristle off his fingers. She didn't look into any more.

The corridor led to the guards' station, a windowless chamber lit by a roaring fire. Instruments hung on a rack: metal tools designed to slice, grip, tear, or simply get red hot. Brother Attor was warming his hands, his back to her. Although the guards had confiscated most of her knives, Megan still had the one strapped to her thigh. She took an experimental step forward.

"Ah, good, you made it," said Brother Attor, turning to face her. "I would have joined you in your cell, but the damp plays havoc with my asthma." He gave a pathetic little cough, like a child feigning illness, and beckoned her over. "Come, warm yourself."

Megan hung back. The fire could warm, but it could also burn. "What's this about?"

"Not shy, are we?"

She thought about the charges he had mentioned, whom she could have murdered. "Brother Brogan did . . . did that to himself."

"Indeed."

"We didn't have anything to do with it," said Megan.

"Not exactly what the witnesses say. Or will say. When it's been explained to them."

Brother Attor pulled up a stool. He wiped its surface with a handkerchief, examined the grime the handkerchief had accumulated on its brief journey, and threw it in the fire. It blackened and shriveled, reduced to nothing in a few seconds.

He sat. The flames cast a warm glow on one half of his handsome face; shadows hid the other half. He gazed on Megan, taking in the contours of her body. Was he planning on seducing her? Was that the price to get out of here? Maybe it wasn't Gwyneth who'd had the crush on him, maybe it was he who had desired her. And now he had found the next best thing. Megan's skin crawled.

"Father Galan wants you executed by dawn tomorrow."

"We don't even get a trial?" said Megan.

"Well, yes, but . . ."

"He's the one trying us."

Brother Attor applauded her answer. The action reminded Megan of being back at school, which reminded her of Brother Brogan, which reminded her of everything else. She slumped against the wall.

"I'm here to offer you a deal," said Brother Attor. "One that will preserve your lives. Yours and your child's."

"And Eleanor's?"

"Two out of three isn't bad."

Here it came. Megan steeled herself, digging her nails into her palms, unsure of her response. How far would she go to save her baby? How far *could* she go?

"You will testify the Endalay woman conspired with thugs and foreigners to overthrow the rightful rulers of God's realm," said Brother Attor, "and in return the High Priest will pardon you."

"What?"

"We know she had made contact with the Sandstriders," said Brother Attor. "We know you hired mercenaries."

"We hired the mercenaries to rescue my sister."

"That's not what their captain says."

"You trust him?" said Megan. "We had to find something else to interest them. They would have cared as much about the plight of one poor girl as you did. They're mercenaries—the solution was obvious."

"Your hired swords were to rendezvous with the Sandstriders in Dustor, from where you would invade the county. Your first target was Trafford's Haven, which you'd already reconnoitered."

"Who on earth would want Trafford's Haven? Even the witches wouldn't go near the place."

Brother Attor twitched. "It was to be a staging post for richer targets elsewhere."

"No, it wasn't," said Megan. "There was no staging post, no invasion, no deal with the Sandstriders. All we want to do is save my sister. She's out there, scared and alone, and I'm the only one who gives a damn about her. Eleanor's not interested in taking back her family's old position. You can keep the power you've done so much to protect."

The priest pulled a rolled-up parchment out of his robe and proffered it to Megan. "Things will be far more pleasant if you confess. Father Galan will absolve you of your sins and we will all lead peaceful lives, satisfied no one is going to take the crown."

"Crown? What? Eleanor? She isn't royal."

"Isn't she?" said Brother Attor. "You know what these aristocrats are like, inbreeding like prize animals. She'll have some connection, somewhere in her family tree. Someone'll dig it up, use it to rally the malcontents, and before you know it we'll have a tyrant queen responsible for the deaths of thousands. This doesn't affect just our sleepy little county, this affects the entire Realm. Please, Megan, confess and take the pardon. It's the only way to save yourself and prevent a war."

Megan shuddered at the sound of her name from the priest's lips. She edged closer to the fire. It warmed her body but couldn't touch her soul. "It's not Eleanor you have to worry about, it's the witches."

"If they are here—"

"They are!"

"If they are here, then the Realm doesn't need the aristocracy making one last desperate grab for power. It needs to be united."

Were the priests really that scared of Eleanor? Her support seemed limited to one dead servant and a widow who was too scared to let them stay a full day.

The people certainly seemed disinterested in having the aristocracy back.

"Why does she matter?" continued Brother Attor. "She'll only see one more sunrise no matter what you say, but you can affect what happens to you. Say the right thing and this can all be over. Think about your sister."

"What?"

"We have ships," said Brother Attor, "disciplined men who won't get homicidal when the promised fortune doesn't materialize. All we need is the will, which you can provide."

"You believe me?"

"We can send a squadron down to Dustor to see if the witches are really there. If your sister's really there. I always did like Gwyneth. Wouldn't like to think of her in the hands of those who would do her harm."

It was all Megan had fought for, the sole purpose of her existence, and this priest was offering it to her with a glib promise. The only cost was betrayal and that was a coin everyone spent in the end. Was it even a betrayal? There was no doubt Eleanor wanted to retake her father's seat, and she *had* met with the Sandstriders. The priests' accusations might be true, in the broader picture if not the details.

A guard appeared. "The High Priest requires your presence," he said to Brother Attor.

"Do you have an answer for him, Megan?"

It would be easy. A few minutes in the great hall of the palace, agree with whatever Father Galan put to her.

It would be easy. Watch Eleanor drop from the scaffold. Megan had seen many people die—enemies, loved ones, friends, strangers—what was one more?

It would be easy. Sit back while the priests' soldiers went to rescue Gwyneth. Why put herself at more risk?

It would be easy. And nothing right ever was.

Megan rose and straightened her clothes. "Remind Father Galan of the sixth Pledge of Faith," she said. *I pledge truth in all I do.*

With that, she spun on her heel and marched back to her cell.


A pair of guards bundled Eleanor into the cell, throwing her onto the floor as if she were the day's trash. The countess winced and held her side as Megan helped her up onto the stone block. Her hair was a ragged curtain across her face. Megan brushed it back. A fresh bruise marred Eleanor's cheek.

"Are you all right?"

"I think so." Eleanor prodded her ribs. "Don't think anything's broken."

"Did they torture you?"

"They didn't even interrogate me. Just a little softening up." She shook her head. "Why do they need to ask questions? Our fate's been determined by God. It doesn't matter what we say. How can we contradict Him?"

"It's not what they told me. The priests think you're planning a coup. They offered me a pardon if I gave you up."

Eleanor brooded for a while. "You should take it," she said eventually.

"What? I can't—"

"What does one more lie mean to me?" said Eleanor. "Take the offer. Save yourself. Save your sister. Save your baby."

"I can't betray you."

"It's not betrayal if I tell you to do it."

"It is to me."

"Are you doing this to make a point?" said Eleanor. "Is your life worth a brief moment of moral superiority?"

"I'm not superior to anyone," said Megan. "No one should die for me." She thought of Silas and mumbled, "No one else."

Eleanor leaned back and stared at the ceiling. Megan knew from her own observations there was nothing up there unless you found algae formations exciting. "At least you'll have a few more months," the countess said.

"What do you mean?"

"They won't execute a pregnant woman."

"Not the impression I'm getting."

"You have told them, haven't you?" Eleanor sat upright and reached out for Megan. "You should. Use the time it gives you."

"They already know. I assumed you . . ." If they hadn't interrogated Eleanor, how could they know about the baby? "This isn't about you."

"No."

"It's about me."

"I'm afraid so."

"They want to kill me and my baby."

"Brother Brogan must have told them, in case his plan failed," said Eleanor.

"But why offer me a pardon to confess we were plotting to overthrow the priests?"

"Because that pardon is as ephemeral as my chances of reclaiming the lands of my ancestors. Your confession would condemn you as surely as it would me. The priests would have a reason to execute you, and no one would have to worry about the witches or the consequences of murdering an innocent girl. The Book of Faith must be obeyed in letter if not in spirit."

"Bastards."

"You've just noticed?"

Eleanor examined the cell, testing the door and the brickwork. "We need to get out of here. Do you still have that knife you stole from Lynette?"

"How did you . . . ?"

"A well-bred girl like you not bringing down her breakfast tray? Obvious you didn't want me to notice there was something missing. Lynette'll be annoyed. They form a set."

Megan slipped a hand inside her pants. The guards had failed to check inside her clothes. She'd tied the knife too well to her thigh though, and it took a few tugs before she was able to yank it free. She paused before handing it to Eleanor, reluctant to give up her last weapon.

"What's the plan?" she asked, massaging her thigh.

"Plan?" said Eleanor, testing the blade of the knife.

"Guess that was asking too much."

"If you don't have a plan, it can't go wrong."

Shouting floated in through the window, the cries of the mob. Had they come to demand the heads of the traitors who had plotted the overthrow of their rulers? If so, who did they view as the traitors and who the rulers?

Eleanor tapped the blade of the knife against her cheek, and then she slipped it inside her sleeve. "All right," she said. "When the guard comes in, you distract him and I'll get stabby."

"They come in pairs."

"Distract *both* of them then."

The yells of the mob were getting louder, more agitated, with one or two screams thrown into the mix. Instinct drew Megan to the window, even though she knew the only thing she'd be able to see through its bars would be the surface of the Speed.

A ship glided into view, tall and sturdy, riding high in the water. It was heading west to east—an arrival from the sea. Men swarmed on its decks. The dying sun glinted off steel. Weapons. The vessel was a warship, but unlike any Megan had ever seen.

The stern became visible, as did the flag it had flying there. A huge cloth, bleached white, and on it a feared symbol: the star-broken circle.

There was a sequence of flashes; a silence that lasted either for a fraction of a second or an eternity; then a roar as the world trembled.

# twenty

Megan and Eleanor clutched onto each other, stabilizing themselves against the shock waves that shuddered through the jail. "The witches," said Megan, digging her nails into Eleanor's arm. "They've come for me."

"You don't know that."

"They show up hours before I'm due to be hanged. Bit of a coincidence, don't you think?"

Booms sounded in sequence. The floor shook beneath their feet. Plaster trickled down from the ceiling of the cell. Megan recognized the smell. Acrid with a hint of rotten egg. The gunpowder at Brother Brogan's. The witches were going to blow the city apart to get to her, steal her baby, crown it monarch of a world they intended to devastate. She needed to run, she needed to hide, she needed to find the blackest hole imaginable and cower in it.

Eleanor flew to the door and hammered on it. "Guards! Guar—"

The door flung open, catching her by surprise. She twisted out of the way, lost her footing on the slimy flagstones, and smacked into the floor. Megan hurried to help her up. A barked order made her freeze.

"Bring them to the place of execution."

A pair of guards piled into the cell, swords slapping their thighs, their crimson jerkins a flash of color amid the gray. Another pair stood outside the door, their pikes ready to impale any who attempted to flee. Eleanor made a move for the knife stashed in her sleeve, but a guard grabbed her arms and pinioned them behind her back, pressing until she cried out. Another guard administered the same treatment to Megan. He wrenched so hard her shoulders almost dislocated.

The guards frog-marched them out into the corridor. Father Galan, the High Priest of Eastport, stood there, clutching the Book of Faith to his enormous belly. His gorgeous robes were stained with wine, his lips with grease. Megan caught his eye. He refused to hold it, and set off down the corridor, intoning as he walked.

"God, born of the eternal universe, ultimate arbiter of man, take these souls we deliver unto You. Show them Your mercy and love and the wonders of Your creation. Rejoice, for though life ends in death, out of death comes life."

The funeral prayer. A chill crept across Megan, as if Death was caressing her, his soon-to-be paramour.

"Please," she said, squirming in the guard's hold. "You can't do this. They're not witches or demons. You must know that. Surely you don't believe your own propaganda. They're men. You can fight them."

"They're not witches?" said Father Galan. "Look what they're doing to the city."

"You think God wants you to murder an innocent child?"

"Innocent?"

Megan turned to the guards. "The priests have been lying to you all these years," she cried, "and now they want to kill—"

Father Galan motioned to the guard holding Megan, who clamped a hand over her mouth. Megan tried to bite it. He squeezed harder. Father Galan repeated his prayer.

"God, born of the eternal universe . . ."

They marched through corridors of clammy limestone, lit by flickering torches whose chief purpose seemed to be to intensify the shadows. The guards bundled Megan and Eleanor down rough-cut steps made slippery by river water seeping through the rock. Rats squeaked at them, protesting at the disturbance. A guard drove his pike down on one of them, shattering its spine.

More booms. Megan swayed with the guard holding her. She amplified the motion, then twisted, throwing him off his feet. He kicked out just as she was grabbing for the dagger hanging at his hip. His boot crashed into her knee. There was an explosion of pain, then nausea. Megan retched, spewing up half-digested lumps of bread.

They resumed their march before she knew what was happening. Two guards had her now, dragging her between them as if she was a stunned animal on its way to the slaughterhouse. Megan tried to keep in step with them, to at least make her final journey on her own two feet, but her knee throbbed every time she put her weight on that leg. Broken or bruised? The least of her problems.

Distant cries greeted them as they emerged into the courtyard, the screams of a terrified city. An orange glow shimmered above the high walls of the jail. Pillars of smoke climbed to the heavens. The city was aflame.

A pair of gallows on a raised platform stood silent sentry in the middle of the square, the ropes dangling from their arms swaying in the wind. Megan pressed into the guards, trying to push them back. Her throat constricted. She couldn't breathe. The guards jerked her onward, jolting breath back into her.

Father Galan, still reciting his prayer, glided to the base of the platform. Eleanor allowed herself be led up the steps, meek as a newborn kitten. Megan continued to struggle, yanking her body this way and that. One of the guards cuffed her, sending her head spinning. They carried her the rest of the way.

Flimsy planks rattled under her feet. *No, no, no.* This couldn't be happening. She was still asleep—at Lynette's, at Silas's, at home. She'd wake any moment now, cold sweat coating her trembling body, the nightmare dispersing like smoke on the wind.

Scratchy hemp bit into her neck. The noose tightened, the embrace of an unwanted lover. Megan tried to loosen it. Her executioner slapped her hands away and called for rope with which to tie her hands.

A guard started to slip the second noose over Eleanor's head. "May I pray first?" she asked, her voice barely above a whisper.

The guard looked to Father Galan, who nodded. Eleanor bowed her head. "God, born of the eternal universe . . ." She craned her head around to address the guard who pinned her arms. "Could you let me make the sign of the circle?"

The guard dropped his hold. Eleanor brought her arms around, made a play of rubbing them to restore the circulation, and made the sign of the circle over her chest. She slipped her hands into her sleeves and cast Megan a sideways glance.

Megan got the message. Hope sparked within her, gave her courage. Her mind raced, searching for a plan.

"Hey!" she called down to Father Galan. "You realize you're going to burn in hell for this, don't you? For a very long time, considering the amount of blubber you're carrying."

The High Priest scowled and reddened. The guards smirked at the childish insult, their attention drawn away from Eleanor for a vital second. The countess whirled around and punched the guard behind her with the underside of her fist. Blood spurted between the hands that flew to his face. He shrieked and kept on shrieking, a cry of horror as much as pain. She had stabbed him in the eye.

The other guards on the platform gawked at their agonized comrade, then at each other. They lunged for Eleanor. Megan grabbed the rope at her neck and swung herself at them, hard as she could. She collided with the rearward one. He careered into his companion. They went flying in a tangle of limbs and landed on the hard stone of the courtyard with a sickening crack. Only one of them attempted to regain his footing.

Megan tugged at the noose, desperate to escape its chokehold. It was too tight. She couldn't move the knot. She steadied herself, found the correct position, and yanked. The rope burned her skin as she dragged her head through it, one last kiss to remember it by.

With a thrust of her knife, Eleanor silenced the guard she had half blinded. She crouched beside him and ransacked his body, relieved him of the weapons he no longer needed. His dagger she slid across to Megan, along with Lynette's knife; his sword she claimed for herself.

Boots stomped up the steps. Eleanor's eyes widened. Megan spun, jerking out of the way as a pike shot toward her, and kept spinning. Her arms whirled as she slashed out at her attacker's unprotected face, first with one knife, then the other. Blood erupted in a fine spray.

There was a boom from the river. A chimney tottered, then crashed into the courtyard in a shower of dust and masonry. The guards who could ran, or rather stumbled away, leaving Megan and Eleanor alone with Father Galan. He brandished the Book of Faith at the women, as if its pages could shield him from their blooded blades.

"Kill me and you betray the Faith," he said.

"You are not the Faith," said Megan.

"That's what the witches claim. Are you one of them?"

Megan raised her knife and prepared to strike. Eleanor grabbed her arm and pulled her back. "Go," she said to Father Galan, "before I let her do something entirely justified."

The High Priest ran, almost tripping over his robes in his haste to escape.

Megan sank to her knees before her legs could give way. She was dizzy, nauseated, breathing too fast. Her brain felt as if someone had chopped it up and shoved it back into her head.

Eleanor put a hand on her shoulder. "Are you all right?"

"Yes. Just need . . . just need . . . not every day you almost get executed."

"I used to think that as well. Until I met you."

Movement in one of the upper-floor windows betrayed a priest watching them. He was too far away and the glass too cloudy to make a positive identification, but Megan thought she recognized the stature and pristine garments of Brother Attor. "Let's get out of here."

Eleanor hurried to the main gates. Megan hobbled after her. Her knee was getting better, but the injury was going to need further running off. She suspected opportunities to do so weren't going to be hard to find.

The gates were locked and barred, the sentry posts abandoned. Eleanor put a token shoulder to the oak, but she might as well have tried to barge her way through the stone walls. She slapped the wood. "There's got to be another way out of here."

"Don't look at me," said Megan. "It was your family who used to live here."

"Ten generations ago. You think floor plans are passed down via race memory?"

The screams and cries and the general sounds of panic made Megan wonder if escaping the palace-cum-jail was such a good idea. It was safe and secure, albeit in the same way as a well-wrapped present: a gift to the witch soldiers who would soon swarm the city. The appeal of escape reasserted itself.

"The High Priest," she said. "He was going . . ."

"Not this way."

They traced the route taken by the High Priest and his guards before him: across the courtyard and into the east wing of the jail. "If you were the way out, where would you be?" said Eleanor.

"Near the exit?"

Their eyes were drawn upward as boots thudded above their heads. Eleanor dashed off in the direction they were heading. Megan limped after her, pointing out the drawbacks in her plan. They collided into two of those drawbacks as they clattered down the stairs.

"They're coming in through the main gates," said Eleanor, bringing herself to her full aristocratic height. "Go quick. Stop them." The two guards dashed off in a direction that led to the main gates only if you included the possibility of circumnavigation. Eleanor and Megan exchanged glances and shrugged. Not quite what Eleanor had intended, but it was good enough. They hastened after them.

The women skidded around a corner, catching sight of the retreating guards squeezing through a postern. The undersize gate slammed after them and bounced back open. Megan and Eleanor didn't need a further invitation.

Several of the buildings around the jail were on fire, the flames devouring the dry wood. No one was attempting to put them out. The population had only one thought: grab anything portable and flee, join the crowds streaming to the gates at the cardinal points of the inner city.

Eleanor and Megan edged along the scarred walls of the jail until they reached the river. An abandoned merchantman was in the process of sinking, its stern sticking out of the water as if making a rude gesture. Out on the Speed, wreathed in smoke, three warships floated, all flying the star-broken circle. One of them was listing, taking on water. Near it, only the masts of the priests' war galley were visible—the rest of the ship was under the surface, the water around it foaming as men kicked for their lives.

Brilliant flashes penetrated the black clouds, heralding explosions of timbers, stone, and dirt on either side of the water. The opposite bank—what Megan could make out of it anyway—had turned from green to brown, verdant fields reduced to churned mud. The setting sun glinted off the armor of soldiers running for the hills; it also glinted off armor that remained entirely stationary.

Rowing boats glided out of the fog: witches heading for the jetties, heading for Megan. Five minutes before they landed, no more. She rubbed her knee. The pain had subsided to a dull ache. She had to get away, lose herself in the crowds fleeing the city. She could beg or buy a ride, a place on a wagon or a fast horse. The priests had confiscated what remained of her silver, but she still had the last sovereign hidden in her clothes. Get out, lie low, and then resume her search for Gwyneth.

Megan looked across the water, realization dawning. Search? She'd already found her. "Gwyneth's on one of those ships," she said. "We've got to get over there."

Eleanor shook her head. "I don't think—"

"Don't you see? If they're sending their soldiers ashore, the ships'll be undefended. We can swim across and rescue her."

"Swim the Speed? Even at the best of times it's a death trap. The currents . . ."

"All right, we'll get a boat. We'll wait until the soldiers are ashore and steal one of theirs."

The first of the boats pulled up alongside a jetty. A couple of men stormed along the pier brandishing sticks at them. Arrows dropped them. The soldiers faced no further resistance.

"Megan, this is a warzone. Do you really think they'll have brought your sister here? She's one of the two most precious things in the world to them and I have no intention of letting them get their hands on the other one."

"I have to try," said Megan. "And it's the last place they'll look for me."

"No."

"It's what we came here for."

"We came here to find an army," said Eleanor.

"The army's running away!"

"You don't think you should take that as a hint?"

Megan jabbed a finger toward the warships. "But if Gwyneth's over there . . ."

"Wherever she is, she's safe. You, on the other hand . . ."

"Is that all you're concerned about?" said Megan. "Keeping me from them? You're still trying to stop Joanne's prophecy."

Eleanor rubbed Megan's arm. "This is about more than rescuing your sister now. I don't know what weapons the witches are using against the city, but it's obvious we can't fight them with a few blades. We need the whole Realm behind us."

Megan let herself be persuaded by Eleanor, though she couldn't say whether logic or fear clinched the argument. They sheathed their weapons and left the river for the chaos of the inner city. Young and old streamed by, rich and poor, escaping the flames that cackled in glee at their retreat. Eleanor pulled Megan out of the way of a collapsing house front. It crashed into the ground, vaporizing into ash and dust. Megan cursed herself. She had brought this on the town. If she had gone elsewhere, Eastport would now be settling down for a peaceful night like it had done thousands of times before.

The East Gate was closest. The road that led from it followed the Speed upstream before turning north at the Washbrook Bridge and heading for the heartlands of the Realm. They would have to reach the bridge before the witches' ships did. She'd seen what they'd done—what they were doing—to the ships on the river, to the garrison, to the city. A bridge wouldn't last long.

Everyone else had the same idea. Megan and Eleanor were carried by the crowd as it surged toward the walls, desperate to stay on their feet and avoid being trampled to death. The street narrowed, squeezing everybody together. An old man cried and stumbled. A panicky washerwoman swatted him aside with a meaty arm. He collapsed into a forest of legs. Megan bent down and tried to help him up. A stray knee slammed into her thigh. Eleanor's arm shot out and grabbed her before she hit the ground. She didn't see what happened to the old man.

The crowd burst into the square outside the East Gate, normally used to hold outgoing traffic while the city guards collected customs duties. Now it held only bodies. Men, women, children, animals. Dismembered, beheaded, peppered with arrows and crossbow bolts. Blood flowed into the drains as if it were rainwater.

Activity at the gates made them back off. Behind the jaws of the portcullis, bowstrings tautened. Soldiers in black armor stepped out of sentry posts, wielding axes smeared with blood and scraps of body tissue.

The witches had sealed the city. They were trapped.

# twenty-one

Megan eased herself into the crowd, cloaking herself in the trembling bodies with their stink of sweat and fear and the stomach-churning stench of burning that brought back memories she wished never to experience again. The soldiers scanned the people for their prey, eyes flicking from face to face. They would know what she looked like: Gwyneth was better than any portrait. Not that the witches were being so subtle: there were no teenage girls among the corpses.

She tried to retreat further. A hand slammed into her shoulders, shoving her forward into the gap between the soldiers and the crowd. Megan whirled her arms, trying to stay on her feet. The gaze of every soldier locked onto her. She froze, swallowed, then broke out into a run.

Barging people out of the way, she sped down the street, only vaguely aware of Eleanor calling after her. Footsteps thundered behind her. Faced with ships spitting death on one side and sharpened steel on the other, the terrified mob was prepared to follow anyone offering direction. The only trouble was they were bringing the soldiers with them.

She ducked off the main street. Smoke was belching out of one of the buildings. A seamstress's—lots of flammable cloth. It didn't look too bad at the moment. The fire must have only just started. Megan dove in, eager to lose her tail. Her panting sucked in the fumes. Maybe she had underestimated the severity. She coughed and dropped to her knees. The air was a little clearer nearer the ground.

She pulled her hood up and crawled through the shop, tucking her hands into her sleeves to protect them from the hot floorboards. Back way, there had to be a back way. A bale tumbled and bounced across her path, trailing burning scraps. She wafted them out of her path and kept on going.

Megan made it into the backyard. She allowed herself a brief pause, to regain her breath and wipe the tears streaming from her eyes, then hauled herself over the wall and into the alley beyond. She'd lost the crowd. She wondered whom they were following now. Whatever sap happened to be in the lead when they had lost sight of her, she guessed.

She considered her options. First she had to find Eleanor, then they had to find a way out of the inner city. The South and West Gates would no doubt be as well guarded as the East Gate, but the wall was old and not well maintained. There were places it was climbable and rumors of holes knocked through where houses backed onto it. They could even risk the river: let the currents carry them beyond the boundary of the western section of the wall; whether they'd be able to make it back to shore again was another matter.

Megan scurried down the alley. She'd have to stick to the shadows, keep to cover whenever possible. Night was coming, which would help, as would all the abandoned buildings. If she could just avoid drawing attention to herself.

She smacked into something solid.

"What have we here?"

Megan looked up. A soldier looked down at her through hooded eyes. His skinny frame was wrapped with a layer of hard muscle, his sunburned skin almost obscuring the tattoos snaking across his face. The ax he grasped was stained with dried blood.

She backed off. A wall impeded her progress. The soldier cocked his head as he examined her. Megan gave thanks her ill-fitting clothes did nothing for her figure.

"Have you seen my mother, sir?" she gabbled, the words tumbling out of her mouth barely had they come to her. "She went looking for our kitten, and you know how cats get scared by big bangs and I haven't seen her since and there's all these nasty men around and . . ."

She started crying. It wasn't hard to fake, not the way things were.

"Calm, little one. There're no nasty men. Just the True. We're here to save you."

"Really?"

"Come with me."

"My mother said I shouldn't go with strange men."

"I'm not strange men."

"You have those strange tattoos."

"They testify to our faith and how we strive to overcome our imperfections."

"Mr. Fluffy has imperfections. There's this black spot under his chin that looks like a badly shaved beard. He likes it if you tickle him there."

The soldier made a grab for Megan. "Look, love, I really couldn't give a toss about your—"

A sword flashed through the air and buried into his neck, all the way to the bone. Blood erupted in a gory fountain, drenching Megan. The soldier keeled over and splashed into a puddle of his own fluids. He convulsed once, twice, then was still.

"Mr. Fluffy?" said Eleanor, wiping her sword on the man's clothes.

"It was the first thing that came to me," said Megan. "If you'd hurried up . . ."

"It's hard to sneak up on someone at full pelt, especially in these boots."

Megan tried to clean some of the blood off her face with her sleeve. "How d'you find me?"

Eleanor began to search the soldier. "I figured out the stupidest thing you could have done and took it from there." She handed his dagger over to Megan, who slipped it into the scabbard dangling from her waist. "A burning building? Really?"

"No one was going to follow me in there, were they?" Megan checked up and down the alley. Figures hurried past the streets at either end but none paid them any attention. "What now?"

"We head for the palace."

"The palace? The High Priest's palace? The guy who wants me dead?"

"It's better than the alternative," said Eleanor. "With any luck he never made it back, and I doubt he let too many people know what he was doing. Anyway, the palace is practically a fortress. My family wasn't universally popular."

"Can't imagine why."

"The witches can't have that many soldiers here. Few hundred at most. If we can hole up somewhere while someone rallies the troops, the priests should be able to raise enough men to retake the city."

"You're forgetting those ships."

"Forgetting?" said Eleanor. "I'd say it was more willful ignorance. Come on."

As they moved away from the waterfront, the damage to the city lessened, the fires became sparser. Whatever it was the ships were firing at Eastport—once, Megan caught the impression of an metal ball the size of a head—they didn't seem able to reach this far inland. It was only a moment's grace though. With no one to fight them, the flames would find their way to all parts of the densely packed city.

Eleanor pulled Megan into a doorway as two of the witch soldiers took up position at the crossroads at the end of the street. One of them peered toward them, trying to make out the shapes in the shadows. Megan pressed into Eleanor. The countess's flesh yielded to her, her pulse racing. Megan's adopted the same pace.

"We'll have to go around," whispered Eleanor.

"How?" As soon as they stepped into the street they'd be spotted.

Eleanor tried the door. Locked. "People are so untrusting these days."

One of the soldiers motioned to the other and they both got on their knees. They each fingered a circle above their hearts, then pounded their armored chests twice with their fists. They closed their eyes and bowed their heads. One started to intone.

"God, born of the eternal universe, give us the strength to deliver to us Your Saviors, that the world may know the path of the True and . . ."

Megan watched the praying soldiers offering up piety amid the violence, the anger boiling inside her. After all they had done, they had the nerve to present themselves to God? She drew her knives and stepped toward them, imagining her blades ripping into unprotected flesh, blood gushing onto her outstretched arms, warm as mother's milk.

". . . give thanks for our victory, which we do in Your . . ."

Eleanor grabbed her and dragged her back into the doorway, clamping a hand over her mouth to stifle her objections. Megan tried to wrench herself out of the embrace, but her strength was no match for Eleanor's. She gave up the struggle and closed her eyes, waiting for the soldiers to finish their indulgence of hypocrisy and for the blood-thirst that made her body tremble to pass.

Eleanor released her. Megan opened her eyes, blinking as she adjusted to the light. The soldiers had moved on.

"You should have let me kill them," she said.

"In cold blood?" said Eleanor. "I don't think you're ready for that."

They crept through the city, flitting from shadow to shadow. In one of the myriad alleys that led to the main square, they came across a family huddled against the walls. A middle-aged mother with bedraggled hair, a baby cradled in her arms; a white-faced father cuddling a daughter, his face covered in bruises; a teenage son, all acne and nerves. They cowered at the women's approach, eyes big at the sight of fresh blood and drawn blades.

"It's all right," said Eleanor. "We won't hurt you."

"I know you won't," said the boy. He produced a wooden mallet, its head caked in stone dust. A mason's tool. "Get lost."

Eleanor brushed past him and glanced out of the alley onto the square beyond. "Looks quiet enough. Oh . . ."

Megan peered over her shoulder. Corpses were scattered around the square, arrow shafts sticking out of them. One of them groaned and crawled toward them, inch by painful inch. Arrows hummed from the surrounding buildings. Most broke on the stone; the ones that didn't, halted the crawler's progress.

"We were going to wait until it was fully dark," said the father, "then try to get to the palace."

"The priests still hold it?" said Eleanor. The father nodded. "What about the temple?"

"The soldiers took it. They hoisted their flag, the . . ." He made the sign of the circle, as if ritual could counter the witches' actions. "There's archers there too." He grasped Megan's arm. "They took her."

"Who?" said Megan.

"My Shelly," said the man.

Megan didn't need further clarification. He had a fourth child. A girl, her age. She patted his shoulder. "I'm sure she's all right."

"How do you know?"

Megan didn't, of course. The witches might release Shelly once they determined she wasn't Megan, or they might find it simpler to slit her throat. "Have faith," she said, wincing at the hollowness of her words. The father snorted.

Eleanor retreated into the alley. "We need to find a back way."

"If we're quick, we can make it across the square," said the boy. "Once we get to the palace, the pillars'll protect us."

"Sure," said Eleanor. "We might only lose one or two of us. Who do you want to sacrifice? Your mother? Your little sister?" The boy glared at Eleanor, his expression leaving no doubt who he'd choose.

Eleanor took the lead, Megan the rear as they wound their way through the alleys that surrounded the palace. The boy barged his way to the front and declared they should go left. His path brought him back out onto the square. Arrows spat at his feet and shattered on the walls around his head. Eleanor yanked him back to safety.

As they passed a ramshackle gate, Megan heard sobbing. She paused, straining her ears. A woman's cry. She eased the gate open. A serving girl—the right age to be a target for the witches—was crouched in a mound of garbage, hugging herself. Megan beckoned to her. She shrank into the rotting vegetables.

Megan crouched in front of her. "What's your name?"

"Daisy."

"Daisy, I'm Megan. Come with me. There's a group of us. We're going to the palace. You'll be safe there."

The girl shook her head. "The priests'll beat me again."

"Why would—"

"Because of you."

Megan recognized Daisy now: the serving girl from the temple library. Blood rushed to her cheeks. Another who had suffered because of her, like the thousands in the city. And, unlike those, here she bore direct responsibility, even if she hadn't struck the actual blows.

"I'm . . . I'm sorry."

"Was it worth it?" asked Daisy.

Megan looked into the scared eyes of the young girl. "No. Nothing's worth this." She held out her hand. "Please. I'll protect you." *This time.*

Daisy allowed Megan to hoist her to her feet. Megan put her hand on her shoulder to steer her out of the gate. Daisy winced and pulled away.

"Is that where they . . . ?"

Daisy nodded.

Megan checked their rear. She thought she saw something, a flicker of movement behind them. The alley appeared deserted. She took Daisy by the hand and hurried after the rest of their party.

They found their way to a side door into the palace. Eleanor hammered on it, demanding to be let in. The occupants rushed to ignore her demands.

"I suppose it'd be too much to ask that you kept the keys," said Megan.

"I think the priests might have changed the locks in the past forty years," said Eleanor. She hammered again. "Open up! We have men and children here!"

"You're drawing attention to us," said the mother.

"That's the idea."

The mother pointed down the alley. A black-armored soldier was marching toward them, cradling a battle-ax. There was no sign of eagerness or worry in his demeanor; he didn't hurry or hold back. He was a man going about his job.

Eleanor's eyes flicked upward to the balcony that jutted above the door. She put the rest of the party behind her. "If this doesn't go well," she said to Megan, "run."

"If what . . . ? You're not going to fight the guy?"

"I'll take him on," said the boy, brandishing the mallet.

"No!" Megan and Eleanor said together.

"Don't worry," said Eleanor. "Remember what I said about this place."

The soldier was almost upon them. The party shuffled away in the opposite direction, hugging the wall of the palace. All except Eleanor, who continued to hold her ground.

"You're all coming with me," said the soldier. "No one'll get hurt."

Eleanor raised her sword. "I don't think so."

The soldier towered over her. A bear versus a fox. Eleanor retreated a couple of steps.

The soldier stepped up to her former position and brought his ax into an offensive stance. There was a hum and a crack. The soldier crumpled to the ground, a crossbow bolt sticking straight up out of his helmet.

Megan hurried back to the door and looked up. The balcony wasn't just a balcony—it was a brattice. Through the arrow slit in the floor above her, she could make out the shape of a man.

Eleanor joined her. "Can you let us in now?" she called up.

"Give me a moment, ma'am."

There was a thud, then a scrape of metal upon metal. Megan and Eleanor ushered their party into the palace. Then, with the help of the corporal of the guards who had shot him, they dragged the soldier inside so his corpse wouldn't attract interest.

They found themselves in an antechamber. Bare stone walls and slits for windows left it cold. A set of footholds cut into the wall led up to the brattice. Weapons were piled in a corner: crossbows, longbows, swords, knives, and maces. All they were lacking was the people to wield them.

"Let's find somewhere to . . ." started Eleanor. Yelling from the alley cut her off.

Megan poked her head out of the door. Two more soldiers were rushing down the alley, chasing a man. He tripped and went sprawling. One of the soldiers pulled in front of his comrade. He was almost on top of his prey.

"There's nothing we can do for him," said Eleanor, attempting to pull Megan inside. "We have to get inside."

The man looked up, a pleading look on his face. Shock ran through her. "It's Damon!" shouted Megan.

"In that case, we definitely have to get inside."

Damon attempted to push himself up. The lead soldier kicked him in the back, sending him flying again. His head hit the cobblestones. Blood gushed from his mouth. The soldiers advanced. Damon picked himself up, stumbled toward Megan, stretched out his hand.

Eleanor pulled Megan back into the antechamber and slammed the door shut.

# twenty-two

The corporal had just finished reloading his crossbow. Megan snatched it off him. Eleanor blocked her way.

"I can't let you go out there," she said. "You're not risking all of us."

"They'll kill him," said Megan.

"I'm not exactly unhappy at the prospect."

The door shuddered against Eleanor's back as Damon hammered on it. "Come on! Let me in! Please!"

Megan clenched the crossbow to her chest, torn over what to do. Could she condemn him to die, even if that was what he had done to her family and friends? Daisy and the family stared at her in silent judgment, not understanding why they had left someone to the mercy of the witches. Damon continued to batter away, his cries becoming ever more desperate.

She pointed the crossbow straight at Eleanor's head. Point-blank range. The bowstring trembled under the tension.

"I won't give them another victim."

Eleanor closed her eyes. Her face was serene, beautiful as a martyr's. Was she going to make Megan shoot her? Could Megan do it—kill one friend to save another, kill one betrayer to save another? And, even if she could, what gave her the right to choose?

Eleanor saved her from the decision. Shaking her head, she stepped aside, pulling the door open as she did so.

Damon tumbled into the antechamber. Behind him, a soldier had his ax raised, midswing.

"Hey!" Megan called out.

The soldier gawked at her and the crossbow she had aimed at his head. Megan fired. The bolt flew into the soldier's mouth, smashing his teeth. He managed a glance down at his unexpected meal before toppling over.

The other soldier charged up and skidded to a halt. Megan brought the crossbow to bear on him, then remembered Eleanor's comments on using a one-shot weapon against two enemies. The soldier cocked his head and smirked. Megan remembered the landlord's response at the burning inn. She hurled the weapon at the soldier, who had to raise his arms to protect his face.

Damon kicked back, knocking the soldier's legs out from under him. Megan grabbed his ax and charged out into the alley. She swung in a low arc. The blade thudded into the back of the man's knee, almost taking the leg off. The soldier's head rolled back as he screamed in agony. Megan wrenched the ax out of flesh and bone and this time aimed at his neck. His agony came to an end.

Damon looked up at Megan, gratitude etched on his face. She caught his eye for a moment, then looked away, her cheeks starting to burn.

"We should . . ." Damon pointed inside the palace. Megan nodded. She threw away the ax and held out her hand, still keeping her eyes from his. Damon hauled himself to his feet.

The corporal slammed the door shut and barred it. "Glad you're on our side," he said.

"We'll see," muttered Megan. She hadn't forgotten who was the master of their sanctuary.

Eleanor brandished her sword at Damon. She beckoned to the boy from the family they had rescued. "Take everyone," she said. "Get them food and water. See if you can find a priest. He might have some news on your sister."

Daisy looked to Megan, eyes widening. "Go with them," Megan said. "You'll be fine."

"But the priests . . ."

"Have more to worry about than one girl they've already chastised."

The party had filed out, keeping a wary eye on Eleanor's drawn blade. She advanced on Damon. "What the hell are you doing here?"

Damon looked down at the blade inches from his throat. He took a step backward; Eleanor took a step forward. Megan moved behind her and held a knife at her back.

"I didn't rescue him so you could kill him," she said.

"I think what Megan is trying to say is that this conversation will go a lot better if it's a lot less pointy."

Eleanor considered for a moment, then sheathed her sword. Megan made a show of waiting a few seconds before sliding her knife back up her sleeve.

Damon wiped his bloody mouth on his sleeve and brushed the dust from his clothes. "Thanks for coming to help me," he said to Eleanor. "Took real guts, that. A sign of a true friend. Oh, wait a minute . . ."

"Are we suppose to believe this is a coincidence?"

"Course not. I've been following you."

"Following . . . ?"

"That hair and exquisite bone structure stand out at a hundred yards," said Damon. "It wasn't hard to pick you up, though I did lose you in all those damn alleyways."

"Why?"

"They keep crisscrossing and doubling back and they all look the same."

Up in the brattice, the corporal whistled to himself. It sounded a little too self-conscious, as if he was making an effort not to listen in on their conversation. Megan wished she had that luxury. She suspected

Eleanor's antagonism to Damon had nothing to do with what *he* had done.

"Why were you following us?" Eleanor said to Damon.

"Thought you might need me."

"What for? Target practice?"

"This is not helping," said Megan.

"If we get in a fight, you'll be ruing your lack of training."

"He was forced to Thicketford by the witches, like Gwyneth was forced to go with them. And he saved my life."

"So he claims."

"*He* never had any intention of harming me."

Damon's brow creased as he caught the emphasis in Megan's words, the look she gave Eleanor. "Am I missing something?"

"No," said Megan. "Nothing that isn't in the past. Right, Eleanor?"

The countess pursed her lips, then nodded. She slunk off to the weapons cache and rummaged around, examining the bows stashed there. She tested their strings, plucking them one by one. A sequence of deep hums echoed around the antechamber as if she were picking out a tune.

Megan stepped close to Damon. "If I find out you're lying," she murmured in his ear, "I've got a knife with your name on it."

"That's not just a dedication, right?"

"No."

"I'm not lying."

Could she believe him? Did her own desire outweigh sense? Despite what he might or might not have done, it was good to see him again—it felt as if Megan had been given something back. It wasn't her grandfather, it wasn't Gwyneth, but it was something.

Something whistled between the two of them and thudded into the door. Eleanor stood holding a long-bow, its string still humming. "Just testing," she said. "Mind if I keep this?" she shouted up to the corporal.

"If I did mind, it wouldn't go well, would it?" the corporal shouted back down.

Eleanor plucked her arrow out of the door and examined the structure. "We need something heavy to barricade this with."

"I'm sure there're plenty of priests around," said Damon.

"Probably best if we don't run into any of them."

"Why are we avoiding priests? Apart from the usual reasons?"

"They know about me," said Megan. She pointed to her stomach. "About . . ."

"And they want to deal with it?"

"More like deal with me."

"Trust a priest to find a way around the Book of Faith," said Damon.

Eleanor pointed at the soldier the corporal had shot in the head. "Help me with him."

The three of them rolled the body across the floor. His armor screeched as it scraped the stone. They tucked him against the door.

"Do you really think that's going to stop the witches?" asked Megan.

"No," said Eleanor. "But it'll confuse the hell out of them if they do break in here."

A squad of soldiers marched into the antechamber and spread out. "They're on the move," said the commander, paying no attention to Megan and the others. "Seal the palace. No one in, no one out." He pointed to one of his subordinates. "You, up and cover the door."

"Already covered, sir," the corporal shouted down from the brattice.

Megan, Eleanor, and Damon tried to slip away. The commander stopped them. "Who are you?" He noticed the body blocking the door. "And who's he? What's he doing there?"

"There was a draft," said Damon.

The commander eyed him with the expression of a man contemplating violence. Megan suspected Damon got that a lot. "Get out of here."

The three of them slipped up their hoods and left the antechamber, making their way into the palace proper. Hundreds of civilians—thousands, perhaps—had found their way inside. Gilded couches served as hospital beds, luxurious tapestries as shrouds. Priests and acolytes scurried through the corridors, tending to those they could help, praying for those they couldn't. Despite the bloodstains, no one paid the trio any attention: they weren't missing any limbs, they weren't catatonic, they weren't screaming in agony or with grief at the loss of a loved one.

Eleanor led them upstairs, squeezing past the shocked and injured. A toothless woman grabbed Megan and babbled incoherently. Spittle ran down her chin; blood streaked her filthy hands; she had lost control of her bowels at some point. Revulsion gripped Megan until she remembered why the witches had descended upon the city. She took the woman's hands in her own and squeezed.

"I'm sorry. I'm so sorry."

Whether the woman's jabbering contained words of condemnation or forgiveness, Megan couldn't determine.

She caught up with her friends. Eleanor was arguing with a guard standing sentry outside an ornate door.

". . . can't go in there. It's Father Galan's private chamber."

Eleanor swept past him. Damon shrugged at the guard, whose pike was no defense against beauty and self-confidence. "What can you do?"

A four-poster bed, large enough to accommodate the three of them plus the guard who was still protesting their trespass, dominated the room beyond. Wisps of incense floated from burners, infusing the air with a heavy spiciness that made Megan want to sleep. Portraits hung from the walls: nubile women in decidedly nonreligious poses.

Megan warmed her hands over the fire burning in the grate. There was a pitcher of water beside the bed. She poured some into a bowl and washed her face and neck, which was still raw from where the noose had bitten into it.

"You have no right to be here," said the guard.

Eleanor pulled down her hood and looked around. "I was born in this room."

"You want us to put up a plaque?" said Damon.

"And my mother died here."

Megan looked up from her washing. Water dribbled down her face and dripped back into the bowl.

Damon looked shamefaced. "Um . . ."

"What he means to say is he's sorry to hear that," said Megan. "Me too."

"Me as well," said the guard. He caught the looks flashed at him. "What? You think because I carry a pike for a living I'm incapable of sympathy?"

Eleanor gave him a sad smile. "You couldn't give me a moment, could you?"

"I don't know . . ."

"Given what's going on outside, do you think your time's really best served protecting the High Priest's underpants?"

"Well . . ."

"Five minutes?" said Eleanor, running a finger down the guard's cheek.

He blushed. "I suppose I could get called away, you know, to help with . . . stuff."

"Stuff's important."

As soon as the guard left, Eleanor hurried to the windows, an intricate sequence of latticework the city's chimneys had left nearly opaque. She counted off the panes and opened the middle window, yanking hard to combat the swollen wood and rusty hinges. It was quiet outside. The boom from the witches' ships had ceased and only the occasional scream made its way to the palace. A light rain had sprung up, dampening the fires.

"Give me a hand," said Eleanor, beckoning to Damon.

"What do you need doing?"

Eleanor grabbed his hand, slipped it into one of her gloves, and formed it into a fist.

"Oh," said Damon, "a literal—"

Eleanor drove his fist through the bottommost pane. Glass shattered and rained on the rug beneath their feet.

Damon yelled and snatched his hand away. "What the . . . ?" He stuck his injured hand under his armpit and squeezed. "I think you broke something."

"That was the idea." Eleanor crouched down and began searching through the remains of the window-pane. "Ah, here we are." She alighted on a chunk of glass the size of a peach pit and held it up to the light of the fire. No, not glass. It was too pure, the colors coruscating from its faces too hypnotic. A diamond.

Damon suspended his agony. "Is that . . . ?"

"The last of the Endalay fortune."

"You said it was gone."

"I wasn't sure if they'd replaced the windows."

"Glass is expensive," said Damon. "Especially diamond-studded glass." He examined the panes. "Any more . . . ?"

"Just the one." Eleanor tossed the precious stone to Megan. "Keep it safe." She poured fresh water into the bowl and washed herself.

"You're giving it to me?"

"Travel expenses."

"You could travel to the Diannon Empire on that."

"You could *buy* the Diannon Empire with that," said Damon. "Well, maybe a small bit of it. An archipelago they're not using."

Megan tucked the diamond into the pouch where she had hidden her last sovereign. "I'll keep it safe."

"I know a fence," said Damon. "Up in Kewley."

"Thought you might," said Eleanor. She turned to Megan. "On no account let him have that."

"Anyone'd think I was untrustworthy." There was silence. "No one rush to deny it."

They left the bedchamber. The guard was hovering outside, affecting nonchalance. Eleanor brushed his cheek with her lips. "Thank you."

"I don't know what you mean, my lady."

"There's a good bed in there, a warm fire. I'm sure you can find someone who needs it."

"Father Galan . . ."

". . . only wants to help those under his care."

"We talking about the same—"

"Hold her!"

They spun around. Brother Attor was advancing down the corridor, his robes billowing behind him. He jabbed furiously in Megan's direction.

"Don't let her get away!"

"I guess the underpants police caught up with us," said Damon. "Usual response?"

"Uh-huh," said Megan.

They ran.


Heads snapped to follow their progress, voices rose in protest at crushed toes and elbowed ribs. Megan had no idea where they were—the palace corridors merged into an infinite line of human suffering— she just knew she had to keep running. She had a baby to protect, a sister to rescue, friends to keep alive.

They skidded into the atrium. Scores of faces snapped up to inspect the newcomers. Guards stepped away from the entrance and advanced on their position. A priest stacked barrels by the huge oak doors in a vain attempt to barricade them.

Megan bent over and rested her hands on her thighs, fighting to regain her breath. Ephemeral patterns snaked across the expanse of marble: torchlight reflected from the glass ceiling down onto the polished floor. "We . . ."

"Wrong turn?" said Damon, his panting worse than Megan's. "We should have stopped off at the gift shop, picked up a map."

They spun on their heels, aiming to backtrack, but Brother Attor had kept up his pursuit. Eleanor strung her bow and leveled it at him. There was a collective gasp from the occupants of the atrium, civilians and guards alike.

Brother Attor held up his hands. "I have no intention of hurting you."

"That's nice," said Damon.

The priest's words had been aimed at Megan, and only at her. "No, it's not," she said.

Eleanor's bow thrummed. The arrow embedded itself in Brother Attor's chest. He stared down, astonished at the red stain blooming across his once-pristine robes. Eleanor notched another arrow and let fly. Brother Attor keeled over. The arrows sticking out of his body snapped under the impact.

Damon stared down at the dead priest. "What the hell?"

"Why do you think he wants Megan unharmed?"

"Well, she's quite personable when she's not . . . oh."

Eleanor restrung her bow and covered the advancing guards. Megan flicked out a knife and held it by her side. The guards exchanged nervous glances. There were eight of them, armed and burly. They'd have no trouble overpowering the trio—or seven of them wouldn't anyway. Was anyone going to volunteer to be the man Eleanor dropped?

"Should I try to look menacing too?" asked Damon.

"We don't want to turn this into a comedy," said Eleanor.

Megan addressed the guards. "He was a witch. A traitor. To the Realm. To the Faith. To everyone."

"And we're expected to take your word for that?" said one of the guards. He had a sergeant's stripes stitched to his sleeves.

"He'll have a tattoo of the star-broken circle," said Eleanor. "Considering his status, somewhere concealed. Check under his hair."

The sergeant sidled around them and knelt by Brother Attor's corpse. He slipped off a glove and fingered the priest's tonsure.

"What happens if he doesn't find one?" murmured Damon.

"We give them you," said Eleanor.

The sergeant shot back, a terrified look in his face. "It's . . . it's there. Like she said."

The civilians huddled together. The guards gripped their weapons and drew into a defensive formation. Several members of the crowd glared at Megan and Eleanor with the suspicious looks of people who associate the bearer of bad news with its cause.

The sergeant regained his composure. "If a priest of the Faith was one of them, anyone could be," he said. "We need to check everyone."

Damon shuffled from foot to foot. "Isn't that a bit over the top?"

"Starting with you."

"There's no need to start a witch hunt." Damon thought about this for a moment. "Well, there is, but you don't really think I'm—"

A new voice made itself heard: loud, clear, used to commanding attention. "I would advise everyone to make their way out of the atrium in a disorganized and panicky fashion." The last of the coarse black powder poured out of the barrel Brother Irwyn cradled in his arms. He tossed it aside and fixed his gaze on Megan. "Especially you, Mother."

Megan's throat dried. Eleanor took in the danger and fired, but she was too hasty to get a steady aim.

The arrow struck the wall above Brother Irwyn's head and clattered to the floor. The priest plucked a burning torch from its sconce. Eleanor fumbled to restring her bow. The guards vacillated, unsure about the new precedent of attacking their masters.

Eleanor's arrow flew past Megan's face and pierced Brother Irwyn's heart. The torch dropped from his grip as he keeled over. The flames caught the trail of powder. It ignited, spitting and hissing like an angry animal.

"Everyone out of here!" yelled Megan. "Now!"

The spark of fire raced along the powder trail, heading for the barrels by the door. Megan and Eleanor threw people toward the corridors that led away from the atrium and into the palace. Panic gripped the crowd even though they didn't know what was coming and they stampeded. The spark was almost at its target. Megan dove for cover and buried her head in her hands.

The intensity of the explosion shattered the divisions between her senses. Light became heat, heat became noise, noise became blinding light. Everything overlapped and merged into chaos as if the universe was being reborn.

Someone helped Megan to her feet. A single scream filled her ears. Warm wind blew dust in her face. Through the haze she could make out flames licking at the remains of the doors. Something else too. Shadows flitting through the clouds, their shapes resolving into armored men forming into two columns, an honor guard for the figure shimmering between them. They each knelt as she passed by, circling their chests and beating their hearts, pledging themselves to the triumphant vision in pure white silk.

Gwyneth.

# twenty-three

Megan thought she was dead, that the single tone she could hear was the heavenly choir, that her sister had come to welcome her to the afterlife. Gwyneth said something to her, but she couldn't hear the words. She hung limp as Gwyneth wrapped her arms around her, too stunned to return the embrace.

Gwyneth skipped out of the atrium, pulling Megan along with her. Soldiers overtook them and cleared their path, not that they needed to. The citizens who had sought sanctuary in the corridors took one look at the armed men and fled. A priest tried to take the head off one of the soldiers with a candlestick; the soldier returned the compliment rather more successfully with an ax. Gwyneth stepped over the decapitated body as if it was nothing more than a fallen branch.

They swept into the great hall, which the priests had converted into a hospital. Screams told Megan her hearing was returning. Soldiers swarmed in and cut down anyone who showed the slightest inclination to resistance. Gwyneth glided through the carnage and ascended to the High Priest's throne. She tucked her legs under herself, a little girl snuggling into her grandfather's chair.

"Clear the room," she said. Was that her voice? It wasn't what Megan remembered. It was harsh and imperious; cold, as if inflected with ice crystals.

The soldiers ushered everyone out, the sick and those who attended to them. One grabbed Eleanor and Damon and dragged them to the door.

Gwyneth held up a finger. "Not them," she said, a sly grin on her face. "I hear you've been making friends, Meg."

Megan finally found her voice. "What the hell is going on, Gwyn?"

"Not hell, Meg. Heaven. Here in the Realm. We're here to show the True way. You and me. And our children."

"I don't know what they've told you, but—"

"You've been searching for me," said Gwyneth. "And I've been searching for you. God has brought us together at last, like I knew He would."

"What are you talking about?" said Megan. "Gwyn, these bastards want our babies to lead them into a war. They want to destroy everything. Wade and Holt tricked us."

Gwyneth curled her lip. "Oh, please. As if that pair of idiots could trick anyone."

"What . . . ? Oh my God."

Realization hit Megan with the force of a crashing sun. Her brain, unable to cope with the implication of Gwyneth's words, shut down. She felt numb. Her legs gave out from under her. One of the soldiers grabbed a chair and helped her onto it. She had no power to resist him.

Gwyneth sashayed off her throne and approached Megan. "I know you're scared, Meg. I was too, when Attor revealed everything to me. Then I realized I'd been chosen—we'd been chosen—and what a privilege that was. The Saviors are coming again, only this time there'll be no priests to pervert their message. They thought to interpose themselves between God and His people."

"You . . ." Megan could hardly get the words out. "You knew about this? You stood back while they . . . ? Why didn't you tell me?"

"I had to spare you the burden, Meg. The knowledge of what I had to do almost crushed me. You wouldn't have been able to cope. If I'd been wrong, well, at least you would have been spared the guilt."

"If you were wrong?"

"I know," said Gwyneth, flicking her hand, "it sounds silly now."

Megan felt sick, dizzy. Her world was collapsing around her. All those late nights and early mornings with Brother Attor. There was no crush, no affair. They had been plotting against the Faith, against the Realm, against Gwyneth's own family.

"You arranged all this," she said, her voice barely more than a whisper.

"God arranged it," said Gwyneth.

"You brought the soldiers to Thicketford."

"To do God's work."

"You had them kill everyone."

"They refused to follow the path of the True."

"Grandfather . . ."

"He raised arms against us during the war. There was only one punishment."

"You had Wade get me pregnant."

"You prefer it was by force?" snapped Gwyneth. "Concentrate on your blessings, Meg. You can have anything you want, anyone you want. We no longer live under the priests' rules but God's." She leaned in. "Ours."

Soldiers were wrenching the knife out of Megan's hand and dragging her away from Gwyneth before she even realized she had attacked her sister. Gwyneth staggered back onto the throne, fingers smearing blood across her cheek. The rage burning inside Megan wanted to slash Gwyneth to ribbons, but she had managed nothing more than a scratch.

A soldier snatched up water and a cloth and tended to the wound. Gwyneth fixed Megan with a hurt look. "How could you?" she said. "I'm your sister."

"You—"

"I shall pray to God for the strength to forgive you," said Gwyneth. "I'm glad I told Attor to exclude you from the planning. You really are too wild and self-centered. Where is he anyway? You—" she pointed at a soldier —"go find him."

Was everything Megan had been through a lie? Should she have been running away from her sister rather than running toward her? There had to be something in there, something of the only person alive she loved, didn't there?

"Please don't do this to me, Gwyn." Megan took a step toward the throne. A pair of soldiers stopped her going any farther. "I traveled the county looking for you."

"I invaded the county looking for you."

Gwyneth straightened on her throne. She could be a queen, beautiful and imperious in her elegant gown. Her black hair shimmered in the light of the chandeliers high above their heads. Her olive skin glowed with the blush of pregnancy.

"Why did you run, Meg? You said you had a headache. Why couldn't you have stayed in your room like a good girl?"

"You would have let everyone live?"

"I've explained that," said Gwyneth, affecting a weary tone. "Besides, we'd heard the priests had dispatched a force to Thicketford. If they found only you and me missing, they might have worked things out, figured out some means to stop the prophecy."

Megan's eyes flicked to Eleanor. "There was no force." Just the Realm's last countess, with a mission she couldn't bring herself to complete.

"Yes, well, we know that now. Tobrytan's intelligence was faulty. This is war though, and there are going to be casualties." Gwyneth leaned forward. "I hear you're not exactly innocent on that score."

"I was forced to—"

"So was I."

Megan found herself shaking her head, as if the denial in the gesture could erase what her sister had done. This was worse than witnessing the death of her grandfather. That had destroyed her future. This destroyed her past as well. "I'll never forgive you for this."

"I am the Mother of the Savior," said Gwyneth. "Nothing I do requires forgiveness."

Megan searched her sister's face for some sign of doubt, some sign of regret. She found none, just the sneer of a coldhearted bitch who saw nothing past her own ambition. Nothing else mattered to Gwyneth, nobody else mattered. The priests had been more right than they had suspected when they accused the witches of following a demon queen—a demon queen who shared Megan's blood. The soldiers were probably looking at them both and seeing no difference. Megan's skin crawled at being likened to Gwyneth, but she had to be, didn't she? They had been together since they were born, grown up together, suffered the same heartaches. Had Gwyneth been faking all that time, or was Megan only waiting for the right circumstances before she exchanged her own soul for power?

Gwyneth looked over Megan's shoulder. "Ah, captain."

Megan looked around. A stern officer marched into the hall, his strides so long the soldiers in his detail had to scurry to keep up with him. He was aged but battle-hardened, skin as tough as the leather under his chain mail, a neat goatee streaked with iron. He looked old enough to have fought in the first war, battered enough that he might have been fighting every day since.

He knelt before Gwyneth. No, not just her. Megan too. "Mothers. We need to leave."

"What is it about you and running away, Tobrytan?" said Gwyneth, beckoning the officer to rise. "If you hadn't panicked in Thicketford, we wouldn't have had to go through all this."

"*I* panicked?" said Tobrytan, his eyebrows rising.

Gwyneth raised her chin, daring him to contradict her. It was a gesture heartbreakingly familiar from many a childhood argument. "The city is ours."

"We don't have the men to hold it."

"Bring the guns from the ships and arrange them on the city walls," said Gwyneth. "They should be enough to hold off any force the priests can put together before the general arrives here with the rest of the fleet."

"The general's days, weeks, away, Mother, and that's assuming the weather holds." Tobrytan curled his lip. "Besides, I have plans for this place."

"Plans?"

"We're going to bombard the city. Raze it to the ground."

Megan gasped. "You can't."

"The general gave no such order," said Gwyneth.

"The general didn't have family at Trafford's Haven," snapped Tobrytan. "The general didn't watch them burn. The general hasn't been waiting forty years to avenge them."

Gwyneth settled back into the throne and brushed invisible dirt from her gown. "Do what you wish."

"What?" Megan couldn't believe this. "You can't let him. There're tens of thousands of people in Eastport."

"There were that many in Trafford's Haven," said Tobrytan.

Megan held out a hand to her sister. "Gwyn, please, stop him. They're innocent. They've done nothing to you. I'll do anything you want. I won't resist anymore. Please let them live."

Gwyneth closed her eyes, bowed her head. "It is God's will."

"God's . . . ? How can you . . . ?" Megan turned to Tobrytan. "Don't do it."

"You cannot order me to—"

"Yes, I can!" yelled Megan. "Do I not carry one of the Saviors?" She straightened herself. "Captain, I order you to call off the bombardment."

"You're not one of us."

"What does it take? Tell me! I'll swear your pledge. What was it? I pledge obedience to God and His Saviors. I pledge. *I pledge!*"

"Meg, you're getting hysterical."

"What about the star-broken circle? You want me to bear it? Give me a knife and I'll carve it over my heart!"

She lunged for Tobrytan. A soldier grabbed her, drew her back, held her while her body trembled from the adrenalin coursing through her veins. Tobrytan looked on for a moment, his face implacable, before striding over to her.

"You have been honored by God," he said, "but you do not yet understand his purpose. You must let yourself be guided."

"By you?" said Eleanor, her voice cutting through the hushed hall. "Wouldn't that make you a priest?"

A soldier smacked her to the floor. Damon went to help her up. He was beaten down for his efforts.

Tobrytan cocked his head as he watched the commotion play out. "Didn't we send you to God out on that beach?" he said to Damon.

"He didn't want me. Next time He'd be happy with socks."

"You think it's a good idea to mock?"

"Someone has to," said Damon. "I forgot how boring you all were."

"Damon," Megan said in a low voice, "don't antagonize them."

Eleanor got to her feet. "Please forgive him, captain."

"And you are?"

"I am Eleanor of the house of Endalay, Countess of Ainsworth, Baroness of Laxton and Herth, First Lady of Kirkland, Overlord of the Spice Isles, and Defender of the Southern Lands."

"Really?" sneered Tobrytan.

Eleanor flushed. "And your little bitch is in my chair."

The captain motioned to the soldier nearest Eleanor. He slammed his fist into her head. She staggered, lost her footing, and dropped to her knees. Her eyes rolled as she tried to get up. She bent over, coughing up bile.

"Take her to my cabin on the *Vengeance*," said the captain. "I'll deal with her personally."

Two soldiers grabbed the woozy countess by the arms and dragged her out of the hall. Gwyneth smirked. Megan despaired. Not so long ago she would have given anything to be with Gwyneth; now she would give anything if she never had to lay eyes on her again. But she had responsibilities. She couldn't save Gwyneth, but she might be able to save the world from her. She had to rescue Eleanor from the witches' ships and then stop those ships from destroying Eastport.

The knife she had stolen from Lynette's was still stashed in her sleeve. Megan palmed it and searched for a target. She'd only have one strike—she'd have to make it count. She couldn't take on Tobrytan, and there were too many soldiers between her and Gwyneth. That left one choice.

Megan held her hands over her groin. This was going to be messy. She braced herself, waited for Gwyneth's attention to flick away, then sliced the top of her thigh. Pain seared through her nerves. Blood gushed, saturating her between the legs. Her cry was not the fake one she had been preparing for, but real.

Megan tucked the knife back in her sleeve and doubled over. "Damon!" she shrieked. "The baby!" She backed off a little, letting the audience in the great hall witness the stain she had left on the marble.

Damon hurried over. Masking her actions with his body, Megan pressed the knife into his hands. There was a brief pause as he assessed the situation, then he stashed the weapon away.

"I think I'm losing the baby," she said. "You need to get me to a hospital."

Damon looked around, at the abandoned stretchers, the bandages and empty bottles of medicines, the drying pools of bodily fluids. "You're kind of in one." He leaned forward and whispered. "Did you think this through?"

"The Sisters of the Faith," Megan whispered back.

Gwyneth barged Damon out of the way. "What is it Meg?" She whitened as she saw the blood between her legs. "Oh my . . ."

Megan wrapped her cloak around her before Gwyneth could notice the torn fabric of her pants. "Get me to the sisters."

"We can take care of you here."

"Brought a midwife with you, did you?" said Damon. He grabbed an abandoned surcoat and maneuvered Gwyneth out of the way. "Let me see to her."

"You?"

"He trained to be a priest," said Megan. "He knows about healing."

Damon staunched Megan's wound with the surcoat. Gwyneth tried to yank him away. "Get out of—"

"I'd stay back if I were you," said Damon. "If she's miscarrying, her blood could be fatal to another pregnant woman."

"I've never—"

"There's stuff in there," said Damon. "Dangerous stuff."

"Stuff?" said Gwyneth, backing off despite her skepticism. "That's your expert opinion?"

"I trained to be a priest—no one ever said I qualified. We need to get her to the Sisters of the Faith. They can tend to her, save the baby. She needs medicine. Willow bark, coca, guarana, hemp leaves, yohimbe, poppy. They have a convent next to the temple. You and you—"

he pointed at two of the soldiers —"grab that stretcher. We have to get her over there right now. There's no time to lose."

Gwyneth shook her head. "You're not taking her out of here."

"Do you want your sister to die? Do you want her baby to die?"

Gwyneth looked over to Tobrytan. He fidgeted with the grip of his sword, but this was one enemy he couldn't hack down. "I'm afraid he's right, Mother."

"We can't trust a priest."

"Not with our souls, no, but with our flesh, yes. They do have knowledge."

"Maybe God spared me for a reason." Damon reached under Megan's cloak to rearrange the surcoat so a dry piece was next to Megan's wound. "You don't have long left, my child. Shall I say the funeral prayer? God, born of the eternal universe . . ."

"All right," snapped Gwyneth. Megan knew her sister had no choice. Her power relied on the baby she was carrying, and that baby was nothing without its cousin. "All right."

The two soldiers hastened over with the stretcher, a homemade affair no doubt constructed to haul one of their victims into the palace. They helped Megan onto it and started for the exit.

"Wait," said Tobrytan. The stretcher party halted. Megan felt for Damon's hand. "You lot. Escort duty."

A quartet of soldiers fell in with them. Megan swore under her breath. They might have been able to fight two soldiers; six gave them little chance.

They left the palace and hurried across the square. Rain pattered down on Megan's upturned face. She squeezed her thighs together, trying to block out the pain from her throbbing leg. Maybe the blood flowing from the wound would take the baby with it; maybe it would take her life with it. Would that stop the killing? Did she have a duty to the Realm—to both the dead and the living—to sacrifice herself? Her child was innocent, no matter what Gwyneth and her fellow delusionals insisted, but by fighting to preserve its life wasn't she as guilty of selfishness as Gwyneth was?

They rounded the temple—dark and silent, more of a necropolis than a place of worship—and reached the house of the Sisters of the Faith. Widows and spinsters, fallen women and women who had refused to fall, those fleeing abuse and those seeking refuge, the sisters admitted all to their order, passing no judgment in exchange for a life devoted to God and the poor. They were based in a converted mansion that some rich merchant had donated in penance for a lifetime of debauchery. Megan wondered if God was so easily bribed.

A peephole opened in response to their hammering and immediately slammed shut. Two of the soldiers set upon the door with their axes, reducing it to firewood.

Damon pushed the remains open. "We have a person—" A crossbow bolt whizzed out of the house and speared one of the soldiers in the shoulder. "We have two people who need your help, sisters."

"Be gone, blasphemers!"

Damon turned to the soldiers. "I think she means you."

"We are sworn to protect the Mother with our lives."

"Why don't you go do it from the pub?" said Damon. "We'll catch up with you."

The lead soldier took up position by the door. "You will heal the Mother or we will burn this place down!" he bellowed into the gloom. He turned to Damon. "And we'll use you as kindling."

"I'm not sure that'll work."

"We'll make it."

A middle-aged woman in the simple gray gown of a sister appeared in the doorway. "We'll treat the girl. You brutes stay outside."

The soldier signaled to the stretcher bearers and pushed the woman aside. "No."

"No weapons may cross the threshold. This is God's house."

"He give dispensation for crossbows?" said Damon.

The sisters kept a plainer house than the priests, with whitewashed walls and timbers treated with shipbuilders' tar. Some citizens had sought sanctuary here rather than the palace. The sisters moved among them, administering aid where it would help, comfort where it wouldn't.

The soldiers bore Megan through a schoolroom decorated with infants' drawings of scenes from the Book of Faith and into a dingy corridor, off which branched the sisters' cells, now occupied by the dead and the dying. They found an empty one—well, it was empty once the soldiers cleared it by ax point—and laid Megan on the narrow bed.

The sister shooed the soldiers out. Their leader grabbed her arm and twisted. "If the baby dies . . ."

"Baby?" The sister glanced over to Megan and the blood between her legs. "Your thuggery doesn't scare me. God watches over us."

"Who do you think sent us?"

He shoved her toward the bed and left. The sister regained her composure with a minimum of fuss. "You need to leave too," she said to Damon.

Megan shook her head. "Let him stay."

"He the father?"

The father. Wade. How complicit had he been in all this? Teenage boys hardly needed encouragement to pursue sex, and Gwyneth would have tutored him in what to say, what to do, without his needing to be aware of her ultimate aim. She recalled their last conversation,

out in the wheat fields when life had last had some
semblance of normality. He'd known something, he
was scared of something. Had he found out about the
witches and their prophecy?

Tears rolled down her face. The sister patted her
arm. "There, there. Don't worry. The child might take
after you."

The sister called for hot water. She peeled away
the fabric sticking to Megan's thighs and brought a
candle closer to the wound. She frowned as she took in
the exact nature of her injuries. "What . . . ?"

Megan pressed her remaining sovereign into the sister's palm. "Clean me up. Stitch and bandage me. Let
us slip away and then get away yourselves. The witches
intend to destroy the city."

The sister contemplated the heavy coin, casting
suspicious looks on Megan and Damon in turn, then
placed it on the rickety table by Megan's bed. "What's
going on here?"

"Nothing you need to know about."

"The threats made against those in my care would
suggest otherwise."

"I . . . it's . . . I don't know how to explain it."

"Have you considered the truth?"

"Not on an exclusive basis," said Damon.

"What did those brutes do to you?"

"They . . ."

The sister looked to Damon. "Hey, it wasn't my doing," he said, before turning away and staring at the floor. "Maybe a little bit."

"We can help you."

Megan weighed the fear of betrayal against the need for assistance. Did the sister not deserve to know why Megan had brought the witches here?

"Swear that you won't let any harm come to my baby."

"Why would I . . . ?"

"Swear!"

"I swear by God, born of the eternal universe, I will not harm your baby."

"Or let anyone else," said Damon. The sister shot him a sour look. He shrugged. "Loopholes make me nervous."

"Very well. I also swear I will not let anyone else harm it. Now, what is going on?"


Five of the six soldiers who had escorted Megan filed into her room; the sisters were treating the other for his crossbow injury. She bid them file into a line by the side of her bed, and examined them in the flickering candlelight. One was in his teens, barely older than Megan; a couple looked to be in their twenties; one was in his midthirties. The senior was a grizzled vet of maybe fifty, the dim flame emphasizing the lines on his face.

Were they believers or mercenaries? Did they trust the baby inside her would offer salvation or were they just in it for the money?

"Mother," said the senior soldier, "are you . . . ?"

"I'm still pregnant."

The soldiers traced a circle over their hearts and thumped their chests twice. The sign of the star-broken circle. Believers, it would seem.

"Do you believe in the cause of the True?" she asked.

"We do," they replied in a discordant chorus.

"Will you fight for it?"

"We will." This time the answer was a little more synchronized.

"Will you die for it?"

"Yes."

That settled it. They couldn't be bribed. Megan tucked the Endalay diamond she'd been clutching back into its pouch and swung her legs out of the bed. She grimaced and squeezed her leg. The wound was a burning highway across her thigh, the suture holes beacons along the way. The herbs the sisters had given her to dull the pain had yet to kick in.

She recalled Gwyneth's attitude, the satisfaction that arose from knowing God's will coincided perfectly with one's own, and cloaked herself in it. "Let us give thanks to God, for preserving our Savior and showing we are worthy of Him."

The soldiers looked at each other, faith conflicting with practicalities. Was she their prisoner or their mistress? Megan knelt in front of them and implored them to do the same. Armor clinked, as one by one they followed her lead.

"God, born of the eternal universe, we praise You for the life of the child growing in my womb and for protecting us from harm." *Though I want a word with you about all the shit you've put me through.* "Continue to favor us with Your blessings and Your love."

As Megan led the soldiers in prayer, five sisters glided into the room, their footsteps silenced by decades of training. They took up position behind Megan's escort, one sister per soldier.

"Give us the strength to strike down our enemies and return the Realm to peace and harmony."

Candlelight caught the blades of unsheathed knives, the glow dancing across the polished steel as if it was alive.

"Know our hearts are true to You and You alone."

The play of hands across the soldiers' faces was a lover's caress, the slash across their throats a sensuous whisper. The sisters embraced them as they convulsed and spluttered, allowing their life's blood to soak into their robes. One by one, the soldiers stilled.

The sisters laid their victims out on the floorboards. Megan contemplated the corpses in front of her, suppressing her revulsion. These were soldiers, whose only purpose had been to kill. They had declared war, and Megan was going to have to fight it.

Damon slipped into the room. "What will you do with the bodies?"

"The sewer flows into the Speed," said one of the sisters.

"You can fit a man down into it?"

"Yes."

"I'm not going to ask how you found that out."

Megan clambered to her feet as the sister started to cart out the dead soldiers. "We have to rescue Eleanor, then figure out some way of saving the city."

"What?" said Damon.

"There's more of us now."

"We're not an army," said the sister.

"We don't have to be an army. We can sneak over to the ships and strike from the shadows."

"And get ourselves killed," said Damon. "Oh, I forgot. *We'll* get ourselves killed attacking a battle fleet; they won't dare touch you."

Megan eased herself onto the edge of the bed and massaged her thigh. "Three ships is hardly a battle fleet."

"All right, a battle fleet-ette. Against you and your pigheadedness."

"Most of the soldiers will be ashore."

"The key word there being *most*," said Damon. "Do you think if you put yourself through enough, you'll get yourself killed?"

"I . . . Don't be ridiculous."

"You wouldn't have to face things then, would you? You'd be noble and brave, a casualty of war."

*And leave everyone else to deal with the nightmare my sister's created*, thought Megan. Was it true? Was she looking for a way out of this, or did she really want to rescue Eleanor?

"What would you do?" she asked.

"I see two options," said Damon. "Running or fleeing."

"They're the same thing."

"Fleeing's more . . . dramatic."

"And drama's important?" said Megan.

"Makes us look as if we know what we're doing," said Damon. "We need to get out of the city while there's still a city to get out of. Which do you think Eleanor would view as more important: your safety or some suicidal rescue mission?"

"That's why I have to make the attempt." It's what made Megan different from Gwyneth. She would sacrifice herself for others; Gwyneth would sacrifice others for herself.

Megan stopped the sisters as they were about to haul the final corpse away. "Do you keep any old clothes? For distributing to the needy?"

"Yes."

"Can you show me them? I'll need something to do my hair with too."

"You think this is the right time to play dress up?" asked Damon.

"Depends who I'm dressing up as."

# twenty-four

Megan turned on the spot. "What do you think?" she said to Damon. "Can I pass for her?"

"Look smugger."

"I'm serious."

"At least it'll be dark." He combed her hair with his fingers. "Pity you're not identical twins."

Megan checked herself. The gown was darker and coarser than Gwyneth's, her hair more unruly. Put the sisters together and it wouldn't trouble anyone to tell them apart; if Megan was on her own though, she might get away with it.

She and Damon were the only two who remained in the convent. The sisters had abandoned it, flitting away with their charges under cover of the night, dispersing to all corners of the city with warnings to escape Eastport. Megan prayed they'd find a way out of the inner city.

"I suppose we should do this," said Damon. They had dispatched a messenger to the palace, informing them that Megan's baby had survived and advising them to stay away for the time being, but it wouldn't be long before Gwyneth sent for further information. "I mean, who wants to see their nineteenth birthday?"

"You're not coming with me."

"I'm not?" He repeated his response, a little less cheery this time. "I'm not?"

"I need you to arrange a boat out of here."

"A boat?"

"Floaty thing."

"How the hell do you expect me to persuade someone to sail with an armada blowing anything that moves out of the water?" said Damon.

"Tell them what the witches have planned for the city. And if that fails . . ." Megan held up the Endalay diamond. She didn't know what glittered most: the precious stone or the avarice in Damon's eyes. "A small boat should be able to sneak out without them noticing."

"And be slow enough to be overhauled once they realize we're missing."

"They have to realize first."

Damon pocketed the diamond. Megan hesitated for a moment, then handed him her last sovereign too. "Just in case," she said. "Besides, I don't have space to carry it."

"No," said Damon. "It'd mean carrying one less knife." Megan had rearmed herself from the soldiers' supplies.

"Meet me at the wall, by Silas's place. Better bring some dry clothes."

"Why's that?"

"We'll be coming the fast way."

Megan headed for the riverside. The rain was coming down steadily now, plastering her hair to her head. The streets were quiet, peaceful even; those citizens who hadn't fled or died were cowering in their homes, praying the witches wouldn't come for them.

A soldier was hunched at a crossroads a hundred yards in front of her, using his pike as a leaning post. Oddly shaped bottles hung from the twin baldrics crisscrossed over the plate that protected his chest. Rain streamed down his helmet and dripped from the rim. His head drooped as he fought a losing battle against sleep.

Megan straightened herself into a haughty pose and marched toward him, her heart racing. "You! With me."

The soldier's head snapped up. "Mother? I—"

"However that sentence ends, I'm not interested."

"It's not safe on the streets."

"No," said Megan. *Because of you.* She swept past the soldier and continued on her way to the river, her boots kicking up surface water.

The soldier hurried after her. "There are still heathens on the prowl. Remnants of the city guard."

"I won't let them harm you."

"Mother, it's not *my* safety I'm worried about."

"It's not your safety I'm worried about either," said Megan. A glimmer of suspicion appeared on the soldier's face. Had she pushed the arrogance too far? "What's your name?"

"Jon," he said. "Without an *h*."

"I wasn't planning on writing to you."

"Of course, Mother."

Megan eked out a mollifying smile. "Take my arm, Jon."

She could have been a niece skipping along with her favorite uncle, if it wasn't for the corpses they had to skirt around and the devastation that became ever more pronounced as they neared the river. Megan forced herself to act like Gwyneth, to treat the dead as if they were nothing more than fallen branches on a woodland path. She gave thanks the cold night justified her trembling, the rain her tears.

They reached the water's edge. The witches' ships lurked on the Speed, the odd flicker of light from their cabins. The one she had seen listing earlier had sunk even farther, its bulwarks dabbing the water like a nervous swimmer. Megan scanned the jetties upriver and down for signs of a boat Damon could buy. Nothing but the occasional flotsam: planks from a hull, a scrap of sail, a pole that could have been a mast or an oar. She told herself it was dark, there were plenty of docks she couldn't see, but that didn't stop her stomach sinking as if she had swallowed lead. Her plan was a failure before it had begun.

"Mother? Are you all right?"

"Yes. Nothing. Morning sickness."

"It's not morning."

No, indeed it wasn't morning. That would offer the first rays of the rising sun, warming her face and encouraging life to the fore. Instead it was night, when monsters stalked your footsteps and your fears crushed you until you wanted nothing but to curl up in a tiny ball and hide from the world.

"Take me across to the *Vengeance*."

"But your cabin's on the *Wrath*."

Megan loaded her voice with scorn. "And?"

"You don't want to . . . ?"

"Is it any concern of yours what I want to do?"

"No, Mother. I'm . . . I'm sorry."

Megan dismissed Jon's apology with a gracious flick of her wrist and headed down the pier to where the witches' rowboats were bobbing on the water. She nodded at the soldiers guarding the craft and climbed down into one of the boats. Jon clambered after her and cast off.

The warships were anchored upriver. Jon's cheeks blew out as he fought the current, his face red with the strain, the eerie silence broken only by his ragged breathing and the splash of oars. Wisps of smoke drifted across the surface of the water, like delinquents on the lookout for opportunities. Rainwater seeped through the sodden bench on which Megan huddled, soaking through her clothes. She was going to have one hell of a cold once this was over.

She pointed at the listing ship. "What happened?"

"One of the *Fury*'s guns blew."

*Vengeance, Wrath, Fury*: Megan detected a theme in the witches' naming conventions—that and a lot of unresolved anger. "Did everyone get off?"

"Those who didn't have hot metal jammed into their skulls, Mother."

A body floated by, the depths that had once been so keen to claim him having grown tired of their plaything. Jon shoved it away with an oar. It caught on one of the Speed's many currents and accelerated downriver, heading for the open sea.

"Why are you doing this?" Megan asked. "Why are you fighting for the wi—the True?"

Jon looked perplexed. "Why wouldn't I?"

"Why you personally?" said Megan. "How did you become one of the True?"

"I've always been one. Since I was born." Jon slowed his strokes to get his breath, keeping them just fast enough to hold their position. "I was a baby when the priests burned Trafford's Haven. My family managed to get away on the flotilla that sailed to the Diannon Empire."

"How many were on this flotilla?"

"A few thousand sailed," said Jon. "A few hundred landed." He picked up his pace. His sentences came between labored breaths. "We survived the ocean, the heat, the thirst, the starvation. It was a test from God. To show we were worthy. To show we were strong enough to protect you and the Saviors."

"And what happens when the Saviors are born?" asked Megan.

"The land will be swept clean until only the True remain."

Megan didn't need to ask how the land would be swept clean. She'd seen it at Thicketford, at Halliwell, here in Eastport. *My God, Gwyneth, what have you brought upon us?* She looked back at the city, serene in the dark, the damage it had suffered disguised by distance. Maybe once the witches found she was missing Tobrytan would hold back from his bombardment, lest she was hiding in the city he wanted to destroy. It was her best hope, unless Eleanor could come up with something better.

They pulled alongside the *Vengeance* and maneuvered along its hull until they reached a rope ladder that slapped against the planks as the ship rocked with the waves. Megan caught the ladder and stood up. The boat lurched at the shift in weight. She had to cling onto it to keep herself upright.

Megan regained her composure. Rain blew in her face as she looked up to contemplate the climb. "No peeking up my gown," she said as she placed her foot on the first rung.

"Mother, I wouldn't . . . I would never . . ."

Megan hauled herself up, past the layer of algae and the row of open ports with their scorched borders. The ladder swung around—back-and-forth, side-to-side—trying to shake her off or slam her into the hull. She had to wrap her hand tightly around each of the rungs to make sure her grip was secure. Each time she let go to reach for the next one she feared the slippery wood would betray her. Before she was even halfway up, her muscles ached with the strain and pleaded for a rest. The gash in her leg screamed in protest, the skin pulling against the stitches like a badly made shirt. But still she kept on climbing.

As she neared the top, a soldier peered over the bulwark. "Mother?"

"I'd appreciate . . ." Megan gasped for breath. "I'd appreciate a lift here."

The soldier leaned over and held out a gloved hand. "Where's everyone else?" he asked.

"They . . . they stayed behind . . . to clean up."

"Clean up?"

"You made an awful mess."

Megan took a firm hold of the soldier's hand and glanced up as she prepared to heave herself onto the ship. The soldier glanced down. She caught the glimmer of nonrecognition in his eyes.

"Wait," he said. "You're not . . ."

Megan didn't have a choice. She grabbed the soldier's collar and let herself drop. The soldier flipped over the bulwark and together they plummeted in a tangle of flailing limbs. Megan tried to arrange her body into some semblance of a dive, but the river came onto them too fast. They smacked into the Speed.

The impact disoriented her. She thrashed in the inky water. Where was she? Where should she go? The river pressed upon her with a power she was incapable of comprehending. She had to fight against it, but her muscles ached and her skin stung and the little breath she retained in her lungs didn't seem worth keeping.

Megan forced herself to move anyway, remembering those who needed her. She kicked through the water, broke the surface, then jerked her head in bewilderment. The ships had gone. She realized she was being stupid and turned around. The *Vengeance* loomed above her, the *Wrath* and the listing *Fury* visible beyond it.

Jon rowed the length of the ship toward her. She headed toward him, though the force of the current meant she could do little more than stay on the spot. The gown didn't help: the wool had bloated in the water and she couldn't kick properly. Still, it was better than armor and its fascination with gravity. There was no sign of the soldier she had dragged down with her.

Jon hoisted her aboard the boat. "What happened up there?"

Megan gasped for breath. "He said . . . he said this gown made my bum look big."

"I thought it was the preg—no, forget I said that, Mother."

Megan told him to row back. Teeth chattering, she squeezed the water out of her clothes. The saturated wool clung to her like Death's clammy hand. She pulled the gown off. It landed on the bottom of the boat with a heavy splat. Jon averted his eyes at the sight of her underwear. The knives strapped to her forearms and shoved into her boots dissuaded leering.

The ladder had doubled in height since Megan had last climbed it. She made a halfhearted grab for it. The rung slipped out of her grasp.

"You haven't got a pick-me-up for a weary girl, have you?"

The soldier unhinged one of the odd-shaped bottles from his baldric. "I've got some Hennigan's Traditional Brain Rotter."

"My grandfather warned me about drinks that promise instant death."

"I wouldn't say it was *instant* . . ."

Megan accepted it anyway. It warmed her stomach, albeit in the same way swallowing burning coals would have. She handed the skin back to the soldier and hauled herself up again.

\*   \*   \*

Megan flipped herself over the bulwark and dropped onto the ship. She crouched, catching her breath and checking her surroundings. Rain polished the deck, making it gleam in the silvery moonlight. What crew was left on the ship had been driven below by the weather.

There was a hatch set into the deck amidships. She hurried across to it, yanked it open, and dropped to the deck below. She found herself in a dark space, barely high enough for her to stand in, with a smoky atmosphere that left a gritty residue on her tongue. It reeked of gunpowder.

Moonlight fingered in through the open ports, illuminating two rows of black cylinders, each four or five feet long and set in a wheeled cradle. Megan tapped one. Iron, warm to the touch. Thin cracks crisscrossed the unfinished metalwork. She pressed her hands on it, banishing the cold from her fingers.

She spotted a crate half-filled with balls the size of melons. It took two hands for her to lift one. They were iron, too. She poked her head around the far end of the cylinder. There was a hole there. The ball fit perfectly. If you tipped some gunpowder in there and lit it, you'd force the ball out at fantastic speeds. It'd wreak havoc wherever it landed. The witches had used these to devastate the city. *Guns*—wasn't that what they'd called them?

The clomping of boots pulled Megan's attention back to her mission. She scurried sternward—heading toward the cabins, she hoped—and pressed against the wall beside the low door set there. Footsteps thudded from the other side. One set, heavy: a soldier. Megan slipped out a knife. She could feel the approach in the rattle of the boards. Ten paces away. Five. Three. One. The door opened.

She whipped her arm around, neck height. The soldier's momentum took him right into the knife. Metal skewered his throat. Megan twisted and yanked, ripping through fat and gristle. There was a wet gargle. The soldier slithered off the blade and crumpled to the floor.

She stepped over the body and found herself in a cramped corridor from which a trio of doors branched off. Megan eased the middle one open an inch and peered inside. A soldier peered back.

"What the . . . ?"

"This isn't the little girls' room?"

"Huh?"

Megan shouldered the door, hard as she could. It flew open, cracking the soldier across the bridge of the nose. He staggered backward into the cabin, clutching his face. Megan slashed at him with a knife. The blade screeched across the armor covering his stomach. He snatched her outstretched arm, pulled her toward him, and punched her in the mouth.

She collapsed to her knees, spitting blood. The soldier grabbed her hair and wrenched her head back. His fist drew back, preparing to slam into her face again. Megan twisted her head, trying to get out of its trajectory.

A voice interrupted them. "Don't you know who she is?" Megan and the soldier turned to its source. Eleanor was spread-eagled across the bed, her wrists tied to the posts. "Look at her."

He did. "You're . . ."

"I'm the other Mother." Megan winced at her unintentional rhyme. "The second Mother. I bear one of the Saviors who will . . . save the True and . . . lead them to . . ."

"Truthiness?" suggested Eleanor.

"That'll do." Next time she was trying to be portentous, Megan vowed to rehearse. She backed away from the soldier. "What do you think will happen to you if you harm me, harm my baby?"

The soldier swallowed, his attention flicking between Megan and the tethered countess. "Any rules against taking you prisoner?" he said.

Megan pulled the knives out of her boots and held them ready. "Try it. One of us will die. If you're lucky, it'll be you."

"Captain Tobrytan . . . orders . . ."

"God's countermanded him."

"How can you know?"

"How can you not?" said Megan. "Go on. Get away from here. Lose yourself in the forest or the mountains or who knows where."

"The captain'll find me. And when he does . . ."

"He might find you," said Megan. "God definitely will."

The soldier fled from the cabin. Megan picked at the knots that secured Eleanor to the bed. The ropes had been pulled tight, the rough hemp scratching the countess's skin. Megan dug her nails in and pulled.

"What are you doing here?" said Eleanor.

"Rescuing you."

"Without your clothes?"

Megan tugged at her underwear. "Hey."

"That only counts as a technicality."

"You try moving about in a dress that weighs half a ton."

"What happened to your leg?"

Attention drawn to its existence, the wound across Megan's thigh started to throb. "It's just a scratch."

The ropes were too secure for her to untie. She selected a knife with a serrated edge and started to saw.

"You should have left me," said Eleanor. "Run away."

"That's what Damon said."

"Much as it pains me to say this: he was right."

"If you're going to keep complaining . . ."

"Might as well go along with you now."

The knot Megan was attacking came apart. She switched her attention to the other one. Eleanor rubbed her raw wrist against her cheek.

"It's not your fault," she said. "You don't have to atone."

"What's not my fault?"

"Your sister. What she did."

"Of course it's not my fault," said Megan, upping the pace of her sawing. "But the fact that you brought it up suggests you at least contemplated it."

"I tried to think what I'd feel like in your position."

Megan slumped by the side of the bed. Eleanor took over the job of freeing herself.

"I don't understand why she did this," said Megan. "We were happy. We didn't need anything, we never went hungry or without. We had a home, a grandfather who loved us, each other. Were we not enough for her?"

"People always want more."

"There's wanting and there's—" Megan threw her hands in the air —"all this."

"You can do anything if you can justify it to yourself."

"I'll remember that the next time I see her."

Eleanor cut herself free, throwing off the remains of the rope as if it was a dead animal. She held a hand out to Megan. "Are we going to get out of here or mope?"

"Mope?"

"Come on."

The two of them snuck out of the cabin and into the corridor beyond. "How long do you think it'll take that soldier to get over his crisis of conscience?" whispered Megan. Approaching footsteps shook the boards. "I wish I hadn't asked that question."

She led Eleanor to the gun deck. The pattering on the planks above their heads was easing off. The rain was stopping, for the moment anyway. The clouds that obscured the moon and cast the interior in near darkness suggested it'd be back soon.

"We should have brought a candle from the captain's cabin," said Eleanor.

"Not with all the gunpowder down here. One stray flame and we go the way of Brother Brogan . . . which might not be a bad thing."

"Don't tell me you're thinking what I think you're thinking."

"All right," said Megan, striding down the central corridor between the guns, "I won't."

Eleanor hurried after her. "You *are* thinking what I think you're thinking."

"You only think that."

Megan ran into what she had been expecting: a stout door at the far end of the deck. She unlatched it. There was a small storeroom beyond. She made out the outlines of dozens of barrels. The smell left no doubt what was in them. Megan's heart raced. She'd seen what one barrel had done to Brother Brogan's house, what a few had done to the gates of the palace. What could all these do? A plan started to formulate in her mind.

Megan wedged her knife into the lid of one and eased it open a couple of inches. "Give me a hand with this," she said.

The two women held the barrel at either end and crept out of the storeroom, leaving a trail of coarse powder in their wake. They stopped underneath the hatch that led to the upper deck and upended the barrel.

"Get topside," Megan said.

"You are going to be right behind me, aren't you?" said Eleanor.

"Of course."

Megan ushered Eleanor up onto the barrel. Eleanor shoved open the hatch and hoisted herself up. Megan groped around. The witches must have had something to ignite the gunpowder. Her hand fell on a battered tin box. Inside were flint and steel. She tucked the box in her boot, then followed Eleanor up to the main deck.

Her blood ran cold. A leviathan was cutting through the gloom, heading for them. It was the *Wrath*, its rigging creaking as it lumbered through the water. Slowly, unstoppably, it maneuvered alongside them. Men became visible on its deck. Soldiers scurrying, forming into a line along the bulwark. A hole had appeared in the clouds, allowing moonlight to glance off the hooks each of them held—the teeth of the beast waiting to attack.

Megan ripped Eleanor's cloak off her and arranged it into a heap by the open hatchway. She struck the steel against the flint. It sparked but the cloak failed to light. Two soldiers emerged from the quarterdeck and advanced, one cautious pace at a time. Eleanor placed herself between them and Megan, her knife at the ready.

The hooks arced over from the *Wrath*, ropes trailing behind them like tails. Metal teeth bit into the bulwarks of the *Vengeance*. Soldiers heaved. The two ships inched closer and closer.

Megan took a moment to steady her hands, then struck again. More sparks. The cloak smoldered. Another strike. A tiny flame ate away at the fabric, bright as a sun in the night. She blew it a kiss to encourage its growth. The flame spread.

"Go!"

Eleanor dashed across the deck and vaulted the bulwark. Megan kicked the burning cloak through the open hatch. The soldiers' faces dropped as they realized what was happening. Megan allowed herself the pleasure of witnessing their panic before following Eleanor and flinging herself off the ship.

The shock wave burst through the river, slamming into Megan. She used its power to propel herself away from the exploding ship, keeping under the surface to shield herself from the debris that rained down. A second blast kicked into her. She tumbled, disoriented, fighting the urge to panic and breathe in the water.

The strain became too much for her. She released the dead air building up in her lungs and followed the trail of bubbles to the surface. She gasped, sucking air into her abused body, then forgot everything as she caught sight of the crippled *Vengeance*, flame and smoke billowing from the massive hole in its bow. Alongside, the *Wrath* too was in trouble. Fires raged across its decks. The explosion on the *Vengeance* must have detonated the gunpowder stored on its sister ship. Both vessels were taking on water, going down fast. A crew member leapt into the Speed. Megan wondered if he'd had the foresight to remove his armor.

Eastport was spared the threat of the witches' guns. There was a horrific satisfaction in witnessing the destruction of one's enemies. Was this how Gwyneth felt, the thrill at the extent of her power? Did Megan's pleasure at watching the ships burn make her as bad as her sister?

The river played with her, hoisting her on its shoulders, then attempting to drag her under. She rode the waves, offering the minimum of resistance, looking everywhere for Eleanor, her teeth chattering as the icy water slid against her bare skin. Where was the countess? How good a swimmer was she?

Her heart leapt as she caught sight of Eleanor approaching, her strokes correct but labored. Megan took a deep breath and kicked toward her.

"Are you . . . are you all right?" she asked.

Eleanor switched to treading water and nodded. "You?" Megan pointed at the sinking ships and nodded in return. "What now?"

"We meet Damon . . ." Megan gasped gulped in air. "We meet Damon by the wall . . . near Silas's. He's getting us a ship."

"Your plan relies on Damon?"

"Only in an essential way."

They kicked off downriver, then let the current take over. Eastport sped by, the ruins of the riverside buildings continuing to smolder. Only the odd flicker in the shadows betrayed any sign of life. How would the city react to the destruction of the invaders' fleet: would they use it as a rallying call or would they continue to cower? How would Gwyneth react? Was she scared? Would she realize God wasn't on her side or would she interpret it as a test, a setback in the war against His enemies, her enemies?

As they reached the city wall, more pressing questions surfaced, like where was Damon and would they survive the freezing water until he showed up? Megan swam against the current to slow herself down. She scanned the river. Silhouettes shimmered in and out of existence, floating past them one moment, revealing nothing but the churning Speed the next.

"We need to get ashore!" Eleanor shouted above the roar of the current. "He's not going to show up!"

"Yes, he is!"

But why would he? Megan's mission had been suicidal. Why not take the diamond and the gold and get
himself out of the city? His conscience wouldn't trouble
him because he hadn't saved a dead girl.

And then, downriver, a light in the black. Megan
slapped the water to get Eleanor's attention and kicked
off. The countess shouted something after her, some
warning, but Megan wasn't listening. She was swim-
ming hard, drawing on her last scraps of strength.

The light resolved into a lantern, its dim glow picking out the shape of a small sailboat. A figure moved
around on its decks. He spotted the disturbance in the
water and waved, called out. Her name? Yes! Damon
was on the boat, beckoning her. Megan flipped onto
her back to make sure Eleanor was following, then
onto her front to cover the final yards.

She drew closer to the vessel, a fishing boat by the
look of it. Damon leaned over the edge and held out
an oar. Megan reached out. The wood brushed her outstretched fingers. She made a second attempt to grab it,
but the current caught her and carried her away. Before
she knew it, she was careering past the hull. Damon
dashed around to the bow and thrust the oar out again.
It smacked the water a yard behind her.

The Speed was living up to its name now, eager to
meet the sea. Megan pushed as hard as she could, but
she couldn't overcome its force. She watched Eleanor

clamber aboard the boat. Her mission was accomplished. She had rescued the countess, saved the city. Surely it was no shame now to rest her weary arms and surrender to the river?

The boat jerked forward. Slow at first, but gaining fast. She'd never be able to intercept it before it shot past, but Megan made the effort anyway. It spat something out. A net ensnared her. Megan yelped, swallowed water, then found herself lurching across the current. She hit something solid.

Damon and another man leaned over the edge of the boat and grabbed her, Megan's flesh so numb from cold it hardly registered the pressure. The men heaved, trying to pull her out of the river. Megan tried to help, but she didn't have the energy to be anything more than deadweight. The men cried out and heaved again. The world lurched as Megan shot over the bulwark. A third pair of hands—Eleanor's—dragged her into the safety of the boat.

Megan collapsed onto the deck, panting as she sucked cold air into her lungs. Water streamed off of her, soaking into the timbers. Up in the sky, a cloud raced across the moon, momentarily darkening the world before leaving a disk of pure silver to light their way.

"Any more?" asked the unfamiliar man.

"That's it," said Damon, panting. "Get us out of here, skipper."

"Aye."

The skipper opened the sail out fully and the boat made another leap forward. Damon pressed a blanket around Megan. He held her tight, absorbing the compulsive shivers that racked her, warming her with his body.

Eleanor perched on the edge of the boat, a blanket draped over her shoulders. "I suppose we should thank you," she said to Damon.

"I was in the area."

"Thank you," said Megan.

"No problem. Well, not entirely. There was this . . . but you don't want to hear about that. Not sober anyway."

Megan squeezed water out of her hair. "Next time we do this, let's pick somewhere drier."

"And warmer," said Eleanor.

"And less warzone-y," said Damon.

He reached behind and grabbed a sack, from which he pulled out wine and bread. Eleanor accepted the loaf from him and ripped it into hunks. Damon uncorked the bottle with his teeth, flashed them a grin, and took a hefty slug before passing it around.

Her body warming, her stomach filling, Megan contemplated her friends. Her friends? They'd tried to kill one another, but they'd saved one another. They'd distrusted one another, but they'd been there for one another. They'd sought out others, but in the end there was only the three of them. She guessed that made them more than friends—they were a family. That was good; she needed a family. Her unborn child needed a family.

The river widened, merging into the sea. The city receded, first until it was a mere smudge on the horizon and then dropping from the world entirely. Megan hunkered down. The boat plowed on, losing itself in the desolate expanse.

# epilogue

Damon had been riding for weeks now, making his way up from New Statham to the county of Keedy in the far north of the Realm, where he was to meet up with Megan and Eleanor. He was in the saddle from sunrise to sunset, a test of endurance that had left his skin raw, his ass numb, and his testicles impacted somewhere around his kidneys. The Kartik Mountains had dominated his horizon for days now, but they never seemed to move any closer. He wondered if he'd ever reach them or if he'd be riding forever.

Finally, he reached his destination: Murray, an anonymous dump of a village Eleanor's mother's family had exploited for generations. He tied his horse up and waddled from house to house, searching for the women. The high-pitched wails of a newborn from a hut on the outskirts led him to the right place. He poked his head inside. The air had the fetid stink of the slaughterhouse: blood, sweat, shit, fear. Megan was sprawled out on the bed, her bleached hair sticking to her face, a baby cradled in her arms. An old woman—the midwife presumably—worked between her legs, doing things that made Damon's balls retreat into his body even further.

He went over to examine the baby. Pink and wrinkly and pissed off with the world. "This is what all the fuss is about?" he said. "Looks like my Great-Uncle Ralph."

"He's a she."

"There were rumors about Great-Uncle Ralph too."

The baby looked up at him with her big brown eyes, and for a moment Damon saw Megan in them—but a Megan without the pain, a Megan with hope and innocence. His heart softened. He kissed Megan's forehead. "Congratulations."

"Thank you."

"What're you calling her?"

"Cate," said Megan. "After my mother."

"Opted against Jolecia, I see?" said Damon. Megan looked unimpressed. "Personally, I would have gone for Damonella."

Eleanor's voice cut out from the shadows. "Are they going to march?"

"I'm fine, thanks. Why would I want a drink after weeks on the road?"

The countess stepped out, knocking back a cup of wine. Even with her dyed hair hanging in lank tails around her face, her eyes bleary and bloodshot, and her clothes stained with the remnants of childbirth, she was still a hundred times more alluring than any other woman he had ever met, or ever even imagined. One day she might start treating him like a real person rather than a servant she couldn't fire.

"What took you so long?" she asked.

"There was a ferrymen's strike. Took me ages to cross Lake Pullar."

"Why the detour?"

Damon helped himself to the half-empty flagon hanging from Eleanor's hand and took a heavy swig straight from it. "The War Council agreed to the Supreme Priest's request," he said. "They're going to raise an army."

"They should have done it months ago."

"Because rushing into a war with the witches has such a good precedent." Damon shrugged and belched. "You know what it's like when you put priests together. The number of arguments increases exponentially."

A week after they had fled Eastport, a much larger witch fleet had arrived in the city to reinforce Gwyneth's forces. While the priests argued, the witches had secured the Speed—isolating Ainsworth from the rest of the Realm—and marched on the rest of the county. Every town, every village, surrendered to them. They had few soldiers to defend them, and no answer to the witches' guns.

Refugees braving the blockade had brought news and also reports on the witches' true nature. The priests modified their propaganda, admitting the witches followed their own version of the Faith, but claiming they had always said that. Claims that Ahebban and Jolecia were demons were lessened or explained away as metaphor. Gwyneth was now the chief object of their condemnation; they appeared ignorant of Megan. Damon suspected both sisters preferred it that way.

That still left what to do with Ainsworth—an unloved corner of the Realm whose sole purpose was to get itself attacked every other generation. Some of the council gathered in New Statham was prepared to write off the county, reach an accommodation with the True; others were keen to raise an army to invade Ainsworth and slaughter every last one of the witches. The latter faction won out.

The call had gone out to the Realm, demanding that every able-bodied man report for service. A war was coming. It would be more terrible than the land had ever witnessed, and Damon had no intention of being a part of it. He'd done his part. He'd helped Megan and Eleanor out of Eastport and spied for them in the capital. Now he deserved a few quiet decades. With the baby to look after, he could persuade the women to remain up here, well out of the action.

The midwife finished with Megan. Eleanor poured herself another drink. "It's taken too long, even for priests."

"What do you mean?" asked Damon.

"Someone's sowing dissent. When I get back, I'll need a list of those priests who were trying to delay action. We'll have to see where their loyalties lie."

"When you get back? Where're you going?"

Eleanor went over to Megan and held out her hands. "It's time."

"Just five more minutes," said Megan, holding her child closer. "Just five more minutes with her."

"And after that? Another five?"

The baby reached out and played with her mother's finger with her own tiny replicas. Megan pulled her hand away, then offered it up again. The baby gurgled. "Would it be so bad?"

"We've discussed this. You know she'll be safer."

Eleanor slipped her hands around the baby. At first, Damon thought Megan was going to resist, but she let Eleanor pluck Cate out of her arms. The baby started crying. Eleanor rocked her.

"Shush, little one."

Eleanor bent over so Megan could give her daughter a final kiss before carrying her out of the hut. Megan buried herself in the crumpled sheets and sobbed. Damon dithered. He took a step toward Megan. Was there anything he could say to ease her pain, anything that wasn't a dismal platitude? He backtracked and went after Eleanor.

"Where're you taking her?"

"I'll be back in a couple of days," said Eleanor, strapping baby Cate to her chest.

"You don't trust me?"

"Not to keep quiet under torture, no."

"I guess I am allergic to red-hot metal."

"Half the Realm wants this little girl dead," said Eleanor, "the other half wants to worship her. I'm going to find someone who'll treat her as a normal child."

"You don't believe she is one of the Saviors reborn, do you?"

"They do; that's what matters." Eleanor hoisted herself up on her horse. "Look after Megan. Don't let her do anything stupid."

"Yeah, because we've both had great success there."

Eleanor gave the horse a gentle tap in the ribs. It broke into a trot, heading north toward the mountains. Damon wondered if she was going to leave the baby on their cold slopes, let God look after it. No, the direction meant nothing. Eleanor was cunning enough to double back once she was out of sight.

He went back inside. Megan was still curled up. The sobbing had stopped, or become inaudible at least. Damon poured her a drink and hovered by the bed.

"How're you doing?"

"I need some fresh air," said Megan, stirring. "Help me outside."

"Shouldn't you rest?"

"It's a few paces."

"She's already gone," said Damon.

"Just help me."

They shuffled outside, Megan leaning heavily against him. He found an old crate and upended it for her to sit on. Together they stared out at the mountains, still capped in snow despite the approaching summer, and watched the sky pale as afternoon transitioned to evening.

"You know," said Megan, "when all this happened I thought at least a little good had come of it. Now I've lost even that."

"It won't be forever."

"It won't?"

"Once the priests' army marches south."

"And gets annihilated by the witches' guns."

"I'm not saying there won't be any casualties," said Damon, "but the numbers are on our side."

Megan grimaced as she shifted on the crate. Sweat prickled her skin despite the cooling day. "When you were in New Statham did you hear anything about . . . about . . . ?"

"Holed up in Eastport," said Damon. "She's all, you know, that thing that pregnant women get."

"Glowing?"

"Lardy."

"Lardy?" said Megan. "Is that what you thought I looked like?"

"No, of course not. You were that other thing. Glowing."

"You think she'll find her a good family?"

It took Damon a moment to match nouns to the pronouns. "I'm sure Eleanor has it all planned."

"Will Cate love them more than she does me?"

"You're her mother."

"She won't know that."

"She will when . . ."

"When I get her back." Megan stiffened, her features hardening. Damon had seen the look before, the cold determination: on her sister in the High Priest's palace. "And I will get her back, even if it means I have to kill Gwyneth and every one of her bastard followers personally. Believe me, I'll do it."

Damon did.

And it scared him.

# acknowledgments

As someone once said—if I wasn't so lazy, I'd look up who—writing a novel is a solitary endeavor, publishing a book is a team exercise. Thanks must go first of all to my agent, Claire Wilson at Rogers, Coleridge and White, without whose tireless work and enthusiasm this book wouldn't exist. For making a lifetime's dream come true, I owe her my eternal gratitude. And 15 percent of my royalties.

Next, I must thank the good people at Quercus, who took such a big leap of faith: my editor, the wonderful Sarah Lambert, for her advice and guidance; my copy editor, Talya Baker, whose appreciation of the semicolon exceeds even my own; Niamh Mulvey, who has generously volunteered to take the blame for any errors; Sean Freeman and Nicola Theobald for their outstanding cover; and all those working to make the book the best it can be. I probably only know a tenth of what you're doing.

Last, but not least, I have to thank my family—my wife, Kirby; my son, Tom; my sister, Lyndsay; my brother, Peter; my parents, Mom and Dad—for their love, patience, and general letting-me-get-on-with-it-ness. This is for you.